"If it hadn't been for that tree, she'd be miles down river by now, we reckon."

One of the uniformed PCs pointed upstream. "Her hair had caught on that tangle of branches. Apart from that she was floating free."

The tree in question must have come down during the winter storms; it projected some fifteen feet into the river, its upper branches submerged and well out into the main current. Inspector Thanet could visualise the scene clearly, the body carried along by the swollen waters, accelerating as it approached the rush of water over the weir, the twisting tumble as it was carried over the lip into the churn of the waters below, the sudden check as the woman's abundant hair caught in a web of branches lying in wait beneath the surface . . .

Bantam Crime Line Books offer the finest in classic and modern British murder mysteries.
Ask your bookseller for the books you have missed.

Agatha Christie

Death on the Nile
A Holiday for Murder
The Mousetrap and Other Plays
The Mysterious Affair at Styles
Poirot Investigates
Postern of Fate
The Secret Adversary
The Seven Dials Mystery
Sleeping Murder

Dorothy Simpson

Last Seen Alive
The Night She Died
Puppet for a Corpse
Six Feet Under
Close Her Eyes
Element of Doubt
Dead on Arrival
Suspicious Death

Elizabeth George

A Great Deliverance
Payment in Blood

Colin Dexter

Last Bus to Woodstock
The Riddle of the Third Mile
The Silent World of Nicholas Quinn
Service of All the Dead
The Dead of Jericho
The Secret of Annexe 3
Last Seen Wearing

Michael Dibdin

Ratking

Liza Cody

Head Case
Stalker
coming soon: Under Contract

Ruth Rendell

A Dark-Adapted Eye
    (writing as Barbara Vine)
A Fatal Inversion
    (writing as Barbara Vine)

Marian Babson

Death in Fashion
Reel Murder
Murder, Murder, Little Star
Murder on a Mystery Tour
Murder Sails at Midnight

Dorothy Cannell

The Widows Club
Down the Garden Path
coming soon: Mum's the Word

Antonia Fraser

Jemima Shore's First Case
Your Royal Hostage
Oxford Blood
A Splash of Red
Quiet as a Nun
coming soon:
Cool Repentance
The Wild Island

Margery Allingham

Death of a Ghost
Police at the Funeral
coming soon:
Tether's End
Traitor's Purse
Pearls Before Swine

A LUKE THANET MYSTERY

SUSPICIOUS DEATH

by
Dorothy Simpson

BANTAM BOOKS
NEW YORK • TORONTO • LONDON • SYDNEY • AUCKLAND

*This edition contains the complete text
of the original hardcover edition.*
NOT ONE WORD HAS BEEN OMITTED.

SUSPICIOUS DEATH

*A Bantam Book / published by arrangement with
Charles Scribner's Sons*

PRINTING HISTORY
*Charles Scribner's edition published November 1988
Bantam edition / February 1990*

ISBN 0-553-28459-2

Published simultaneously in the United States and Canada

Bantam Books are published by Bantam Books, a division of Bantam Doubleday
Dell Publishing Group, Inc. Its trademark, consisting of the words "Bantam
Books" and the portrayal of a rooster, is Registered in U.S. Patent and Trademark
Office and in other countries. Marca Registrada. Bantam Books, 666 Fifth Avenue,
New York, New York 10103.

PRINTED IN THE UNITED STATES OF AMERICA

KRI   0 9 8 7 6 5 4 3 2 1

To Mark and Janet

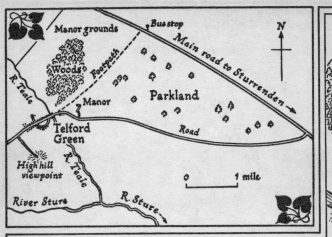

Manor grounds
Bus stop
N

Woods
Footpath
Main road to Sturrenden

R. Teale
Manor
Parkland

Telford Green
Road

High hill viewpoint
R. Teale

River Sture
R. Sture

0   1 mile

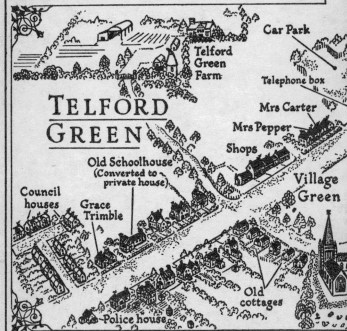

Car Park

Telford Green Farm

Telephone box

TELFORD GREEN

Mrs Carter

Mrs Pepper

Shops

Old Schoolhouse
(Converted to private house)

Village Green

Council houses

Grace Trimble

Old cottages

Police house

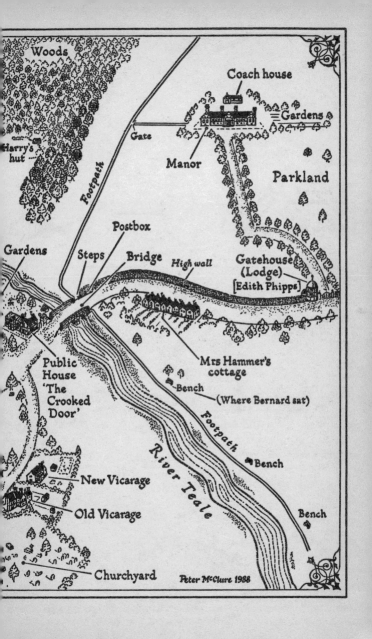

Woods

Coach house

Gardens

Harry's hut

Manor

Gate

Parkland

Postbox

Gardens

Steps

Bridge

High wall

Gatehouse (Lodge)
[Edith Phipps]

Public House 'The Crooked Door'

Mrs Hammer's cottage

Bench

(Where Bernard sat)

Footpath

Bench

New Vicarage

Old Vicarage

River Teale

Bench

Churchyard

Peter McClure 1988

ONE

Thanet lay awake, staring into the darkness, ears tuned to catch the slightest sound from along the corridor. Beside him, Joan's deep, even breathing told him that she was sound asleep. He glanced at the luminous dial of the clock. Midnight.

This was ridiculous.

Moving stealthily, so as not to disturb her, he set aside the bedclothes and padded to the door, shivering slightly as the cold night air penetrated his pyjamas. No one would have believed it was April. Since the rain stopped at around six o'clock the temperature had rapidly plummeted to below freezing point and the house was cooling fast. All the more reason to take a firm stand now.

He eased the door open and glanced along the corridor to Bridget's room. Yes, as he thought, she was still up.

She was sitting at her desk, staring at the open book before her. Not by look, word or gesture did she acknowledge his presence as he came in.

"Sprig," he said softly, the memory of past confrontations causing his resolution to crumble. "Don't you think it's time you gave up for the night?"

She stirred, then, like someone awakening from a long sleep, and glanced up at him. "I haven't finished yet."

"But it's past midnight!"

Her mouth set stubbornly. "I must finish this section."

"What is it?"

"Biology. I told you. We've got this massive test tomorrow."

"But . . ."

"Dad, leave it alone, will you? If it's got to be done, it's got to be done. If I go to bed without finishing I'll never get to sleep."

Her voice was rising, the familiar edge of near-hysteria, near-desperation creeping in, and once again, in the face of it, he was powerless.

"All right. But try not to be too long." He bent to kiss the top of her head and switched on the electric fire before leaving.

What else could he have done? he asked himself as he returned to his own bed, snuggling up to Joan's comforting warmth. If he had persisted there would have been floods of tears and when Bridget did get to bed she would have been too upset to sleep. How many other parents all over the country, he wondered, were at this very moment faced by precisely the same dilemma? He had heard plenty of tales of pre-examination traumas, but who could have guessed that the imminence of GCSEs would turn his cheerful, extrovert Bridget into a wan, anxiety-ridden ghost of her former self? The situation had been deteriorating steadily since Christmas, when she had failed several of her "mocks," and lately a combination of overwork, lack of sleep and general listlessness had been giving Thanet and Joan real cause for worry. Endless discussions had brought them no nearer a solution and time and again they had reached the unsatisfactory conclusion that there was nothing they could do other than offer her reassurance and moral support, grit their teeth and stick it out.

Another couple of months and it would all be over, Thanet told himself yet again as he tried to compose himself for sleep. Until it was Ben's turn . . .

Next morning Joan and Ben were brisk and energetic, Thanet and Bridget heavy-eyed and lethargic. It was Thanet's turn to do the school run and when he dropped the children off he again noted Bridget's dragging reluctance as she headed for the school gates. If only there were something he could do to help her. But you couldn't fight all your children's battles for them, he reminded himself as he drove off. Learning to cope alone was part of the painful process of growing up.

At this point, normally, his spirits would begin to rise. He loved his work, enjoyed the constant and varying challenge of it, the comforting familiarity of well-known faces, long-term relationships. But at the moment even this solace was denied him. After twenty years Superintendent Parker had retired, and the winds of change were sweeping through the subdivisional police headquarters of Sturrenden, the small country town in Kent where Thanet lived and worked, in the shape of Superintendent Draco, a Welshman recently promoted from Cardiff.

Thanet glanced at his watch. He'd better get a move on, or

he'd be late for the 8:45 morning meeting which Draco had instituted as part of the new regime.

Pater, the duty officer, greeted him with a grin. "Morning, sir. You'll be pleased to hear they've decided to start on redecorating your office today."

"Oh, no . . . I thought it wasn't going to be till next month."

"Change of plan, sir. DS Lineham is directing operations."

"What do you mean, 'directing operations'?"

"They thought it would be quicker and easier if your desks were moved next door."

"Oh, great."

Upstairs the CID section was a hive of activity. In the main room a corner was being cleared to accommodate Thanet and Lineham and the corridor was crowded with desks, chairs, filing cabinets, noticeboards, stacks of files and decorators' equipment.

Detective Sergeant Lineham, carrying a chin-high stack of folders, grimaced as Thanet advanced, scowling.

"How are we supposed to get any work done, with all this going on?"

"It won't take long, sir. By the time you're back from the meeting, we'll be more or less straight."

"There are times, Mike, when I find your optimism positively nauseating. How long will they take to do our office?"

"Two days, they say. Cheer up, sir, it's all part of our new image." But all these upheavals were having an effect even upon the normally cheerful Lineham. His usual mischievous grin was conspicuous by its absence.

Thanet snorted in disgust. "New image! Stop provoking me, Mike. I was perfectly happy with things as they were."

"I must admit I'll miss the map of Australia on the ceiling myself."

"Anything important come in since last night? I'm due at the meeting in five minutes."

There was only routine stuff, however, and Thanet's report to Draco was brief. He had to admit that the new Superintendent was efficient, and seemed to know exactly what he was trying to achieve. If only he didn't have the unfortunate knack of putting people's backs up . . .

"One last point . . ." Draco's eyes, dark and diamond-bright as the anthracite in his native hills, glittered as he glanced from one man to the next, deliberately allowing his gaze to rest for a moment on each one. "I've said it before and I'll say it again: I want to know everything that goes on in my patch. Everything.

So if someone nicks an old lady's pension book or there's a fight in a school playground, I want to be told about it. Vigilance is the key word, vigilance and efficiency. And efficiency, as far as we are concerned, means reports. Detailed, literate and accurate reports, which we will all actually read. So just make sure that everyone gets the message. That's all for today. Thank you for your time."

The phone rang as they began to file out and he snatched it up. "Draco." He listened for a moment then covered the receiver and called Thanet back, waving him into a chair.

Thanet studied him as he waited. Typically Celtish in appearance, Draco was short—barely regulation height, Thanet guessed—and thick-set, with close-cropped curly black hair and sallow skin. Even when, as now, he was in a passive role, he emanated controlled energy. It was in the tilt of his head, the intensity of his concentration, the rhythmic tapping of his forefinger on his desk.

"Yes. Yes, I see. When was this? Yes . . . Yes . . . Definitely. Inform the SOCO and the CCTV sergeant . . ."

Thanet's interest sharpened. If the Scenes-of-Crime Officer and Closed Circuit Television operative were being notified, it could only mean . . .

"Yes, of course, the police surgeon too. DI Thanet will be along shortly. Yes."

The phone went down and Draco focussed his attention on Thanet. "As you'll have gathered, there's been a suspicious death. Woman pulled out of the river at Donnington Weir. Found by an old lady walking her dog. You'd better get over there."

"Any sign of foul play, sir?"

"That," said Draco, impaling Thanet with his glittering stare, "is what you're going to find out."

"Yes, sir." Thanet turned to leave.

"Oh, and Thanet . . ."

"Yes, sir?"

"When you have found out, I want to know about it. The lot."

"Right, sir."

As he hurried upstairs, Thanet spared a moment to wonder if Draco was going to be able to content himself with being a mere administrator. This was what had always deterred Thanet from seeking promotion. He loved the investigative side of his work, the interviewing of witnesses and suspects, the intellectual challenge and supreme satisfaction of solving a difficult puzzle. To have found himself stuck behind a desk for most of his working life would be anathema to him. At this moment, he wouldn't have changed places with Draco for all the incentives in the world.

In the CID room Lineham had managed to establish some sort of order and was busy sorting through files on Thanet's desk. Thanet glanced around. All six Detective Constables were present, each conspicuously busy.

Thanet addressed the room at large. "Well, it looks as though we're going to be stuck with each other for the next two days, and we'll just have to make the best of it. Anyway, with any luck you won't be seeing much of me. There's been a suspicious death. A woman's body, pulled out of the weir at Donnington."

Heads turned and glances were exchanged as a ripple of excitement ran around the room. The unspoken word vibrated in the air. *Murder?*

"Of course," Thanet went on, "we have no idea yet whether it was accident, suicide or murder, so don't get too excited about it. Initially, Lineham and I will go and take a look, and Bentley and Swift will come with us." Swift was new to the section and his thin, dark face lit up with a look of ill-concealed satisfaction. Bentley, his usual phlegmatic self, merely nodded. Thanet tried to ignore the others' evident disappointment. It was understandable, of course. Sturrenden was a fairly law-abiding community and possible murder cases were few and far between. "Naturally, if this turns out to be a potential murder investigation, you'll all be involved, one way or another. So get your heads down and clear off as much routine stuff as possible." He turned to Lineham. "Anything urgent we've got to deal with before we go?"

"Not really, sir, no."

"Right. We'll be off, then."

Thanet and Lineham took one car, Bentley and Swift another, in case they needed to divide forces later. It was market day in Sturrenden and the town was crowded with pedestrians thronging down the High Street to the large cobbled area of the Market Square, where traders who made their living moving from market to market would have been setting up their stalls since early morning. Donnington Weir was about two miles out of town but unfortunately was accessible by road only from the far side of the river. It was therefore necessary to cross the one and only river bridge, which as usual on market days was congested with traffic.

"About time they found a new site for the market, if you ask me," grumbled Lineham as they queued to cross the river.

The policeman in Thanet agreed with Lineham, the private citizen thought that it would be a shame to sweep away a centuries-old tradition merely because of the inconvenience it caused. He contented himself with a non-committal grunt. In any case, there was no desperate rush. The SOCO and CCTV officer would have to get to Donnington and carry out their routine procedures before Thanet and his men could do very much. He gazed around at the colourful market scene. After yesterday's rain it was good to see blue skies and sunshine. Canvas awnings flapped, clothes on display swung to and fro on their hangars in the brisk wind which had sprung up overnight and puffy white clouds scudded gaily eastwards towards the coast and the sea. Thanet spotted Helen Mallard, the wife of the police surgeon, buying fruit from one of the stalls and according its selection her customary care. A professional writer of cookery books, she shared with Bridget, Thanet's daughter, a passionate interest in anything and everything to do with the preparation of food. She saw him and waved, came across.

He wound down the window.

"Hello, Luke, how are you all? I haven't seen Bridget for ages."

Until Christmas she and Bridget used to get together once a week for what they called their "creative evenings." It was also through Helen Mallard that Bridget had managed to land a commission to write a children's cookery corner in the *Kent Messenger*. Lately, Thanet thought sadly, her interest even in that had waned.

He pulled a face. "The prospect of GCSEs is really getting her down."

"I gathered as much. Well, if she wants me, she knows where to find me. It might make a change, for her to come over one evening."

"I'll mention it to her. Thanks, Helen."

The car in front began to move.

"See you."

" 'Bye, Luke. Love to Joan."

Ten minutes later they turned off the main road and drove down the gentle incline into the large public car park at Donnington Weir, a well-known local beauty spot on the river Sture. A grassy meadow studded with mature oaks stretches between car park and river, and on the far side the land rises in a wide landscape of gently rolling pastureland scattered with farms, oast houses, barns and cottages. It is a favourite place, especially in summer, for family picnics and local artists. On this brisk April morning, however, the parking area was occupied only by a few police cars, an ambulance and the old Rover which Doctor Mallard, Helen's husband, stubbornly refused to part with.

Bentley and Swift pulled in alongside them and all four men put on wellington boots.

Thanet greeted the uniformed PC on duty beside the swing gate leading into the field. "Morning, Weaver. Which way?" Thanet had been scanning the wide, grassy expanse, but could see no sign of activity. From here the river was invisible.

"Over there, sir." Weaver pointed to a small stand of trees over to the left.

"Right."

The heavy frost had thawed, but the wind had not yet dried out the residual moisture and their boots made a swishing, squelching sound as they moved through ankle-high grass across ground still sodden from the winter rains. Nearer the water the ground fell away, sloping down to the footpath along the river bank which in summer was rarely without its complement of dog-walkers and strolling couples. This morning it was deserted save for the flurry of activity near the trees. A small, nattily dressed figure was approaching, bald head gleaming and half-moons twinkling in the sunshine.

"Ah, reinforcements have arrived. Morning, everyone."

"Morning, Doc," they said, Thanet smiling with genuine pleasure. He was very fond of the little police surgeon, whom he had known since boyhood, and it always delighted him to see Mallard in the ebullient mood which had enveloped him since his second marriage. For many years before that Mallard had been a lonely embittered figure after the lingering death of his first wife.

"You beat us to it, I see," said Thanet. "What's the story?"

"Well, she's dead, all right." Mallard peered mischievously at Thanet over his glasses. "That what you wanted to know?"

Thanet tutted. "Come on, Doc, stop playing games."

"The young are always so impatient," murmured Mallard, putting down his bag and pulling out a notebook. He flipped it open. "Female, white, mid-forties, height 5'6", weight about 9 stone, cause of death . . ." He paused.

"Well?" demanded Thanet.

Mallard shut his notebook with a snap. "I'm not too sure I want to commit myself, as yet."

"She didn't drown, then?"

"She might have. On the other hand, she . . ."

". . . might not have!" finished Thanet.

"Precisely. Look, I'm sorry, but I can't pronounce yet on this one. You know how tricky drownings can be. She might have had a cardiac arrest or a laryngeal spasm as a result of the shock of falling into the water, or . . ."

"Or?"

Mallard shrugged. "There's a nasty gash on the right temple. It's difficult to tell, at the moment, whether or not she got it before or after she went into the river."

"You'll do a diatom test?"

"Definitely, yes."

Thanet knew that this test would settle whether or not the woman had died before or after entering the water. Diatoms are microscopic algae, found in both sea and fresh water. Water is sucked into the lungs during drowning, and diatoms enter the bloodstream and are pumped to the heart, entering the body tissues. The presence of diatoms in these is therefore proof that the victim was alive on entering the water.

"How long had she been in the river?"

Mallard shrugged. "Difficult to tell. But by the condition of her hands and feet . . . she went in some time last night, I'd guess." The doctor picked up his bag. "Well, must go now. See you later."

As they made for the trees, Thanet was interested to note that he was feeling none of his usual qualms at viewing the body. The first sight of a corpse normally filled him with a complex and uncomfortable mixture of emotions, soon past but hard to endure while they lasted. This morning, however, his stomach was steady, his mind clear of the customary clogging apprehension. Why was that? he wondered. Because all signs of violence would have been washed away by long immersion? Or was it possible that at last he had outgrown his weakness?

Trace, the Scenes-of-Crime Officer, came to meet them. "Morning, sir. It looks as though she went into the water somewhere further up river. The undergrowth along the bank just here is pretty dense and there's no way anyone could have dragged her through and dumped her without leaving traces of her passage. I understand they had problems enough getting her out . . ."

Thanet nodded a greeting at the two ambulancemen waiting

near by before moving towards the body which was stretched out at the foot of a tree. Mallard's description had told him what to expect, but the bald facts had conveyed no image of the reality. The woman, even in death, had an interesting face: high cheek-boned, with jutting nose and powerful jaw. Deep vertical creases between her eyebrows hinted at bad temper, short sight or periods of intense concentration. A strong character, he guessed, and perhaps a difficult one. He noted the gash on the right temple, mentioned by Doc Mallard, and stooped to look more closely. Yes, it had been quite a nasty blow. Her long hair, he saw, had been dyed; it darkened perceptibly at the roots.

Closer proximity made him notice her jewellery too: large, tear-drop pearl earrings with gold mounts and a triple choker of pearls. If genuine, they would cost a packet. He glanced at her left hand. Yes, there was a wedding ring, plain gold, and a modest engagement ring with three small diamonds. On the same hand she wore two other rings, both apparently gold, one of a twisted rope design, the other elaborately chased. And on her right hand she wore a large diamond cluster which, again if genuine, would probably pay the deposit on a modest house.

Her shoes were missing but her clothes, too, were interesting: a quilted anorak over a peacock blue cocktail dress with a heavily beaded and sequinned top. A strange combination, surely? He pointed it out to Lineham.

"Hardly the sort of coat to wear over a dress like that."

Lineham frowned. "Perhaps she was entertaining at home and just slung the anorak on to go outside for some reason?"

"Possibly." Thanet glanced up at Trace, who was watching him. "Anything in the pockets?"

"Just a handkerchief and a set of car keys, sir."

"Car keys . . . Did you notice any cars belonging to members of the public back there, Mike?"

Lineham invariably noticed cars.

The sergeant shook his head. "No, sir."

"We'll check on the way back. So," mused Thanet, "no means of identification, so far."

"Sir?" It was Swift, looking uncomfortable.

"Yes?"

"I don't know whether I ought to say anything, as it's so vague, but . . . I'm sure I've seen this woman before, somewhere."

"But you can't remember where?"

"No sir. It's so frustrating. I've been racking my brains."

Swift stared down at the dead face, as if willing it to provide him with the information. He shook his head. "It's no good."

Thanet clapped him on the shoulder. "Don't worry, it'll come. Just put it out of your mind, that's the best way." He walked across to the river bank. To his right, a couple of hundred yards upstream, was the weir; eight or ten feet below him the swollen waters of the Sture, obscured by a dense tangle of undergrowth. Broken branches and trampled twigs confirmed Trace's words about the difficulties of retrieving the body. "This where you got her out?"

"Yes, sir." One of the uniformed PCs pointed. "If it hadn't been for that tree, she'd be miles down river by now, we reckon. Her hair had caught on that tangle of branches. Apart from that she was floating free."

The tree in question must have come down during the winter storms; it projected some fifteen feet into the river, its upper branches submerged and well out into the main current. Thanet could visualise the scene clearly, the body carried along by the swollen waters, accelerating as it approached the rush of water over the weir, the twisting tumble as it was carried over the lip into the churn of waters below, the sudden check as the woman's abundant hair caught in the web of branches lying in wait beneath the surface . . .

"Have you checked the bank upstream?"

"We had a quick look, sir, but there's no sign of a struggle, or of anything out of the ordinary."

"Good." But they would take another look all the same, thought Thanet. In any case, there was little point in cordoning off the area or setting up screens. He told the ambulancemen they could take the body away, then turned back to the uniformed men. "Who was first on the scene?"

"We were, sir."

Thanet addressed the older of the two patrolmen. "I assume it was a member of the public who discovered the body?"

"Yes, a woman out walking her dog, sir. She lives in the cottage on the corner just up there, where you turn off the Sturrenden road to come down to the car park. We thought it would be OK for her to wait at home to give her statement. She was pretty shaken."

"Fine. Right. So this is what we do."

Thanet despatched young Swift to take a statement from the witness, then ordered a further search of the river bank upstream, both above and below the weir.

"Any news, report back to me. DS Lineham and I are going back to headquarters."

Trudging back across the field Lineham said, "Looks as though we might have a problem with identification, sir."

"Mmm. I don't know. It wouldn't surprise me if it's not too long before someone reports her missing. She looks pretty well-heeled, don't you think? I should say she's come up in the world."

"What makes you say that?"

"Those rings. Modest engagement ring, the rest of her jewellery—if it's genuine—pretty expensive. Either her husband has had a successful career, or she has."

"She could have come downriver for miles," said Lineham.

Something in the Sergeant's tone made Thanet glance at him sharply. Now that he came to think about it, Lineham had been unusually subdued all morning. Normally the prospect of a possible murder investigation aroused all the Sergeant's enthusiasm.

"Anything the matter, Mike?"

"No. Why?"

Now Thanet was certain. He knew Lineham too well. But if the Sergeant didn't want to talk about it . . . "Just wondered . . . Anyway, I think we'd better take a good look at a map. Come on."

Back in the CID room they were still studying a large-scale map of the area when Pater, the Station Officer, came on the line. "I've got someone on the phone, sir, says his wife is missing. Sounds as though she could be the woman we pulled out of the river this morning."

"What's his name?"

"Salden, sir. Lives at Telford Green."

Which was in the right direction, upriver from Sturrenden on the river Teale, a main tributary of the Sture. "Put him on."

"Mr. Salden? Detective Inspector Thanet here. I understand your wife is missing?"

"Yes. I didn't find out till this morning, but her bed hasn't been slept in."

"I wonder, could you describe her for me?"

"She's five six, slim, long blonde hair, brown eyes . . ."

"How old is she?"

"Forty-five."

"I see. And do you happen to know what she was wearing last night?"

There was a pause. Then, "A deep blue cocktail dress, with those shiny things on the top . . . What d'you call them . . . ?"

"Sequins?"

"Yes, that's right, sequins." The man's voice suddenly sharpened. "Why?"

Thanet sighed. This was one of the worst parts of his job, and he especially hated having to communicate news like this over the telephone. But it would be unfair and rather pointless to keep Salden in suspense while they drove out to Telford Green.

"I'm sorry, Mr. Salden, but I'm afraid I might have some bad news for you."

TWO

"Here we are, sir."

For the last few minutes the two police cars had been running alongside the tall red brick wall of Telford Green Manor, where Salden lived, and now the gates had come into view. Lineham turned in past the little octagonal gatehouse and as arranged the other car continued on into the village.

Salden was due back shortly from a visit to the mortuary where, Thanet knew, he had confirmed that the dead woman was his wife. Thanet wasn't looking forward to the interview. Above all things he hated questioning the newly bereaved, having to probe at a raw wound when the witness was least able to bear the pain. It had to be done, however, and if this turned out to be a murder case . . . well, Thanet was as aware as the next man that in cases of domestic murder it is the husband who is the most likely suspect.

Meanwhile, he and Lineham had been doing their homework and studying a large-scale map of the Telford Green area. The main road to Sturrenden, which lay five miles to the east, ran at this point more or less parallel to the river Teale, which flowed into the Sture two miles downriver. The road to Telford Green, a small community with a population of around 500, cut away diagonally, crossing the Teale in the centre of the village. The Manor grounds were sandwiched between the two roads and ran right down to the Teale on the far side of the bridge in the village.

The rest of Thanet's team had been detailed to go into the centre of the village and work their way along the river bank, looking for signs of anything out of the ordinary.

The driveway to the Manor was about half a mile long, curving to the left between impressive mature oaks and copper beeches before straightening out in an avenue which afforded a fine view of the house, which was black and white, long, low and timbered.

Lineham whistled as it came into sight.

"They can't be short of a penny."

As this was the Sergeant's standard reaction to every dwelling bigger than a four-bedroomed detached, Thanet ignored it. What interested him much more was what was going on in front of it. A bulldozer was parked between a car and a police motorcycle, and a group consisting of a uniformed policeman, three men and two women seemed to be having a heated discussion. All six turned to look as Thanet's car approached.

"Wonder what's up?" said Lineham, parking neatly alongside the bulldozer.

They both got out.

"Detective Inspector Thanet, Sturrenden CID," said Thanet, addressing the company at large. "What's going on?"

They all started to speak at once, and Thanet raised a hand. "One at a time, please."

One of the women stepped forward. "Is it true?" she said. "About Mrs. Salden?"

She was around fifty, short and dumpy, with untidy fluffy brown hair, a round ingenuous face and unfashionably uptilted spectacles. Her clothes were drab—brown tweed skirt, cream blouse with Peter Pan collar and a shapeless brown speckled cardigan.

"Sorry," said Thanet, "you're . . . ?"

The woman flushed, an ugly brick red. "Edith Phipps," she said. "I'm Mrs. Salden's secretary. And this is Mrs. Pantry, the housekeeper. And will you please tell these men that in the circumstances nothing can be done, for the moment, now that . . . Is it true?" she repeated. "Is Mrs. Salden really . . . ?"

Thanet dragged his attention back from the fact that, without a single word being exchanged, he had taken an instinctive dislike to Mrs. Pantry the housekeeper. "Er . . . yes, Miss Phipps, I'm afraid it has been confirmed. Mrs. Salden is dead."

"Then I should think that settles it," said the uniformed PC to the other three men. "Sorry, sir, PC Kimberley. This is my patch, and Miss Phipps called me in to try and settle a dispute. These men are bailiffs. Mrs. Salden has an order for possession against a chap called Greenleaf who's been living in her woods and they've come to enforce it, as he's been refusing to move after the notice expired."

"And the bulldozer?" said Thanet.

"Greenleaf lives in a ramshackle sort of hut, sir, that he built himself. The bulldozer was to demolish it."

"And I'm simply saying," broke in Edith Phipps, "that they can't go on with this, now that the circumstances have changed." She was holding herself under a tight control, her hands, tightly clasped and white-knuckled, betrayed her agitation. "We don't know if Mr. Salden will still want to go ahead, and anyway he certainly won't feel like being bothered with all this, when he gets back, he'll be too upset. Please," she said to Thanet, "send them away. Otherwise there'll be so much trouble . . ."

"Trouble?" Thanet looked at PC Kimberley.

"The village people are opposed to the eviction, sir. A number of them are waiting down in the woods, near Harry's—Greenleaf's hut. I've sent to headquarters for reinforcements."

"Then I agree," said Thanet. "The eviction should be postponed. Mr. Salden will have too much on his mind to be bothered with this sort of problem."

The taller of the two bailiffs shrugged. "So long as you're willing to take the responsibility, Inspector."

"I am."

"OK." He glanced around, as if reassuring himself that there were plenty of witnesses, then said, "Come on then, Ted, we'll be off." And to the bulldozer driver, who had been standing by smoking a cigarette and looking bored, "You too, mate."

The bailiffs got into their car and drove off. The other man shrugged, took his cigarette out of his mouth, spat, replaced the cigarette and then climbed into the seat of his cab.

"Right," said Thanet. "If you'd just wait here, Kimberley, I'd appreciate a word with you later." He turned to the two women. "Shall we go indoors?"

His words were drowned by the full-throated roar of the bulldozer starting up, and he had to repeat them. Mrs. Pantry led the way through the heavy oak front door into a huge entrance hall open right up to the roof rafters. A wide, highly polished oak staircase led up to a galleried landing. The stone-flagged floor was incongruously adorned with a modern bordered carpet square in strident tones of orange and green.

"May I enquire which of you two ladies saw Mrs. Salden last?"

The women looked at each other.

"I did," said the housekeeper, reluctantly.

"What time would that have been?"

"About twenty to ten last night, when she left to visit her mother, in the village."

"I haven't seen her since yesterday afternoon," said the secretary.

"Right, well perhaps I could have a word with you later, Miss Phipps." He looked at the housekeeper. "Is there somewhere private, where we could talk?"

"We could go into the kitchen."

"Fine."

Thanet's sitting-room and dining-room would both have fitted comfortably into the kitchen, which had evidently been built on to the house in the days when there was no servant problem and there would probably have been eight or ten people sitting down for meals at the long pine table. A row of bells, each labelled with the name of a room, hung near the door. Apart from its size it would be a pleasant room to work in, with a chestnut brown Aga exuding a comforting warmth, a more than adequate supply of oak-faced units, and yellow and white checked curtains at the windows, which looked out on to the back garden. A smell of baking hung in the air.

They all sat down at one end of the table.

"Now then," said Thanet, "perhaps you could tell us about last night?"

While she talked he studied the housekeeper, seeking a reason for that apparently irrational recoil he had experienced upon being introduced to her. She was a big, raw-boned woman in her sixties, heavily built and . . . no, not clumsy, exactly . . . He sought the word. Graceless, yes, that was it, graceless in all her movements. Although she was wearing a flowered dress beneath a blue nylon overall she looked as though she would have been much more at home in trousers, her feet planted firmly apart on the quarry-tiled floor. Her hair was cropped, the ends chunky and uneven as though she had cut it herself, standing in front of a mirror. It was an unbecoming style, emphasising the strong masculine planes of her face, the heavily unplucked brows and beginnings of a moustache. Thanet wondered about the circumstances that had brought her here. Was she a live-in housekeeper or a daily, imported from the village? He asked her.

"Oh, I'm full-time, live-in."

"And how long have you been with the Saldens?"

"Eighteen months, now."

Thanet was intrigued by the note of bitterness in her voice and he glanced at Lineham. *Take over*. He and Mike had worked together for so long they were like an old married couple, Thanet reflected as Lineham went smoothly into action. In this sort of situation there was rarely a need for them to communicate in words and Lineham was used to having to take over without warning. Thanet knew that one can often learn more about a witness by watching and listening than by conducting the interview oneself.

Mrs. Salden's disappearance had apparently been discovered at 7:30 a.m. when Mrs. Pantry took up a tray of early morning tea. Her bed had not been slept in and although the housekeeper was surprised she was not really alarmed. She simply thought that Mrs. Salden must have spent the night at her mother's cottage in the village. It had happened before, from time to time.

"Where was Mr. Salden?"

"They have separate rooms." The housekeeper's mouth tightened in disapproval.

"So what did he say, when you told him that his wife's bed hadn't been slept in?"

"He seemed, well, confused, like. Put his hand to his forehead, as if he was trying to pull his thoughts together. He had just woken up, you know," she added defensively.

So Mrs. Pantry's loyalty lay with Salden rather than his wife, thought Thanet. Interesting, but scarcely surprising. Remembering the dead woman's strong, determined face, he couldn't really imagine her getting on well with this woman. What had soured the housekeeper so? he wondered. He tried to imagine her face transfigured by a smile or softened by tenderness, and failed. What a joyless life she must lead.

"In fact, he told me he hadn't got home till four this morning," she added.

"Where had he been?"

"At his mother-in-law's place. She died about half-past three."

"And his wife was there, too?"

"No. But I didn't know that then, did I?"

"Look," said the sergeant, "I'm getting a bit confused. Let's go back, start at the beginning. Were Mr. and Mrs. Salden both here last evening?"

"Early on, yes. They was having a dinner party, see."

Hence the beaded dress, thought Thanet.

"Many guests?" said Lineham.

"No, only two. Mr. Lomax and . . . *Miss* Trimble."

An interestingly scornful inflection, there, Thanet thought.

Lineham frowned. "Lomax . . . An unusual name . . . That

wouldn't be Mr. Douglas Lomax, the borough councillor, by any
chance?''

"Yes, that's right."

Well done, Mike.

"And Miss Trimble?"

"Lives in the village. She's always round here. Mrs. Salden
encouraged her." Mrs. Pantry gave a disapproving sniff and
brushed an imaginary piece of fluff off her nylon overall as if
dismissing the undesirable Miss Trimble as of no importance.

"She works here?"

A derisive snort. "She's a hairdresser in Sturrenden. That
unisex place at the bottom of the High Street."

It certainly sounded an ill-assorted dinner party, thought Thanet.
With an unusually small number of guests. A married couple
might invite another couple for an informal supper, but to give a
dinner party for a borough councillor and a hairdresser . . . He
scented intrigue. What had been going on?

"I see," said Lineham. "So what time did these guests
arrive?"

"Josie—Miss Trimble—came first. Bang on 7:30." *Unfashionably punctual,* her expression said. "Mr. Lomax got here
about a quarter of an hour later."

Mrs. Salden, it seemed, had come downstairs shortly after
Josie's arrival and had come into the kitchen to tell Mrs. Pantry
that dinner might have to be delayed, as the nurse had rung from
old Mrs. Carter's cottage to say that the old lady was asking for
Mr. Salden. He had left at once, having arranged to ring at about
eight to tell his wife what time he was likely to be back.

"Odd, wasn't it?" said Lineham. "Asking for him, rather
than for her daughter?"

A reproving look. "Mrs. Carter was very fond of Mr. Salden.
Like a son he was, to her."

"I see. So it wasn't unusual for the nurse to ring up and ask
him to go and see the old lady?"

"Well . . ." For the first time, Mrs. Pantry seemed unsure of
her ground. "I dunno. I can't say, I'm sure. I don't know what
half their phone calls is about. It's just that last night I had to
know, see, because of dinner getting spoiled."

"Quite . . . So what happened then?"

At eight o'clock Mr. Salden had rung to say that he would be
staying on at the cottage for a while, and that dinner should
proceed without him.

"Mrs. Salden didn't think of cancelling the dinner party?" said Lineham.

"Oh no. Why should she? She wasn't to know it'd be any different this time. Mrs. Carter has been ill for over a year, very ill . . . Cancer . . . There's been many, many times when they thought she wouldn't last the night, but she did. And when that keeps on happening, you get to expect just another false alarm, don't you?"

Lineham nodded. "True."

Mrs. Pantry had then served dinner, and as soon as they had finished the last course, at about half-past nine, Mrs. Salden had apparently rung the cottage, because a few minutes later she had come into the kitchen to say that she was just going to pop down to see her mother and to ask Mrs. Pantry to serve coffee in the drawing-room. She didn't expect to be long.

"The guests didn't leave at that point?"

A disapproving sniff. "Not they. Anyway," she added grudgingly, "as I was carrying the tray of coffee through I did hear Mrs. Salden ask that Josie to wait till she got back, as she especially wanted to speak to her."

"But she didn't come back?"

"Not to my knowledge. Mr. Lomax left about a quarter or twenty past ten, and I went to bed soon after."

"So you didn't hear either Mr. or Mrs. Salden come in, or Miss Trimble leave?"

"No. But she stayed till eleven, I believe."

"What makes you say that?"

"There's a note for Mr. Salden, on the table in the hall. I was dusting," she added defensively, "and couldn't help seeing it."

Lineham was looking at Thanet. *Anything else you want to ask?*

Thanet gave an imperceptible shake of the head and stood up. "This note, Mrs. Pantry. Is it still on the table in the hall?"

"I think so, yes."

"Let's go and see, shall we?"

He waited while she reluctantly dragged herself to her feet.

THREE

Mrs. Pantry led them to a long oak table set against the wall at the far side of the hall and picked up a piece of paper. "Here it is." She handed it to Thanet.

10:35. *Marcia*.
Bernard rang. Is staying on at Holly Cottage. Don't wait up.
                                        Josie.

P.S.
Waited until 11 p.m. then gave up. See you tomorrow,
after work.
                                        J.

Edith Phipps had been hovering near the stairs and now she approached them. "Excuse me, Inspector. I thought you'd like to know. Mr. Salden's home."

Thanet turned. "Oh, thank you. Where is he?"

"In the drawing-room. Through there." She pointed.

A knock at the door, then a second, brought no response. Thanet waited a moment longer, then lifted the latch and went in.

The room was long and low, ceiling and walls striped with ancient, honey-coloured oak beams infilled with white-painted plaster. Thanet didn't think much of Marcia Salden's taste; instead of the old rugs, mellow colours and antique furniture which the room demanded, it was furnished with a heavily patterned fitted carpet, modern dralon three-piece suite and—most incongruous of all—in the far corner, a cocktail bar. Salden was slumped in an armchair beside the inglenook fireplace. As they came in he raised his head in a dazed fashion and then put his hands on the arms of the chair preparatory to levering himself up, as if his legs alone were incapable of taking the strain.

"Please," said Thanet, trying not to stare too obviously at an enlarged photograph hanging on the wall near by. Surely that was Princess Anne shaking hands with Salden? "Don't get up."

He introduced himself and he and Lineham sat down.

"I understand that you have identified your wife?"

Salden nodded.

"I'm sorry."

Salden said nothing. He was considerably older than his wife, in his late fifties, Thanet guessed. Short and overweight, with round face, thinning hair and an aura of soft living, he would have passed unnoticed in any group of middle-aged business-men, his conventional dark suit, sober tie and well-polished shoes almost the uniform of his class and status. Only the dazed look of someone in shock would have singled him out.

"I don't understand," he said. For the first time his eyes focussed on Thanet's face. "What happened?"

Thanet shook his head. "That's what we're trying to find out. Do you feel you can answer a few questions?"

A nod.

"When did you last see your wife, Mr. Salden?"

Salden's forehead wrinkled, as if this were an impossibly difficult question. "I . . . Oh God, I can't seem to think straight. I'm sorry." He rubbed his hand across his eyes. "It must have been, oh, between a quarter and half-past seven last night."

"When you left to go down to the village, to visit your mother-in-law?"

"Yes."

"But you spoke to Mrs. Salden after that, I understand."

Salden stared at Thanet. "Did I? Oh, yes, you're right, I did. On the phone. I rang to tell her not to hold dinner for me. We had guests, you see."

"You were sufficiently worried about your mother-in-law not to want to leave her?"

"Well, it was partly that. But she'd been asking for me, and when I got to the cottage she was asleep. I thought I'd better wait until she woke up. Over these last few months there's been little enough we could do for her except be there, when she wanted us."

"Yes, I see. But you spoke to your wife again later, I believe?"

"Did I?" repeated Salden. He frowned, shook his head. "No I didn't. I'm sure I didn't."

"Didn't she ring the cottage herself, soon after half-past nine?"

"Ah, I see what you mean. Yes, Mrs. Pantry told me . . . No, she must have spoken to Nurse Lint. I'd gone out, by then."

"But I understood you stayed with your mother-in-law until she died, in the early hours of this morning."

"Yes, I did. But I went out for a walk, earlier. Just for some fresh air . . ."

"So you didn't see your wife, when she went down to the cottage, after dinner?"

"No. Nurse Lint told me she'd left shortly before I got back."

"And then you decided to stay on at the cottage."

"That's right. It seemed to me that my mother-in-law had taken a turn for the worse, so I rang home to tell Marcia—my wife—not to wait up for me. But she hadn't arrived back, so I left a message with Josie—Josie Trimble, one of our guests."

"You wouldn't have expected her to want to come back down to the cottage herself, to be with her mother?"

"No. It was my turn, you see. Win—my mother-in-law—had cancer, the lingering sort, and over the last few months we've both spent many nights at the cottage, thinking that she wouldn't last until morning. In the end we arranged that we'd take it in turns to sit with her. I assure you that my wife did everything possible to make her mother's life as comfortable as she could. She even got her a full-time nurse, to live in . . ."

"Please, Mr. Salden . . . I wasn't criticising your wife, merely trying to understand what happened last night. So you're saying that she left your mother-in-law's house at—what time?"

"I'm not sure. Nurse Lint would be able to tell you, I expect. Before I got back from my walk at about half-past ten, anyway."

"And how would she have got there?"

Salden frowned. "Well, normally she would have gone by car. But there must be something wrong with it. It's still in the garage. It was the first thing I checked this morning, when we found she was missing, and I tried it. It wouldn't start."

"These keys were in her pocket."

Salden leaned forward to look at them. "Yes, those are hers. So she must have decided to walk. It only takes a few minutes to get to the village, cutting across by the footpath. And I noticed the torch was missing from her car."

A footpath . . . "Does it run near the river, at any point?"

"Yes. It emerges into the village just beside the bridge."

Salden's gaze suddenly became blank, fixed. His mouth quivered. Then slowly, almost imperceptibly at first, the contours of his face began to blur and slacken. His eyes glistened, then tears began to spill out and trickle down his cheeks.

"Mr. Salden . . ."

Salden gave no sign of having heard. The silent tears continued to run unchecked down the plump, quivering cheeks and then, abruptly, his face contorting into a gargoyle mask of grief, he dropped his head into his hands and began to sob, a harsh, broken, ugly sound.

Any further questioning of Salden would have to wait for the moment. Thanet glanced at Lineham then rose and crossed to lay a consoling hand on the man's shoulder. After all these years in the force he still found the sight of naked grief hard to bear.

In the hall Mrs. Pantry was just answering the front door. "Oh, Mr. Fothergill. Do come in."

"Thank you." The small, wiry figure of a man in his late twenties stepped briskly into the hall. He was wearing corduroys, a tweed sports jacket and a clerical collar. "Is this true, what Jack Kimberley tells me? That Mrs. Salden has been drowned?"

The vicar had presumably run into PC Kimberley outside.

The housekeeper nodded.

Thanet came forward. "I'm afraid so. I'm Detective Inspector Thanet of Sturrenden CID, and this is Sergeant Lineham."

Mrs. Pantry quietly withdrew.

"Richard Fothergill. Vicar of Telford Green." He extended a hand and Thanet shook it.

"I'd just come to offer my condolences to Mrs. Salden, on her mother's death. But this . . . This is terrible. Terrible." The thin mobile face was clouded with genuine distress. "First Mrs. Hammer, then Mrs. Carter, now Mrs. Salden. Three deaths in one week . . ."

"Mrs. Hammer?"

"An old lady who lived in the village. She'd been failing for some time, like Mrs. Carter, Mrs. Salden's mother. But Mrs. Salden . . . This is terrible," he repeated. "What happened?"

"She was pulled out of the river at Donnington Weir this morning. The police surgeon thinks she must have gone in some time last night. More than that we don't know, as yet."

"And Bernard . . . Mr. Salden? How is he? How is he taking it?"

"Badly, by the look of it. He seems very distressed. I'm glad you've come, perhaps you'll be able to help him."

"Of course. I'll call the doctor, if necessary. And between us

Edith Phipps and I will be able to manage the administration to do with his mother-in-law's death, arrange for the undertakers to come and remove her body and so on. Where is he?''

"In the drawing-room . . .''

Thanet watched the vicar knock softly on the door and go in, then turned to Lineham. "Did you notice where Miss Phipps disappeared to, Mike?''

"In there." The Sergeant nodded at a door on the opposite side of the hall.

"Right. Look, give these keys to Kimberley and ask him to see if he can get Mrs. Salden's car started. Tell him I want to talk to him after I've seen Miss Phipps. Then join me.''

"Right, sir.''

Thanet crossed the hall and knocked at the door Lineham had indicated.

"Come in.''

FOUR

It was another beautiful room, with leaded lights, huge fireplace and oak-panelled walls. Thanet guessed that it had once been a dining-room, or a library, perhaps. Now it had been downgraded to an office, and Edith Phipps, surrounded by all the paraphernalia of a thriving business, was seated at a modern desk using a computer.

The desk looked strangely askew, thought Thanet. Then he realised why: there was a second desk in the room, Marcia Salden's, presumably, and Miss Phipps had pushed hers into a position where she would no longer permanently have it in her field of vision.

She rose, looking apprehensive, as Thanet came in, and he waved her back to her seat. "Please . . ."

He crossed to the window and stood with his back to the room gazing out. The avenue of tall trees was immediately ahead, and to the left there was a fine view across sweeping lawns flanked with shrub borders to parkland dotted with mature specimen trees. Over to the extreme right was a wood.

Thanet nodded towards it. "That where Harry Greenleaf lives?"

Miss Phipps looked surprised at the unexpected question. "Yes."

"How long has he been there?"

"About ten years, I suppose. He just sort of, well, materialised. One day we just heard he was living there, and he's been there ever since. Mr. Gentry—the former owner of the Manor—didn't mind."

"There was no formal tenancy agreement?"

"Oh no, nothing like that."

"I see. And the Saldens, I understand, have been here only eighteen months or so."

"That's right."

25

"Which is why local feeling is so strongly on his side? I suppose people feel he has a prior claim, so to speak."

Miss Phipps hesitated. "It's not that, exactly. It's difficult to explain, really. I suppose they feel that Harry isn't doing anyone any harm and there's no reason why he shouldn't be left in peace. He keeps himself to himself, seems quite content with his chickens and his goat . . . And I suppose people feel sorry for him, too."

"Why?"

"He was in some sort of accident . . . A fire . . . Nobody knows the details. But it must have been a bad one. He had to have plastic surgery, and the result is . . . Well, I think he's probably pretty self-conscious about it. People can understand him wanting to live like a hermit . . ."

"So why was Mrs. Salden so determined to evict him?"

Miss Phipps shook her head. "I'm not sure."

"You must have some idea, surely?" He glanced at the other desk. "As her secretary you'll have spent a good deal of time together. She must have talked to you about it?"

There was a knock at the door. It was Lineham.

"Sit down, Sergeant. We were just talking about Harry Greenleaf." Thanet sat down himself, in one of the chairs provided for visitors, swivelling it around so that he was facing her.

"Yes, she did, of course." Miss Phipps was leafing through some papers. "But she never actually told me why she was so keen to get rid of him. You might like to see this." She held out a single sheet. "I typed it yesterday afternoon."

Thanet took the paper but did not look at it immediately. "She may not have told you, but I suspect you had a pretty shrewd idea . . . ?"

Miss Phipps lowered her eyes, gave a self-deprecating little smile and began to fiddle with a loose thread on one of the buttons of her cardigan. "Well . . ."

Thanet waited.

She darted a brief, assessing glance at him. "It's only a guess, mind . . ."

Thanet gave an understanding nod.

"I think," she said, abandoning the button and meeting Thanet's gaze squarely, "I *think* it was because . . . Marcia liked to be in control, you see. She liked things to go her way . . . I think the fact that Harry was living on her land, cocking a snoot at her, so to speak, if you'll forgive the expression . . . She didn't like it. He was a, well, a thorn in her flesh."

Thanet was nodding. "Yes, I see . . . Thank you." He glanced down at the paper in his hand. It was a carbon copy of a letter from Marcia Salden to Harry Greenleaf pointing out that it was now two weeks past the date when he should have left her land and informing him that she had taken steps to enforce the court order. Bailiffs would therefore arrive to evict him tomorrow morning and they would be accompanied by a bulldozer which would demolish the hut in which he lived.

"How would she have got this to him? Did the postman deliver?"

Miss Phipps looked amused, displaying an irregular and mis-shapen set of teeth. "Oh no. I shouldn't think Harry ever has any letters. No, Marcia—Mrs. Salden—was going to walk down and give him the news in person. I typed the letter so that, if he were out, she'd be able to leave it there for him to see. She wasn't taking any chances that he could claim he hadn't been informed."

"Why do it herself? Why not send someone else?"

Miss Phipps shrugged. "No idea. Except that getting rid of Harry had become something of an obsession with her."

"So when did she intend going down?"

"After tea, yesterday afternoon."

"Do you know if she did?"

"No. But I assume so. If Marcia said she was going to do something, she did it."

Interesting overtones there, thought Thanet. A hint of—what? Suppressed emotion of some kind, certainly. "Are you thinking of anything specific?"

"Oh no. No. But this business with Harry Greenleaf was typical. If she set her mind on something, nothing would sway her."

The denial had been too swift, too emphatic. There was more, Thanet could tell. He was about to pursue the matter when she distracted him by adding, "She's always been the same."

"What do you mean? Did you know her before she moved into the village?"

Edith Phipps gave a superior, knowing smile. "I certainly did. I can see you don't know . . . What you said just now about the Saldens being relative newcomers wasn't strictly true. Not as far as Marcia was concerned, anyway. She was a local girl, born and bred in one of those little terraced cottages next to the pub in Telford Green. We went to school together. The village school . . ." She paused, watching him to gauge the effect of what she was telling him. "Yes, Marcia certainly came up in the world, didn't she? But then, she always said she would. Take this house, for instance . . . She always loved it, admired it, from a distance. I think that's why she cultivated me, as a friend. I had access to the grounds, you see, because of my father . . . He was head gardener here, in the days when there were proper gardens, extensive glass houses and so on. We lived in the gatehouse—still do. Mr. Gentry let us stay on, my mother and I, when Father died. Marcia never got tired of wandering around the gardens. She'd lie for hours in the grass, just gazing at the house . . . Mrs. Gentry complained about it once, to my father, and after that we were careful to keep out of sight. We weren't allowed indoors, of course, except for the kitchen . . . Marcia always said she'd live here one day, and I just used to laugh at her. But she did, didn't she? That's what I mean about determination."

"So how did she bring about this dramatic change in her circumstances?" Thanet already had a good idea of what she would say. DC Swift had remembered where he had seen Marcia Salden before—in a TVS series on success stories of the South-east.

"She and Bernard own a chain of health food shops. They started with one, back in 1963, now they have a chain, all over the South-east. Marcia foresaw the health food boom, she had an almost uncanny ability to see which way the wind would blow tomorrow, as far as business was concerned. Together with an eye for an opportunity, when it presented itself, and a tremendous capacity for hard work . . ." Edith shrugged. "She was a very successful businesswoman, believe me."

"Would you say she was ruthless?"

"Oh yes, undoubtedly."

And there was no love lost between you, thought Thanet. He would be willing to bet that Edith Phipps had at some time been one of the victims of that ruthlessness.

"Ruthless people tend to make enemies," he said. "Did Mrs. Salden?"

She hesitated, and a wary look crept into her eyes. "Why do you ask?"

"We have to take into account the possibility that her death may not have been an accident."

Thanet watched a slow tide of colour creep up Edith Phipps's neck and into her face. She took out a handkerchief and pressed it against her upper lip. Did that flush have any significance? Thanet wondered, or was she going through the menopause? She was the right age.

"You're not implying that . . . that it could have been murder?"

Thanet admired her for managing to bring the word out. Most people shied away from actually saying it.

There was a knock at the door. It was Mrs. Pantry, with a tray.

"I thought you might like some coffee."

"Very kind of you."

The housekeeper poured in silence, handed the cups around and was about to leave when Thanet thought of a question he wanted to ask her.

She shook her head. No, Mrs. Salden hadn't come back into the house last night to say the car wouldn't start. Mr. Salden had tried it this morning, though, it was the first thing he thought of checking, and he'd said he couldn't get it to go.

"Thank you."

As soon as she had gone Edith Phipps said, "Inspector?"

"Officially," said Thanet, "this is a suspicious death, and we are treating it as such. It could be accident, it could be suicide, or it could be murder. We shan't know for sure until after the *post mortem*, and we can't afford to waste the interim period doing nothing."

"But you must have some reason, for thinking it might have been . . ."

"I'm sorry, I can't tell you any more."

"Marcia would never have committed suicide. Not in a thousand years."

"That's what people usually say."

"But it's true. If you'd ever met her you'd agree with me."

"Perhaps. But if so, we're down to two alternatives, aren't we? Could Mrs. Salden swim?"

She shook her head. "No. She hated the water."

She fell silent, staring at him, eyes blank. If only he could have known what she was thinking . . .

"So one of the things we have to do is try to build up some sort of picture of Mrs. Salden's movements yesterday. Perhaps you could help us there?"

Edith gave her head a little shake, as if to tug her attention back to the present, and reached for a book at the edge of her desk. "Yes, of course. This is Mrs. Salden's appointment book."

"May I see?"

She handed it to him. It was a conventional desk diary. Some of the entries were made in a neat, precise script, some in a bold scrawl. He glanced quickly through it. Marcia Salden seemed to have led a very busy life.

The previous day held several entries. In the morning there were three: Tunbridge Wells, Tonbridge and Sevenoaks, all bracketed together. At 12:30 she had met someone called J for lunch. The afternoon was blank except for the scrawl: Deliver letter Greenleaf.

Edith Phipps explained. Marcia made a point of visiting all her shops at least once a fortnight. It kept her managers on their toes, she said. Accordingly, every morning was spent in a different area of the South-east and yesterday had been the turn of Tunbridge Wells, Tonbridge and Sevenoaks. J was Janet, the manageress of the Sevenoaks shop. Marcia always called on the shops in a different order, and made a practice of taking the manager of the last shop visited in the morning out to lunch. It made for good public relations, she believed, as well as keeping her up to date with local problems. In the afternoons Marcia would work here, dealing with administration.

"And Mr. Salden? You seemed to imply just now that they owned the businesses jointly. Does he take an active part, or is he a sleeping partner?"

"Oh active. He deals with the financial side—he's a chartered accountant. There's plenty for him to do, believe me."

"I can imagine. We must be talking about substantial sums of money."

"There's an annual turnover of just over £2.5 million."

"I see." He also saw that as sole owner Bernard Salden would now be a wealthy man.

"Husbands and wives don't always find it easy to work together," he said cautiously.

"True. But Marcia and Bernard seemed to get along pretty well. I think because they had clear demarcation lines, and didn't actually spend much time together during the day. Bernard has a separate office."

"Did they never disagree about policy?"

She hesitated. "Not usually, no."

"But sometimes?"

"Not as far as the business was concerned, no."

"But in other ways?" he pressed.

Colour stained her neck and face yet again, and once more she dabbed a folded handkerchief at her upper lip and at the sides of her nose with quick, almost furtive movements.

"I'm sorry," she said primly. "I don't mind answering questions about the business, but I'm not prepared to talk about their private life."

"Even if it does turn out to be murder?"

"If it does . . . then I'll have to reconsider, won't I?"

"Very well . . . Though there is one question about Mr. Salden I shouldn't think you'd mind answering . . . Sheer curiosity on my part, really . . . There's a photograph in the drawing-room. Is that Princess Anne, shaking hands with him?"

She smiled and the atmosphere in the room lightened, as Thanet had hoped it would. "Yes. Bernard is heavily involved in children's charities and as I'm sure you know the Princess Royal is chairman of the Save the Children Fund. The picture was taken at a fund-raising event last year."

"I see. Thank you. Well, I think there's just one other matter, Miss Phipps . . . You yourself last saw Mrs. Salden—when?"

"At half-past five yesterday afternoon, when I finished work."

"How did she seem?"

"Fine. She said she was just going to have a cup of tea, then she was going to walk down and see Harry Greenleaf."

"And you went home to the gatehouse."

"That's right."

"You live with your mother, you said?"

"Yes. She is elderly and unable to look after herself. It's very convenient, living so close, it means I can pop home in the lunch hour to see her. We were very lucky, being able to stay on when Mrs. Gentry sold the house to Marcia, after Mr. Gentry died. I used to do secretarial work for him and Marcia needed a secretary on the spot. There I was, so . . ." She shrugged. "She sort of inherited me, so to speak."

"Very convenient for both of you."

"Quite."

"Did you find it difficult, working for an old school friend?"

She looked surprised. "No, not at all . . . I was only too thankful to be able to stay on."

But there was a reservation in her voice. What was she holding back?

Thanet rose. "Well, I think that really is all for the moment, Miss Phipps." He and Lineham handed her their empty cups and she put them on the tray.

As they walked to the door Thanet said, "Mrs. Pantry tells me she has been with the Saldens for about eighteen months. I assume they engaged her when they moved in."

"That's right, yes."

"She seems . . . Well, I know we couldn't expect her to be

very cheerful this morning, in view of what's happened, but she does strike me as being a rather unhappy person.''

Miss Phipps grimaced. "Yes, she is. She had rather a bad time of it before she came here.''

"Oh?''

"I believe her husband left her. It was a tied cottage and she found herself homeless. She went to live with an unmarried daughter, who then got married. The new son-in-law and Phyllis—Mrs. Pantry—didn't get on, so she decided to find a live-in job as housekeeper—she'd trained as one when she was younger. I believe she had one or two jobs before coming here. She may seem a bit, well, dour, on first acquaintance, but she's all right when you get to know her.''

They had reached the door and Thanet turned. "Oh, there was just one other point . . .''

"Yes?''

"As you live in the gatehouse . . . When you're at home, I suppose you must be aware of the comings and goings at the Manor?''

"To a certain extent, I suppose, if I happen to be in the kitchen, which looks out on to the drive. But there's quite a lot of traffic noise from the road to the village, you can't always distinguish.''

"I can imagine. But in the evening . . .''

"It's pretty quiet, yes.''

"And you were in, last night?''

"Oh yes.''

"All evening?''

She nodded.

Had there been the merest hesitation there?

"So, did you hear any vehicles at all entering or leaving the Manor drive last night?''

She considered, head on one side. "I saw Bernard—Mr. Salden—drive out just before half-past seven. I was in the kitchen, washing up after supper. And then I saw Mr. Lomax's car drive in, about twenty minutes later. But that's all.''

Thanet was more convinced than ever that she was holding something back.

FIVE

In the hall Lineham said, "What now, sir?"

What Thanet would really have liked was a good, long discussion with Lineham about his impressions so far, but that would have to wait. "Down to the . . ."

"Oh, Inspector . . ." Edith Phipps had appeared at the door of the room they had just left. "I forgot to tell you . . . I hope you don't mind, but I took it upon myself to telephone Nurse Lint and tell her about Mrs. Salden. I thought she ought to know, because of Mrs. Carter, and the arrangements that have to be made."

"I believe the Vicar is going to have a word with you about that. What, exactly, did you tell Nurse Lint?"

"Only that Mrs. Salden has been drowned. And I asked her to stay on at the cottage until the undertakers have been."

Thanet smiled. "Good. That's fine."

Edith Phipps gave a satisfied little nod and retreated into her office.

"You were saying . . . ?" said Lineham.

"Mmm? Ah, yes. That I think we ought to take a stroll across to the wood."

"Take a look at this chap Greenleaf?"

"Amongst other things, yes. And I'd like to see the lie of the land, especially around the river, and have a chat with Kimberley to get some local background . . ."

PC Kimberley was waiting patiently outside. He was in his early thirties, tall and well-built, with thick straight fair hair and broad flattened features. At first sight he could well have been taken for a lingering shade of the archetypal rural PC Plod, but Thanet had already noted the alertness of those sharp blue eyes and guessed that there was more to Kimberley than first impressions conveyed.

"Been having some interesting thoughts, Kimberley?" said Thanet.

Kimberley grinned. "Some, sir."

"Then I'd like to hear them. Manage to get that car started?"

"No, I think the battery's flat." He handed the keys back to Thanet.

"Hmm. Well, it seems that Mrs. Salden was last seen alive just after half-past nine last night, when she left to go to the village to see her mother—who, incidentally, died in the early hours of this morning."

"Yes, I'd heard, sir. She's been very ill for some time."

"So I understand. Anyway, Mr. Salden seems to think that if Mrs. Salden couldn't start her car she'd have walked to the village via a footpath. A torch is missing from her car and of course she'd be familiar with the terrain."

"Probably, sir. It wouldn't take much more than five minutes."

"Does this footpath run anywhere near where Harry Greenleaf lives?"

"Depends what you mean by near. He lives in that wood over there. The footpath runs direct to the village. I suppose it passes within, oh, let me see, perhaps four hundred yards of Harry's hut, as the crow flies."

"I see. Fine. So we'll be able to kill two birds with one stone. Come on."

"You want me to come too, sir?"

"Of course. To show us the way . . . And give me a chance to pick your brains, as well."

Kimberley fell in alongside them with alacrity.

"You lead the way, then."

"Right."

Kimberley set off at a brisk pace along the broad path in front of the house and across the lawn beyond. Thanet inhaled appreciatively. It was good to be out in the open air on such a fresh spring morning. Fallen blossom from a flowering cherry tree lay scattered like confetti on the grass, a few tenacious clusters of the delicate sugar-pink petals still clinging obstinately to the branches which here and there were breaking into leaf.

Beyond the lawn Kimberley cut around the end of a border of tall shrubs and they came to a high hawthorn hedge on which the buds were just bursting into tender green, the dense thicket of spiky branches broken by a small flimsy rustic gate made of split chestnut palings and secured only by a metal hook and eye. Kimberley unhooked the latter and pushed it open.

"This is the footpath, sir."

"Don't think much of their security," muttered Lineham as they stepped through. The path was of beaten earth and although muddy after yesterday's rain was well-maintained, clear of weeds and encroaching branches. On the other side of it a stretch of open grass sloped gently up to the edge of the wood.

Thanet glanced to the right. "I presume the footpath goes across to the Sturrenden road?"

"That's right, sir."

"Used a lot, is it?"

Kimberley grimaced. "That's a bit of a sore point locally. Mrs. Salden has just closed it to the public."

"Can she do that? I thought it was virtually impossible to close a public right of way."

"Well, it was all gone into, as you can imagine. Apparently, if a specific route has been in regular use for in excess of twenty years, then that's it, a public right of way is presumed, *unless* there is a notice on the path saying Private, or Permitted Path. In which case, permission can be withdrawn at the owner's discretion."

Thanet turned left and the others fell in, one on each side. "I gather there is such a notice?"

Kimberley sighed. "Oh yes. There's a rotting signboard at each end. They must have been there since the year dot. I don't think anyone's really noticed them for years but of course, when this business came up, we couldn't deny that they were there, even if they were barely legible. There was quite an uproar about it in the village, they even had a public meeting. There's no bus service through Telford Green any more, so people without cars have to walk to the Sturrenden road to catch a bus into the town. This footpath saves a good mile or more."

"And now you say they're up in arms over this Harry Greenleaf business?"

"They certainly are. They can't see any reason why Harry should be made to go. He's absolutely harmless, never bothers anybody, just seems perfectly content to keep himself to himself. You'd hardly know he was there, really . . . To be honest, sir, Mrs. Salden seems to have managed to stir up an awful lot of bad feeling in the time she's been here."

"You're not telling me there's more?"

"Where would you like me to start?" said Kimberley with a grin.

"Good grief." Thanet waved a hand. "Wherever you like."

"Well, the latest thing is Telford Green Farm."

"What about it? Where is it?"

"Ah, well, that's the point. It's where it is that's caused the trouble." Kimberley came to a halt and pointed. "You see those farm buildings, over the other side of the river?"

Thanet and Lineham looked. The hawthorn hedge on their left had ended abruptly, giving way to open parkland across which in the distance could be seen the avenue of trees leading up to the Manor. Half a mile ahead of them in the shallow valley of the Teale lay the village of Telford Green, its mellow roofs strung out on both sides of the old stone bridge for which the footpath was obviously heading. It was almost certainly somewhere along this stretch of water that Marcia Salden had gone in. To the right the wood which Thanet by now thought of as "Harry's Wood" curved gently away, petering out a couple of hundred yards short of the river. From here this was glimpsed merely as a sparkle of fast-flowing water between the trees and shrubs which lined its banks. In the open space between woodland and river was a small group of perhaps ten to fifteen people, all staring up in Thanet's direction. This, he realised, must be the welcoming committee prepared for the bailiffs, on Harry Greenleaf's behalf. Kimberley's request for reinforcements had been met; two uniformed policemen were standing by.

Thanet followed the direction of Kimberley's pointing finger. On the far side of the river, opposite Harry's Wood and between the line of village houses and the water, was a cluster of farm buildings surrounded by neatly fenced fields—empty fields, Thanet realised. The place, in fact, looked deserted.

"Old Mr. Tiller died about six months ago," said Kimberley, "and Mrs. Tiller sold up. Went to live with her daughter the other side of Sturrenden . . . You couldn't blame her, of course, for taking what she could get."

"What do you mean?" said Lineham.

"Well, the village has never had a hall and they've been fund-raising for years and years. Apparently, if a village has no hall the County Council will help out with grants and loans to build one, but you've got to have a certain amount of money in hand and of course you've also got to have the land on which to put it, first. So the Parish Council negotiated with Mr. Tiller for a piece of land behind the pub—the Crooked Door, look, you can see it there, right next to the bridge. It would have been an ideal spot, right in the centre of the village. But before the negotiations were complete Mr. Tiller died. Everyone naturally

thought that the deal would still go ahead, but unfortunately that
was where Mrs. Salden stepped in. As soon as the farm was put
up for sale she offered to buy it well above the asking price, on
one condition—that Mrs. Tiller also sell her the piece of land
earmarked for the village hall.'' Kimberley shrugged. ''I suppose, as I said, you couldn't blame the old lady for accepting. It
wasn't as if she was going to go on living here any more—and,
to tell you the truth, I think she was in such a daze she didn't
really realise what she was doing, it all happened so fast. Anyway, you can imagine how people in the village felt, when they
heard.''

Two people, a man and a woman, had detached themselves
from the group by the river and started up the slope towards
Thanet. The man was carrying something bulky.

''But why was Mrs. Salden so determined to get that one little
bit of land?'' said Lineham.

''Ever heard of Naboth's vineyard, Mike?'' said Thanet with a
grin.

''She made it quite clear why she wanted it, sir. She hoped to
get planning permission to build over the entire farm. The village
hall, she said, would lower the value of the properties—there's
always a certain amount of noise from discos, cars starting up
late at night and so on . . . A delegation from the Parish Council
went to see her, and she was quite blunt about it. Wouldn't
budge an inch, apparently.''

''She certainly seemed to have the knack of making herself
unpopular, didn't she?'' Had this knack extended to her personal
relationships? Thanet wondered. If Marcia Salden had trampled
carelessly all over the feelings of those closest to her in the same
way as she had totally disregarded the local climate of opinion, it
wasn't perhaps surprising that she had ended up in the river.

''Went out of her way looking for it, if you ask me,'' said
Lineham.

The bulky object, Thanet now saw, was a hand-held television
camera. No doubt TVS had been told of the eviction and had
come along to film the fun. There was no way that the film unit
van could have gained access to the site of Harry's hut, he
realised, without entering the Manor gates and driving across the
open parkland of the Manor grounds. No doubt these two had
decided to proceed on foot via the footpath from the bridge. For
the first time he wondered how, if the hut was deep in the
woods, the bulldozer would have got to it.

''Anyway, she'd never have got planning permission to build

there, surely," Lineham went on. "I mean, it's prime agricul-
tural land and outside the village envelope . . ."

"Hmm. I don't know," said Thanet. "Controls are not quite
as strict as they used to be. And I remember my mother-in-law
telling me that someone she knew of had got a planning permission everyone had thought was out of the question because he
had donated part of the land to the community for a village hall
and children's playground."

"You think that's what Mrs. Salden might have had in mind?"
said Kimberley.

"Could be why she was so insistent on wanting that bit of
land too. If she could swing the larger issue by appearing to be a
public benefactor . . ."

Lineham was looking puzzled. "I don't get it."

"Well," said Thanet, "as I understand it, in order to get
planning permission you have to get first the approval of the
Parish Council, then of the Borough Council. I'm just saying
that maybe Mrs. Salden was determined to have the village hall
site included in her purchase of the farm because she wanted
later to be able to offer it as a gift to the Parish Council as an
inducement to them to approve her application for planning
permission on the rest of the land."

"I see what you mean," said Lineham. "It would certainly be
worth her while financially. How big is the farm?"

"Three hundred acres," said Kimberley.

Lineham whistled. "If she paid two thousand an acre and
got—what?—a hundred thousand an acre, with planning permission . . ."

"Big money," said Thanet. It had just occurred to him.
Wasn't Lomax chairman of the borough planning committee?
Surely, if Marcia had been hoping to influence him, she would
have been more discreet than to invite him openly to her house?
Suddenly that odd dinner party began to make rather unpleasant
sense.

The girl reporter, wearing what she no doubt considered to be
appropriate country gear of green wellies, Burberry and a checked
scarf which matched the lining of her raincoat, reached them
first.

"Tessa Barclay, TVS. Can you tell us what's happening?" She
had selected PC Kimberley as being in charge, no doubt because
of his uniform.

Perhaps, thought Thanet with amusement, she thought that he
and Lineham were bailiffs. She was a good candidate for the

small screen, with excellent bone structure, winning smile and pleasant manner. She must be new. He knew most of the regular TVS *Coast to Coast* reporters.

The photographer came puffing up beside her. "Cor," he said, patting the flabby flesh which hung over the waistband of his trousers, "it really is time I started to lose some weight." He was older than the girl, in his forties, perhaps, and beginning to lose his hair.

The girl flashed him an impatient smile and turned back to PC Kimberley. "Can you?"

Kimberley glanced at Thanet, who hesitated. He didn't really want to find himself giving a television interview on the subject of Marcia's death just yet. On the other hand, the villagers down there were not going to disperse without being given a good reason why the eviction had, temporarily at least, been postponed. "There'll be no eviction today."

"Why is that—sorry, Mr. . . . ?"

Thanet sighed. "Detective Inspector Thanet, Sturrenden CID." He saw the hungry look flare in the girl's eyes as she scented news. She glanced at the man beside her and the camera swung up.

"What are you doing here, Inspector?"

He could give some evasive answer, of course, but she would no doubt find out about Marcia Salden later today in any case. And it was never wise to antagonise the media, particularly TVS, who were always very helpful towards the police, both in putting out bulletins when necessary and in *Police 5,* a weekly programme dedicated to solving crime by the reconstruction of past cases. "Mrs. Salden was found drowned this morning."

The girl glanced down the slope at the river. "Down there?"

"No, at Donnington Weir."

"It was Mrs. Salden who was going to evict Harry Greenleaf and bulldoze the little hut he built, and in which he has been living for ten years?"

She was spelling it out for her potential viewers, Thanet realised.

"Yes."

"And you suspect foul play?"

"We suspect nothing and no one at the moment. All cases of sudden death have to be investigated, as you know. We are merely trying to find out how it happened."

"And Mr. Salden has called off the eviction?"

"Mr. Salden is in no state to make any kind of decision, as

you can imagine, or to deal with the kind of problems that might have arisen if the eviction had gone ahead. I gave the authorisation for the eviction to be postponed.''

"Postponed . . . Then does that mean . . . ?''

"I'm sorry. I really can't say any more at the moment. Excuse me.''

Thanet set off down the slope at a brisk pace, Lineham and Kimberley following. The cameraman trotted alongside him on one side, the girl on the other, alternately speaking into the microphone and holding it out in front of his face.

"Who found the body, Inspector?''

"Where, exactly, was it found?''

"What time was it found?''

Thanet stopped, turned to face her. "Look, Miss Barclay . . .''

"Tessa,'' said the girl, showing very white teeth in a ravishing smile.

" . . . I really cannot release any more information at the moment. And I have a great deal to do, so . . .''

"OK.'' She shrugged, turning up her hands in a gesture of surrender. "I give in. If we could interview you later . . . ?''

"Ring my office, late this afternoon,'' said Thanet, privately resolving not to go anywhere near Headquarters at that time.

"Right.'' Another melting smile. "Thanks.''

She fell back, allowing Lineham and Kimberley to flank him once more.

Kimberley at once left the footpath and cut off diagonally down the slope. The villagers, Thanet noted, had disappeared. A minute or two later, he saw why. As he rounded the edge of the trees near the river he saw that to his right a long tongue of grassy meadow protruded into the wood. At its tip, some two hundred yards away where the trees began again, was a ramshackle wooden hut of tarred boards, with a corrugated iron roof. Harry's no doubt. And now he saw where the people had gone. They had obviously assumed that he and Lineham were bailiffs. Strung out across the width of the meadow, sitting cross-legged on the ground, hands linked, they were waiting in silent protest for the confrontation to begin. Here and there a hand-held notice sprouted: HANDS OFF HARRY; HAL'S OUR PAL; JUSTICE NOT LAW. Fleetingly, Thanet wondered how they had heard about the eviction. From Edith Phipps? From Marcia herself? (Unlikely, surely.) From Harry? For the first time he began to wonder what sort of man this was, that he could arouse such strong feelings of loyalty. Or was it simply that he had, by virtue of his peculiarly unfortunate circumstances, unwittingly enlisted the crackpots, the sensation-seekers and the misguided?

Thanet stopped, raised a hand in greeting to the two uniformed men waiting nearby and, cupping his hands around his mouth, called, "All right, you can go home now. The eviction's been postponed."

A buzz of excitement ran along the line, like lightning conducted through their linked hands. But no one moved.

"It's true." Thanet waved a hand. "You all know PC Kimberley. Ask him."

"Is it, Jack?" shouted one of the men in the middle of the line, a stringy man in his sixties, wearing (symbolically?) a combat jacket and ancient corduroys.

Kimberley nodded. "True enough."

Looks were exchanged, then the line broke up as people began to struggle to their feet.

Their self-appointed spokesman was the first to reach them.

"Why?" he demanded. "What made 'er change 'er mind? Get cold feet, did she?"

"You'll wish you hadn't said that, Dan," said Kimberley. He raised an eyebrow at Thanet, who nodded. "This is Detective Inspector Thanet, Sturrenden CID. Mrs. Salden is dead."

The word caused a sudden hush, and an uneasy exchange of glances. Most of the villagers, Thanet noted, were either pensioners or middle-aged women, with a sprinkling of presumably unemployed youths.

The man's hairy eyebrows met in a fierce frown. "Dead, you say?"

Kimberley nodded. "She was pulled out of the river at Donnington Weir this morning."

" 'Ow did it 'appen?"

"Your guess is as good as mine. But as Inspector Thanet says, there'll be no eviction today. You can all go home."

However anti-Marcia they had been, the news had subdued them and they began to drift off in twos and threes. The man called Dan, however, began to march purposefully off up the slope towards Greenleaf's hut.

"Just a moment," Thanet said.

The man halted. "I was only going to tell 'Arry. It does concern 'im, you know."

Thanet ignored the sarcasm. "I'll do it myself."

The man's lips tightened but he said nothing, turning away and hurrying to catch up with some of the others.

"Right, the excitement's over," said Thanet to the uniformed policemen. "You can get off back to Headquarters. Have you seen any of my team?"

"Only in the distance, working along the river bank."

"Where are they now, do you know?"

"They only came a short distance from the village, then turned back."

It looked as though they might have found something. "Tell them I'll be along shortly, will you? I just want a word with Greenleaf, first. Kimberley, I'd like you to stay with us for the time being."

"Sir . . ." said Kimberley as they started up the grassy slope to Harry's hut.

"What?"

"I just thought you might like to know . . ."

"Well? Come on, spit it out, man."

"I saw Mr. Salden last night."

Thanet stopped walking. "Oh, where?"

"In the pub. Must have been somewhere between half-past eight and nine."

"Was he alone?"

"Yes. Looked a bit down, I thought."

"Does he often go to the pub?"

Kimberley shrugged. "From time to time."

"By himself?"

"Usually. But he'll have a pint and a chat. Last night he . . . Well, he gave out the impression that he didn't want to be sociable. Nothing was said, but it was interesting that apart from saying hello, people gave him a wide berth. And I noticed he was drinking whisky. Doubles."

"Don't miss much, do you?"

Kimberley grinned. "Try not to, sir."

"He'd just have come from his mother-in-law's house," said Lineham. "Remember, he said he went out for a walk."

"Yes . . . Did anyone in the pub comment, Kimberley?"

The policeman shrugged. "I imagine they just assumed, as I did, that he was upset because of Mrs. Carter. It was common knowledge that he was very fond of her—his own mother's long dead, I believe—and she thought the sun shone out of his eyes, by all accounts."

"They wouldn't have thought he'd had a row with his wife?"

"No, I'm pretty sure not. I haven't heard any rumours in that direction."

"How long did he stay in the pub?"

"Not much more than twenty minutes, I'd say."

"And he had how many drinks?"

Kimberley thought. "Three."

Thanet turned and began walking up the slope again. "What's he like?"

"I don't know him that well, but he's pretty well liked in the village."

"Unlike his wife."

"Yes. I don't know if you realised, sir, but Mrs. Salden was a local girl."

"Miss Phipps told me."

"I think people found it difficult to accept her as lady of the manor, so to speak. And she made it worse by not making any attempt to enter village life. I mean, she didn't come to church or take part in any village events, or offer the Manor grounds for the village fête, or buy her groceries at the village shop . . . And of course, there's been all that trouble over the footpath and the village hall and now over Harry. Mr. Salden is a different matter—he's on the PCC, gives a hand at village events . . ."

"And patronises the village pub," Thanet said absentmindedly. His attention was now focussed on the hut, about twenty yards away.

Throughout the brief conversation with Kimberley he had been keeping an eye on the primitive structure, but had so far detected no sign of life. It was about fifteen feet long, the boarded wall punctuated only by a window festooned with what looked like an old army blanket. In front a neat little vegetable patch had been carved out of the meadow: weedless rows of spring cauliflowers and sprouting broccoli and a seedbed with a row of fluttering seed packets at one end stood as mute testimony to the care lavished upon it. Over to the left, tethered by a long rope to a stout post hammered into the ground, was a goat, and to the right of the hut was a wired-off enclosure where chickens scratched in the earth around a large chicken hut.

The door, which was on the right-hand side of the hut, facing the chickens, was shut and padlocked. They looked around, but there was no other entrance, the window was not made to open and any view of the interior was obscured by the blanket.

"He's gone, then," said Lineham.

Their eyes met, each knowing what the other was thinking. Had Harry left because of the bailiffs, or because he was implicated in Marcia's death?

Beside the door was a worm-eaten Windsor armchair with broken slats, its surface bleached grey by exposure to wind and rain. Thanet could imagine the old man sitting in it, gazing contentedly down the slope to the river and across to the rising land on the other side. His seemed a harmless enough existence. Why had Marcia been so determined to get rid of him?

SIX

"We think we've found where she went in, sir." Swift was looking very pleased with himself.

It was half an hour later. Thanet had decided that, in view of the fact that Harry no doubt knew the woods like the back of his hand, it would be a waste of time for just three of them to search for him, so they had retraced their steps to the footpath, then continued on to the village. Swift had come to meet them.

Ahead of them to the left of the bridge the high brick wall which edged the grounds of the Manor delineated the road to the village. At this end of the bridge, near an ominous gap in the parapet, the rest of Thanet's men were awaiting his arrival. A number of people, many of whom Thanet recognised as Harry Greenleaf's supporters, were lined up along the parapet at the far end, gaping at the policemen.

"I assume you're talking about the broken parapet." Thanet glanced at Kimberley. He had been impressed by the local man and was surprised and slightly disappointed that such an obvious possibility had not been put forward. Kimberley flushed and opened his mouth to speak, but Swift forestalled him.

"Yes, sir. A heavy lorry skidded into the wall in all that rain yesterday, apparently."

They had reached a short flight of stone steps leading up on to the road at the damaged end of the bridge, and Thanet stopped to take a good look. The parapet was of Kentish ragstone and a section about five feet long had been broken clean off, right down to road level. The chunk of masonry which had fallen out was visible in the river below.

"Hope it's not going to be another 'Did she fall or was she pushed?' case," muttered Lineham, gazing up at the gap.

He was referring, Thanet knew, to the Tarrant case, a murder they had solved the previous year in which the wife of an eminent local surgeon had fallen to her death from the balcony of her bedroom.

"Somewhat different circumstances, Mike."

Kimberley was now very much on the defensive. "Sir . . . I personally checked the safety precautions after the incident with the lorry yesterday. You can come and see for yourself. The Highways Authority put up a temporary barrier and promised to give priority to the repairs, to come back today if possible."

They climbed up on to the road.

"Look, there's a POLICE ACCIDENT sign, and a big DANGER sign on the road at both approaches to the bridge, warning lamps around the gap and a temporary barrier—"

Kimberley broke off, and it was obvious why. Two metal rods had been driven into the road, one on either side of the gap, and ropes had been strung between them, one at the top, one halfway up. The latter must have been carelessly attached; one end was trailing loose, exposing a three-foot gap.

"Not your fault," said Thanet, after a glance at Kimberley's appalled expression.

"I should have checked this morning."

"You had your hands full, with Harry Greenleaf's eviction. And the erection of the barrier was not your responsibility."

"All the same . . ."

Thanet squatted to examine the gap more closely. Halfway down the broken section of wall a solitary spike of rock stuck out, some five inches long. Caught in a split in it were some long blonde hairs and its tip was discoloured by a brownish stain. He peered down into the river below. At the edge of the water, at the bottom of the river bank, was a woman's brown walking shoe.

Marcia Salden's?

It certainly seemed likely that this was where she had met her death.

Thanet stood back and tried to visualise what had happened. Was it possible that it had been a simple accident? Surely not. Anyone walking across the bridge from the village towards the entrance to the footpath in the dark would obviously have to be careful, yes, but Marcia would have known of the danger; she would have seen the damage and the warning lights on her way to her mother's cottage. Unless the accident had happened while she was there, of course. He turned to Kimberley and asked the obvious question.

"At 4 p.m. yesterday afternoon, sir."

"And it took you how long to get it sorted out?"

"A couple of hours."

So the temporary barriers would have been up by about six. Thanet glanced at Lineham. "What do you think, Mike?"

"I really don't see how she could have fallen in by accident. Those red lights are a good three feet out into the road."

"She could have stepped back to avoid a car?"

"Only a lunatic would drive fast over this bridge, especially at the moment, with all these warning signs."

"Oh come on, Mike. There are plenty of lunatics about, as we know too well."

"True. But surely anyone walking across this bridge and knowing about that gap in the parapet is going to be hyper-careful. He probably wouldn't even walk on that side of the road."

"Unless he—or she, as we're talking about Mrs. Salden—had to pass that gap, in order to get to the top of the steps leading down to the footpath."

"Even so . . ."

"And the road might well have been icy, remember, Mike. The temperature dropped like a stone last night, and after all that rain . . ."

"Well, I suppose it's just possible she could have slipped," said Lineham doubtfully. "But one thing's certain. If anyone wanted to get rid of her, he would have had the perfect opportunity, with the parapet down and a slippery road surface. One little shove and she'd be gone."

"Yes, well, obviously we'll have to go on considering the possibility, so we'd better go through the motions and get the rest of the team out. The CCTV team as well as the SOCOs. They've been warned they might be needed." His stomach gave a loud, protesting rumble and he glanced at his watch. A quarter to four. He'd had no idea it was so late.

"Have you all had something to eat?"

"We took it in turns to have sandwiches in the pub."

"Sir . . ." It was Kimberley. "If you and the Sergeant would like a bite . . . I'm sure my wife wouldn't mind rustling up a few sandwiches."

"You're sure?" It was a tempting thought. Thanet suspected that they would be here for hours yet and the pub wouldn't be open again until six.

"Absolutely."

Thanet issued his instructions: house to house enquiries were to begin, and the river bank was to be searched when the SOCOs and CCTV crew had finished. A couple of divers were to search the river bed and Mrs. Pantry asked if she could identify the shoe. Also, someone must fetch his car and Kimberley's motorcycle from the Manor. "We'll walk to your house. I want to take a closer look at the village."

Most of Telford Green lay on the far side of the bridge. Only a few cottages straggled back along the road opposite the boundary wall of the Manor. Behind them lay open fields through which the Teale rushed eagerly towards its union with the Sture.

Once past the bridge, the road widened. On the right the pub, the Crooked Door, lived up to its name, the hinges on the front door sloping downwards in a way reminiscent of the famous door of the old King's School shop in Canterbury. The black and white building itself was equally eccentric, with every wall out of true and a roof which looked in imminent danger of collapse. Thanet suspected that this quaintness had been carefully nurtured as an attraction to customers, and Kimberley confirmed this. Behind it, well-tended lawns optimistically sprinkled with benches and parasolled tables led down to the river.

Facing the pub was the village green, the road dividing to sweep around it in a half-circle and join up again further on. On the far side of the expanse of rough grass was the church, flanked on one side by a couple of large detached houses, one of which was presumably the vicarage, and on the other by a row of pretty brick and tile-hung cottages with white picket fences and well-tended gardens.

On the right past the pub were two short rows of terraced cottages, with four houses in each. In the second cottage of the first terrace, Kimberley told them, had lived Mrs. Carter, Marcia Salden's mother. It stood out by virtue of its well-groomed air—its crisp paintwork, newly pointed brickwork and neat front garden now a mass of many-coloured wallflowers. Their sweet, musky scent, liberated by the sun, drifted out to greet the policemen as they passed. All eight cottages had once belonged to Telford Green Farm, having been built for the men who worked on it, but Marcia had bought her mother's cottage from Mr. Tiller some years ago—at a grossly inflated price, rumour had it. The rest of the cottages were still tenanted and now presumably belonged to Bernard Salden. Just beyond them was a narrow metalled road leading to the farm—Thanet could just glimpse the conical roof of an oast house with its white-painted cowl sticking up beyond some trees. Beyond the green, on both sides of the road, were some rather larger houses, a mixture of old and new, the latter, Thanet guessed, having been built in the gardens of the former, this being the only possible way these days to acquire building plots in rural areas. The village ended with the usual cul-de-sac of council houses. Opposite them was the police house, a typically unimaginative square brick box, with a noticeboard outside.

Mrs. Kimberley, a plump little woman with a frizz of black hair and bright dark eyes welcomed them warmly and half an hour later, fortified by roast beef and pickles with homemade bread, Thanet and Lineham set off with renewed enthusiasm to interview Nurse Lint.

From some distance away they could see that a hearse was parked in front of old Mrs. Carter's cottage, and as they approached two men carried a canvas stretcher bag out of the front door, deposited their burden in the van and drove off.

"The undertakers," said Lineham.

"Mmm. The doctor must already have been and signed the death certificate."

A woman in nurse's uniform had been standing at the front gate gazing after the departing vehicle and now she went back into the cottage and shut the door. A minute or two later, when she answered Thanet's knock, he could see that she had been crying.

"Mrs. Lint?"

"Miss."

He introduced himself and Lineham and she stood back. "Come in."

The front door led directly into a small sitting-room with a brightly patterned brown, orange and yellow carpet, green curtains and a mustard-coloured settee and matching armchair. Thanet wondered how people could stand the effect of so much pattern and colour in so small a space. He found it overwhelming, claustrophobic, even.

She blew her nose and perched on the edge of the chair, gesturing at the settee. "Do sit down."

"Thank you."

Thanet could see that she was making an effort to compose herself. She was much younger than he had expected. He had visualised a plump, matronly woman, a widow perhaps, whose children had grown up and moved away and was therefore free to devote all her time to a patient. Nursing someone terminally ill in a village miles from anywhere wouldn't have much appeal for most young people. Presumably this girl preferred to work in a one-to-one situation. She was in her late twenties and woefully plain, with lank brown hair caught back at the nape of her neck with an elastic band, and metal-rimmed glasses.

"It's about Mrs. Salden's death, I suppose. Miss Phipps rang . . ."

"Yes. We're trying to find out what happened—" He broke off. "What's that?" There was a scratching sound at the door which presumably led to the kitchen.

"Oh, that's Spot. Mrs. Carter's dog. He's upset, he knows something's wrong. I don't know what I'm going to do with him. D'you mind if I let him in?"

"Not at all. Perhaps," Thanet added as she got up and opened the door, "Mr. Salden will take him."

It was a mournful-looking spaniel, ears down and tail drooping. It followed Nurse Lint back to her chair and flopped down beside her, burying its nose in its paws.

"Possibly. But I don't feel I can bother him at a time like this; he'll have enough to worry about as it is." She rubbed her eyes wearily before leaning over to stroke the dog's head. "Perhaps Mrs. Pepper will look after you for a few days, eh, boy? At least you're used to her."

"Mrs. Pepper?"

"Mrs. Carter's friend. She lives next door. She used to take over, from time to time, so that I could get out. They're old friends, they've known each other for years."

She stroked the dog for a moment or two longer, then looked up at Thanet. "I'm sorry, what were you saying?"

"Only that we're trying to work out Mrs. Salden's movements last night. She came here to visit her mother, I believe?"

"That's right."

"What time did she arrive?"

The girl frowned. "I'm not sure." She rubbed her eyes again. "Sorry, I didn't get much sleep last night."

"So I gathered. Surely you're not on duty night and day?"

A shadow of a smile. "More or less."

"But that's ridiculous!"

"No, not really. It's not as bad as it sounds. In fact Mrs. Carter didn't need a lot of attention during the night. And she was a very easy patient, a real sweetie, so looking after her wasn't the strain it sometimes is."

"You were fond of her."

"It's difficult to live with someone as nice as she is for nearly a year and not get fond of them. Oh, I know nurses aren't supposed to become emotionally involved with their patients, but when there's only one, and you spend all your time with her . . . It's easier said than done.''

"I can imagine . . . Look, it really is rather important that we work out the timings of Mrs. Salden's movements last night. Perhaps it would help you to remember if you started earlier in the evening, and worked on from, say, when you rang Mr. Salden, to tell him Mrs. Carter wanted to see him. That wasn't unusual, I understand?''

"Oh, no. She was very fond of Mr. Salden, he was more of a son . . . more like a son than a son-in-law.''

Had she been going to say "more of a son than Mrs. Salden was a daughter''? Thanet wondered.

"And he of her, I believe.''

"Yes. Mind, she didn't often actually ask him to come. He used to call in regularly anyway, so there was no need.''

"When did he last come, before yesterday?''

"The previous day. Yes, he was here at teatime.''

"Do you know what she wanted to see him about last night?''

"No.'' She hesitated. "She'd been restless all afternoon. I think she knew, really, that she was near the end.'' She bit her lip. "I think she just wanted to say goodbye.''

"To him and not to her daughter?''

She shook her head. "She knew Mrs. Salden had a dinner party, and she wouldn't have wanted to upset that. She was . . . proud, like that. Hated to ask.''

"She was prepared to ask Mr. Salden.''

"Yes.'' Miss Lint considered. "I know it sounds odd if you didn't know her, but she was like that, where Mrs. Salden was concerned. I imagine she probably thought that if Mr. Salden saw how poorly she was he'd go back and tell Mrs. Salden and she would come.''

"You're saying it was an indirect means of getting her daughter to come?''

"Yes. Don't misunderstand me, Mrs. Salden was very good to her, bought her this house, I understand, and made sure she had everything she could possibly want . . . Including,'' she finished, with an attempt at a smile, "me.'' She leant over to pat the dog again. "Didn't she, Spot?''

Thanet returned the smile, glad to see that the girl was becoming a little less stiff. And now indeed she did relax, sitting back in the chair for the first time and leaning her head against the back. She looked very tired. The last twenty-four hours must have been a strain.

"And of course that is precisely what did happen, isn't it?"

She frowned. "Well, not exactly. By the time Mr. Salden got here, Mrs. Carter had drifted off to sleep, and he didn't want to wake her up. So he hung around until she did wake."

"Perhaps we could just recap a little. What time did Mr. Salden arrive?"

"I rang the Manor at twenty past seven. I remember that, because I looked at the clock. I was wondering if he'd have time to get down and back before the guests arrived. And he came straight away, so he must have got here about half-past. Unfortunately, as I said, Mrs. Carter had dropped off to sleep by then. I told him I was sure she wouldn't mind if he woke her up—she had been asking for him, after all, but he said no, he'd wait. He'd promised to ring Mrs. Salden at eight, so he did. I heard him say not to wait dinner." She glanced at the telephone, which stood on a small table near the door to the kitchen. "I couldn't help hearing. This is a very small house."

Thanet nodded. "So then what happened?"

"Mrs. Carter went on sleeping for a little while longer, another twenty minutes, perhaps, and then she rang the bell. She has—had—an electric buzzer, Mrs. Salden had it put in for her. Mr. Salden had come downstairs and I'd made him a coffee, while he waited. I went upstairs, to make sure she was all right, and she asked if he'd come. I said yes, and she asked me to fetch him. So I did."

"How long was he with her?"

"A quarter of an hour or so. When he came down he was upset, I could tell. He looked sort of . . . as if he was trying hard not to show what he was feeling, you know what I mean? He didn't say anything, just grabbed his coat and went out. To be honest, I thought he might be going to cry and wanted to get out of the house quickly, so I wouldn't see. Men don't like crying in front of women, do they? I know that, from other jobs I've done."

Thanet remembered what Kimberley had told him. In fact, Salden must have gone straight to the pub.

"What did you do then?"

"I went up to make sure Mrs. Carter was all right. She was sleeping again."

"Did you expect Mr. Salden to come back?"

She shrugged. "I suppose I half thought he might. I wondered if he might go and fetch Mrs. Salden, but he didn't, apparently. When she rang at half-past nine she hadn't heard from him. He told me later he'd been walking. Said he wanted to come back later to see how Mrs. Carter was, and couldn't face going home and being sociable in between."

"What did Mrs. Salden say, when she rang?"

"She asked to speak to her husband."

"I'm afraid he's not here, Mrs. Salden."

"Not here? What time did he leave?"

"About three quarters of an hour ago."

"Did he say where he was going?"

"No. I'm sorry. I assumed he was going home . . . He seemed rather upset."

"About my mother?"

"Yes. She . . . I'm afraid she doesn't look too good."

"Oh God. You think I ought to come down?"

"It's up to you, Mrs. Salden."

"Does she look any worse than she has before, when we've . . . When she's been OK, afterwards?"

"It's awfully difficult to judge. But I am quite worried about her."

"I'd better pop down. Just for a few minutes, to see for myself. I'll be there in five minutes."

"And was she?" said Thanet.

"No. Nearer ten or fifteen, I'd say. She had to walk. Her car wouldn't start, she said."

"Did you tell Mr. Salden that?"

"No. Should I have?"

"I just wondered . . . So she came via the footpath?"

"She didn't say. I assume so. It would have taken her much longer, if she'd walked all the way down the Manor drive and along the road."

"So she must have arrived at what time? Around a quarter to ten?"

"I suppose so, yes."

"How long did she stay?"

"Getting on for half an hour, I should think."

"Until a quarter past ten, then?"

"Must have been. Perhaps Mrs. Pepper can be more precise."

"She was here?"

"She popped in five minutes or so before Mrs. Salden left. She stayed about half an hour till around a quarter to eleven."

"If Mrs. Carter was as ill as that, why didn't Mrs. Salden stay longer?"

"I think she thought it was another false alarm . . . We've had a number of them. And on the face of it there wasn't really much point in her staying. Her mother was asleep when she got here, and didn't wake up all the while she was here."

"And then Mr. Salden got back, I gather?"

"That's right. Not long after she left."

"How long, do you think?"

Nurse Lint put up a hand and began to massage her right temple. "Sorry, I've got a bit of a headache . . ." She frowned, her mouth turning down at the corners. "Ten or fifteen minutes?"

Perhaps Mrs. Pepper could confirm that. And if so . . . Sitting close to Lineham on the small settee, arms touching, Thanet was aware of the involuntary tremor of excitement which had passed through the Sergeant's body. He knew what Lineham was thinking. If Marcia Salden had left only ten or fifteen minutes before her husband arrived back, it was quite feasible that they could have passed each other on the bridge. Say that they quarreled . . .

"Bernard! Where the hell have you been?"

"I went for a walk."

"A walk?"

"I repeat, a walk. I was . . . upset."

"Look, I didn't mind you deserting our guests to visit my mother . . ."

"I should hope not!"

" . . . but I think it's a bit much to spend the rest of the evening going for a walk!"

"Oh, you do, do you? May I ask where you're going now?"

"Home, of course."

"I see. Home. We mustn't be rude to our guests, of course, even if our mother is dying. My God, if they had any sensitivity they'd have taken themselves off hours ago."

"As a matter of fact they offered to leave, but I asked them to stay on. And aren't you being a little melodramatic? If we dropped everything, cancelled everything, every time my mother rings up, we'd have given up living our own lives a year ago, and camped on her doorstep. Anyway, you know perfectly well that after all the false alarms we've had we agreed to take it in *turns to sit up with her. And in case you've forgotten, it happens to be your turn."*

"No, I hadn't forgotten. But this isn't just another false alarm."

"How can you be so sure?

"It just isn't. I know it, she knows it, Nurse Lint knows it . . ."

"What nonsense! How can you possibly 'know.' "

"Please, Marcia, I'm serious. Let's sit up with her together tonight."

"Look, I left her just a few moments ago, and she was sleeping peacefully . . . Let go of my arm, please."

"Marcia, I am dead serious. I want you to come with me. Please?"

"No! I'm going home. I asked Josie to wait till I got back."

"Never mind Josie. You can ring her from the cottage."

"How many times have we been through this? It's pointless both of us staying . . ."

"Marcia . . ."

"Let go of my arm."

"Please . . ."

"Let go, will you?"

"Marcia? Marcia? Oh, my God . . ."

Thanet blinked. The whole conversation had been so convincing that it was difficult to believe he had imagined it. Words hung in the air, and both Nurse Lint and Lineham were staring at him. "Sorry?"

"I said, I told him he'd just missed his wife."

"What did he say?"

"He asked me how long she'd stayed, and whether Mrs. Carter had woken up while Mrs. Salden was here. I said no, she hadn't, which was why Mrs. Salden only stayed half an hour or so, then decided to go home."

"Did you tell him Mrs. Salden's car wouldn't start, and she'd had to walk down?"

"No. He was already halfway up the stairs by then, and I went into the kitchen. Mrs. Pepper was making a pot of tea. A minute later he came down again and made a phone call."

"You heard what was said?"

"No. Mrs. Pepper was clattering cups and saucers. But he came into the kitchen when he'd finished and said he'd rung home to say he was going to stay on here . . . He sat up with Mrs. Carter until she died, you know."

"What time was that?"

"Twenty-five to four. All those hours, he just sat there, holding her hand . . ."

"When he told you he'd rung home, did he say that he'd had to leave a message for Mrs. Salden because she hadn't yet arrived back?"

"No." *Why should he?* her expression said.

Why, indeed? Nurse Lint was his employee. He owed her no such explanations.

And of course he wouldn't have wanted to draw attention to Marcia's absence, if he'd known that she was already at the bottom of the river.

SEVEN

As they emerged from the front door of Mrs. Carter's cottage a loud backfire from across the green, followed by a throaty roar and a cloud of exhaust smoke, caused Lineham to pause and click his tongue in disapproval. Putting his hand up to shade his eyes, he squinted in that direction.

Apart from that brief frisson of excitement a few minutes ago, when they had realised that Bernard Salden had been in the right place at the right time to have murdered his wife, this was the first spontaneous sign of animation that the Sergeant had shown all day. He had functioned efficiently, true, but his enthusiasm, one of his most endearing qualities, had been conspicuous by its absence and Thanet was beginning to find his unnatural silence unnerving. What on earth could be the matter?

For the second time today he decided to try to find out.

"Mike, are you sure you're all right?"

"Yes, fine, thanks." A brief, flickering glance. *How much does he know?*

Come on, Luke, Thanet told himself. You're imagining things. What could Lineham possibly have to hide? The most obvious answer was marital problems. Louise, Lineham's wife, was anything but easy to live with. Bossy and demanding, when they married she had taken over where Lineham's domineering mother had left off. It was a mystery to Thanet why the Sergeant should have chosen a wife so similar in nature to the mother whose rule he had found so irksome. Presumably there was something in him that needed to be dominated—or at least needed to kick against being dominated. In any case, Thanet had no intention of prying. If Lineham wanted to confide in him, well and good; if not, there was nothing he could do about it.

The offending car was heading in their direction and now screeched to a halt by Mrs. Carter's gate, belching noxious fumes. It was, Thanet saw, an ancient Mini, painted what Ben would have called puke green, and it was driven by the Vicar.

"Afternoon, Inspector, Sergeant." Fothergill glanced at their faces and clowned disappointment. "Don't you like her?" He stuck his arm out of the car window and patted its flank. "Don't be insulted, old girl, they're just jealous." Then he put his hand up to his mouth and hissed. "Don't want to upset her, just got her back from the garage."

Thanet had been wondering how they could possibly have missed noticing this car up at the Manor this morning. All was now explained. Fothergill must have gone up on foot or by bicycle, the "old girl" being out of action at the time.

"Got her *back*!" said Lineham.

"Certainly. Have to maintain an appropriately poverty-stricken image, you know, Sergeant. Doesn't do for the clergy to appear too affluent, people don't like it."

"There must be a happy medium," said Thanet, smiling.

"This is it." Fothergill's expression changed. "How's it going?"

"Slowly. Nothing definite yet. Except that we think we know where she went into the river."

Fothergill nodded. "The broken parapet. It did cross my mind, this morning. But the warnings and barriers were so obvious I didn't really consider it a serious possibility. Though the road was very icy last night . . . You're satisfied that it was an accident, then?"

"We still have to try and find out exactly what happened, if anyone saw her, and so on," said Thanet, neatly side-stepping. The manoeuvre had not been missed by Fothergill, he noticed. The Vicar was no fool.

"Yes, well . . . I did what I could for Bernard Salden, by the way. He'd calmed down by the time I left. I got his doctor to come and take a look at him and he gave him a sedative. I gather the undertakers have been to collect Mrs. Carter. We've postponed making the arrangements for her funeral until tomorrow or the next day."

"Very sensible."

"Well, better get on. Got a meeting in Maidstone."

And with a smile and a wave he was off, leaving a trail of black smoke behind him.

Thanet and Lineham stepped back to avoid the fumes, waving their hands in front of their faces and coughing.

"Ought to be in the scrapyard, if you ask me," said Lineham. "I'm sure we could get him for public nuisance."

"If we didn't have better things to do, Mike. Come on, I want a word with Mrs. Pepper." Thanet had high hopes of Mrs. Pepper. If she and Mrs. Carter had been friends for as long as Nurse Lint seemed to think, the old lady might be able to fill him in on Marcia's background.

This cottage, being tenanted, was not in such good structural repair as Mrs. Carter's next door, but the little front garden was ablaze with the purple spires of honesty and regimented rows of pink and scarlet tulips. A straggling bush of *Kerria japonica*, most of its yellow globes now faded, was tied up against the wall between door and window. There was not a weed to be seen.

The woman who answered the door looked as though she would have no problem in buying her clothes from the children's sections of department stores. She was well under five feet tall and although she must have been in her late sixties was wearing what Bridget would call a jumpsuit, an all-in-one sort of tracksuit in vivid green with orange trimmings at shoulders and neck. Her hair was dyed orange. To match? Thanet was relieved to see that her eyes were bright, her manner alert. Excellent. She should make a good witness.

Formalities over, she led them into the sitting-room. It was immediately obvious that Mrs. Pepper had two passions: indoor plants and crochet. The former all but obscured the light from the window, scrambled up the walls and trailed from the numerous containers suspended from the overhead beams, and the latter greeted the eye wherever it happened to fall, in gaily coloured circular woollen cushion covers crocheted in concentric rings, lacy white antimacassars on the backs of chairs and little round mats on every horizontal surface. Mrs. Pepper had evidently found a solution to the problem which dogs every such hobby, that of what to do with the end product: on a table in the window were perhaps a dozen piles of crocheted squares in different colours.

"Blankets," she said, following his gaze. "For Age Concern. They're always desperate for them, come January."

She insisted on providing them with a cup of tea. There was one in the pot, she assured them, she'd just made some for herself. A steaming cup on the arm of the chair beside the fireplace confirmed this. Finally they were all seated, sipping.

"Very welcome, Mrs. Pepper," said Lineham.

"Nothing like a nice cup of tea, I always say . . . I suppose you've come about Marcia—Mrs. Salden. I've seen your men about all over the village."

"That's right, yes. We understand you saw her briefly last night."

"When I went next door to see Win—Mrs. Carter, that is. Yes." Mrs. Pepper's mouth quivered and she set down her cup, picked up a large ball of green wool with a crochet hook stuck through it and began to work. "You don't mind? It helps to keep my mind off . . ." She compressed her lips and shook her head fiercely as if to frighten grief away. "Win—Mrs. Carter—and me had been friends for getting on for fifty years."

"That's a very long time," said Thanet gently.

"It certainly is. I can hardly imagine life without her . . . Yes, I did see Marcia last night."

"I don't suppose you realise this, but in fact you must have been one of the last people to see her alive."

"Really?" The crochet needle was temporarily stilled as she took this in.

It didn't take long to check that the information Nurse Lint had given them was correct: Marcia had been at the cottage when Mrs. Pepper arrived, and had left about five minutes later, at a quarter past ten. Mrs. Pepper was fairly sure of the time because she had watched the headlines on *News at Ten* before going next door. Bernard Salden had arrived about ten or fifteen minutes after his wife left. His car had been parked outside all evening, since half-past seven or so, and had stayed there until a quarter to four in the morning. She had looked at her clock when she heard the engine start up—she hadn't been able to sleep because she had been worried about Win and feared that his departure in the early hours could mean that her friend had died. In the past, when Bernard had sat up with his mother-in-law, he had always stayed all night.

"Really loved her, he did. Like she was his own mum. He'll be ever so upset . . . And now this, with Marcia. Poor Bernard, I feel really sorry for him. He hasn't had much luck."

"Oh, I don't know. He doesn't seem to have done too badly up to now," put in Lineham.

She sniffed. "Oh, him and Marcia have done very well in their business, I grant you that, but money isn't everything, it don't bring you happiness, do it?"

Knowing the value of silence, Thanet said nothing, praying that Lineham would also keep quiet. He was well aware that if he appeared too curious Mrs. Pepper might well clam up, whereas nothing encourages confidences more than a sympathetic and attentive listener.

It worked.

"No," she said, answering her own question. "It don't. And Bernard's had a lot of bad luck. I mean, we all have to go through it, don't we, one way or the other, none of us can get away without losing someone we love, but Bernard . . . His parents were both killed when he was just a young lad, you know, and he didn't have no brothers or sisters, neither, so he was all alone, with no one to fall back on. But he stuck to his studies and got his accountant's exams, and got married—no, not to Marcia, he was married before, you know. But they'd only been married a couple of years and she died, having a baby. Hardly ever happens these days, of course, but this was over thirty years ago. The baby was still-born. Win told me all this later, when the other little girl died. I don't know why I'm telling you all this."

Thanet ignored this last remark. Mrs. Pepper, he knew, was now well launched, and needed only a guarantee of her audience's interest to continue. "Other little girl?"

"Him and Marcia's. So you see what I mean, don't you? He seems to lose everyone he loves, his parents, his first wife, his first baby, his second baby, his mother-in-law what he loved like a son, his second wife . . ."

It was indeed an appalling catalogue of death.

She shook her head. "I don't know how he survives, I'm sure."

"I didn't know he and Mrs. Salden had had a baby."

"Oh yes, they did. Clare, she was called. Well, I don't suppose there's many around here would even know about her or care if they did, but I know because I went to the funeral."

Their rapt attention encouraged her to elaborate and she stuck the needle back in the ball of green wool and laid down her work.

"You see, what happened was this. When Marcia and Bernard got married—she was only eighteen at the time, and pretty as a picture. A lovely bride she was, I went to the wedding. Got a picture somewhere . . ." She looked vaguely around as if it might materialise, but made no effort to get up and show it to them, she was too engrossed in her story.

Thanet would have liked to see it, to have looked upon that dead face when it was still young and vital with all life's promise still untapped, but he was afraid of disturbing the flow of reminiscence. It was clear that, like so many elderly people, Mrs. Pepper rarely had such a receptive audience and that on this particular occasion she especially welcomed the opportunity to be distracted for a short while from her grief over her friend's death.

"Anyway, like I said, when they got married they moved up North. Bernard had been a lecturer, see, at the college where Marcia went to night school. He was one of her teachers, and of course it would have been a bit awkward for him to stay on there, marrying one of his students and all that. I don't suppose people'd pay all that much attention nowadays, but things was different then. So he got himself a job up North and it wasn't long before Marcia fell for the baby. I don't think she was too pleased at first, it being so quick and all, but of course she soon got used to the idea, like they all do, and the following year the little girl was born. Bernard was like a dog with two tails, Win said, absolutely over the moon. He's always loved kids and of course, with his first one being still-born . . . Well, you can imagine, can't you?

"Anyway, a couple of months later he was sent abroad by his firm, and while he was away, the baby died."

Mrs. Pepper paused for an appropriate reaction.

Thanet had no problem in showing his very real sympathy for the man. "That's terrible. What happened?"

"She got pneumonia. But the worst of it was, Bernard couldn't come home for the funeral. He'd been in a car crash and fractured his pelvis and he was stuck in hospital abroad for months. And Win couldn't go, either, she was in bed with 'flu, it was a terrible winter, that one, people dying like flies . . . Poor Marcia had to cope all by herself, and she was in such a state, well, you can imagine, can't you? The next we knew, she was on Win's doorstep, ashes and all. Said she couldn't stand being all by herself up North a minute longer, she hated it, especially with no hope of Bernard being back for months and she'd decided the only thing to do was come home . . . It's the only time I've really felt sorry for Marcia. To tell you the truth, I've never had much time for her, hard as nails she was, but that time . . . I saw her, the day she got here. Thin as a rake and looking as though she hadn't slept for a month, and clutching that box with the baby's ashes in it. D'you know, she'd just walked out of her house, shut the front door behind her and left it all. Just like that. No arrangements made, nothing. And she never did go back. Said Bernard could see to it all when he came home but nothing would induce her to set foot over the threshold ever again. Nothing but bad luck it had brought her, she said, which was why she'd brought the baby's ashes home. She wanted them to be buried here, in Telford Green. Mr. Greenhorn was vicar here at the time, I remember. Lovely service it was, too.''

"Why didn't you like her, Mrs. Pepper?''

"Marcia?" She wrinkled her nose and turned up her upper lip, as if she'd just come across a bad smell. "I told you, hard as nails, she was. Never did have much time for her mother—No, I tell a lie. She did care about her, must have, since she made a lot of money she's been very generous, bought Win everything she could possibly need. But the truth is—though it took me a long time to work it out—Marcia never really forgave her mother for not standing up to her father." She rolled her eyes. "Now there was a right one, believe me."

"In what way?''

"Drink, mostly. He didn't earn much—him and Bert, my husband God rest his soul, both worked on the farm, so they got the same wages and, believe me, the money didn't go far—and George, Win's husband, used to pour most of it into the pockets of the landlord of the Crooked Door on a Friday night. Then he'd come home and beat Win up. Our bedrooms was next to each other on either side of the party wall and many's the Friday I've lain with the bedclothes pulled up over me head to shut out the noise. Nowadays, of course, people call in the police over that sort of thing but forty or fifty years ago it'd never have entered your head to do that. You never heard about "battered wives" and such like in those days. Anyway, the point was, Marcia really"—she paused, seeking the right word—"despised," she brought out triumphantly, "yes, despised her mother for putting up with it. I heard her going on at her about it more than once. "Why on earth don't you stand up to him?" she used to say. "He's only a bully, and bullies turn tail when you stand up to them." She proved it, too, as she got older. Many's the time I've seen her stick up for herself, and for her mother, too, and George'd shout and bluster, but she'd get away with it. But Win never could, she was too gentle. I always thought that was why Marcia got married so young."

"To get away from home, you mean?"

Mrs. Pepper nodded. "Couldn't wait to be independent. And that was Bernard's attraction for her, I reckon. He was able to afford a wife. I mean, he was much older than her, he had a house, a car . . . It was just too good an opportunity to miss. And Marcia always was ambitious. Determined to make her way in the world."

"And she certainly did," said Lineham. "How did she manage it?"

Something in the Sergeant's tone made Thanet glance at him sharply.

"Well," said Mrs. Pepper, picking up her ball of wool again, "it was like this. After the baby died and Marcia came home, she didn't do nothing for a while. To give her credit, she'd always been a hard worker, went on working right up till six weeks before the baby was born . . ."

"What sort of work did she do?" asked Lineham.

"Secretarial. She always was bright, did well at school—wanted to stay on after her O levels, but her father wouldn't let her, said she was sixteen and it was time she got out in the world and started to earn a living. Terrible rows there was about it, but he wouldn't give in. So when she left school she got a job as a receptionist in some office, but she enrolled straight away at night school, like I told you, for a course in—what do they call it?—business studies. Yes. Like I said, that was where she met Bernard. Anyway, after they got married she found a good job as a secretary up North, but after the baby died and she come home, she just used to sit about all day doing nothing, staring into space. Often I'd go in there and she'd just be sitting there with the tears rolling down her cheeks, not making a sound. Win was that worried about her."

It sounded like a bad case of post-natal depression, exacerbated by grief at losing the baby, thought Thanet.

"What did the doctor say?"

"Gave her tablets and that, but they didn't seem to do much good."

"What about her father?"

"Oh, he was dead by then. Died not long after she got married, as a matter of fact, in an accident on the farm. His tractor overturned and of course in them days there was no safety cabs. He was crushed to death."

"Nasty . . . Sorry, I didn't mean to interrupt. You were saying, about Marcia . . ."

"Well, she went on like that for months, we was beginning to wonder if she'd ever come out of it, and then at last she started to improve. Not long after, Bernard came home and took her off abroad for a holiday. He was still walking on sticks at the time, but he could get about all right and off they went. It worked wonders for her. By the time they came back she had it all worked out. They would sell their house up North and move back down here, because that's where the money was. They would buy the lease on a shop with a flat above, and open a health food shop. We thought she was mad at the time, but when Marcia set her mind on something nothing would budge her and of course she was right, wasn't she? Look at the business now!''

Marcia must really have got in on the ground floor, thought Thanet. The health food business had boomed in recent years, especially since the Government had started taking an interest in the nation's health and had launched the campaign for healthy eating. But in the late sixties it had been an unusual choice to make.

Lineham's thoughts had been running along similar lines. "Whatever gave her the idea?'' he said.

"No idea. But she was sharp, Marcia, very sharp. I remember she talked a lot about a gap in the market. And of course, once she was launched, nothing could stop her.''

"They didn't want any more children?'' said Thanet.

"Oh yes, I think so. Bernard was very keen, I know. But they just never seemed to come along. After a while he even suggested adopting one, but Marcia didn't want to do that, said she'd never given up hope of having another of her own, but it wasn't to be.''

So Salden had turned to charity work with children as second best, thought Thanet. He'd certainly had more than his fair share of grief. He stood up, ducking to avoid a trailing spider plant. "Well, Mrs. Pepper, I really am very grateful to you for filling us in like this.''

She came to her feet slowly, one hand in the small of her back, betraying her age for the first time. "I really have been rambling on, haven't I?''

"Not at all.''

"It's very kind of you to say so. But I can't see that it has anything to do with Marcia's accident.''

If it was an accident, thought Thanet.

The more he heard about Marcia Salden, the more likely a murder victim she seemed.

EIGHT

They paused outside Mrs. Pepper's gate.

"What now?" said Lineham.

"I think it would be a good idea if we chewed things over a bit." Thanet took out his pipe, inspected the bowl, scraped it out, inspected it again, blew through it a couple of times and started to fill it. Lineham watched him with resignation.

"Back to headquarters, then?" The Sergeant glanced at his watch. "You realise it's nearly half-past five, sir? You did tell that TVS reporter to contact your office late in the afternoon."

"Ah, but I didn't say I'd be there, did I? Anyway, we can't talk properly cramped up in the corner of the main CID room with phones ringing and people going in and out . . ." Thanet lit up. "No, we need somewhere nice and quiet. The car's as good a place as any, I suppose."

The car was in the pub car park, as arranged, with a piece of paper tucked under the windscreen wipers. *Keys in pub.*

Lineham fetched them. "D'you want to stay here and talk?" he asked. With a glance at Thanet's pipe, he wound down the window. "Or go somewhere else?"

"Somewhere else, I think. I never have found brick and tarmac very inspiring."

"I know a place that'd do."

Instead of turning left over the bridge towards the Sturrenden road, Lineham turned right. Shortly after leaving the village he swung left into a narrow rising lane, the branches of the trees on either side meeting overhead to form a tunnel. The sun was sinking but still bright and the road surface ahead was dappled with pools and patches of light laced with intricate patterns of shadow cast by still-bare twigs and branches. In summer it must be even more beautiful, thought Thanet, and promised himself that one sunny afternoon he'd bring Joan to see it.

"Where are we going, exactly?"

Lineham grinned. "Nearly there."

A few minutes later the trees gave way to hedges and they emerged into a wide expanse of open fields dotted with sheep and cattle. The lane bore around in a wide arc to the left and a few hundred yards further on Lineham pulled into the entrance to a tractor lane and switched off the engine.

"This do?"

Thanet said nothing, simply nodded then sat taking in the view, which was as fine as any he had seen in Kent. They were now looking at the valley of the Teale below them from the opposite direction, and from much higher up. To right and left the river wound lazily away into the distance, its surface mirror-bright and stained with the colours of the setting sun, the road through the village bisecting it at the bridge in a graceful curve. Immediately below them was the church, its spire casting a long shadow on the green beyond, the roofs of the cottages to either side russet red tinged here and there with purple, ochre and a rich, warm sepia. To the left, in the fields between village and river, lay Telford Green Farm, and beyond, on the far side of the Teale, the densely packed trees of Harry Greenleaf's wood. Thanet's gaze lingered here; a tiny figure was walking up the tongue of meadow which led up to the hut. Greenleaf, secure now in the knowledge that his sanctuary was safe for at least a little while longer? Thanet transferred his attention to the Manor, serene in its setting of gardens and parkland and wondered whether Salden had yet awoken from his drug-induced sleep and if he would proceed with the eviction now that Marcia was dead.

Here, spread out for his inspection, was Marcia Salden's world—or part of it, at least, the part in which she had functioned as a private individual. Was her murderer also a part of this tranquil scene, even now going about his daily tasks beneath one of those roofs down there and wondering if his crime would be detected?

Lineham's voice broke into his thoughts. "Beautiful, isn't it?"

In deference to the Sergeant's aversion to pipe smoke Thanet wound down his window. The brisk wind of earlier in the day had abated and a light, cool breeze blew in, redolent of earth, trees, cattle and young green crops.

"How did you discover this place?"

"We were out looking for a picnic spot one day, years ago.

I'd forgotten about it until we drove into the village this morning, I can't think why. It would be hard to find a better."

"I agree . . ." Thanet wrenched his eyes away from the
landscape below and looked at Lineham. "Well, Mike, what do
you think? Have we got a case, or haven't we?"

The Sergeant was gazing straight ahead out of the window.
Free to study his profile at close quarters, Thanet took in Lineham's
pallor, the fine lines of strain around eyes and mouth, the restless
tapping of his fingers on the steering wheel. What *was* the matter
with him? Normally, at this stage, the Sergeant would be bub-
bling over with ideas, suggestions.

"I'm not sure." He turned to face Thanet, leaning back
against the driving door. "What do you think, sir?"

"Oh come on, Mike, don't throw it back at me like that. I'm
asking for your opinion and I want to know what it is."

"But that is it. I just can't make up my mind. Perhaps when
we've got a bit more evidence . . ."

"Evidence, evidence . . . What's got into you, Mike? I'm
usually the one falling over backwards saying take it easy, don't
let's jump to conclusions . . . Of course we haven't got any
evidence yet. If it's there to be found, we'll find it sooner or
later. Meanwhile, you know perfectly well I'm not talking about
evidence, I'm talking about impressions of people, about possible motives, opportunities."

Lineham shifted uneasily in his seat and his eyes drifted away
from Thanet's. "Sorry." He frowned, obviously making an
effort to focus his mind.

Thanet opened the car door, put one foot out and emptied his
pipe by tapping it against his heel. The familiar action soothed
him a little, but he still couldn't entirely suppress the anger in his
voice as he said, "I don't know what sort of a fool you take me
for, Mike, but it's as plain as a pikestaff that something's wrong
and I'm fed up with asking what it is. Now, your private life is
your own affair and I have no wish to pry. If something's wrong
between you and Louise, then it's up to you to take steps to sort
it out. But your work's another matter. In this state you're as
much use to me as a wet flannel and I feel I have every right to
ask. So come on, tell me. What's the matter?"

While Thanet was speaking Lineham had been looking more
and more uncomfortable. Now he glanced uneasily at Thanet,
opened his mouth, shut it again.

"Mike . . . Come on, man. Spit it out."

Thanet waited. He was sympathetic to the Sergeant's predicament, acutely conscious of the conflict raging in his mind, but he could say no more. The issue had been brought out into the open and if Lineham still chose not to confide in him there was nothing he could do about it.

Lineham was staring down at his hands, picking away at a piece of loose skin alongside the thumbnail of his right hand. The silence stretched out and Thanet was just beginning to think his appeal had failed when the Sergeant stirred.

"Louise wants me to leave the force," he muttered. He glanced briefly at Thanet's blank face, then down at his hands again.

Thanet was first astounded and then, as the shock receded, furiously angry with Lineham's wife. His lips tightened as if to contain the spate of words which threatened to tumble out. Here was a minefield and he would have to tread carefully indeed.

"I see."

Lineham glanced at him again, assessingly this time.

With an effort, Thanet kept his voice non-committal. "May I ask why?"

Lineham shrugged, grimaced. "The usual reasons, I imagine. Long, unpredictable, anti-social hours . . . But mainly, I think, the fact that the prospects are poor."

I might have guessed, of course, thought Thanet. He had always suspected Louise of being ambitious. A couple of years back Lineham had sought promotion to Inspector. Thanet hadn't been surprised when he failed to get it. Lineham was an excellent second-in-command, but had always lacked that extra edge which would lift him above the rank of Sergeant. Thanet had thought at the time that it had been Louise who had pushed Lineham into applying, and he had sympathised with the demoralising effect the failure had had upon Lineham, privately approved the Sergeant's decision not to try again. It was obvious that Louise, balked at having one avenue closed, had determined upon another.

On impulse, Thanet swung open the car door and got out. "Let's walk for a while, shall we? The car should be all right; I shouldn't think there'll be many tractors around at this time of night."

Without speaking, Lineham followed suit, and they set off at a leisurely pace along the narrow lane between tall country hedges of hawthorn and blackthorn, field maple, dogwood and hazel, some distinguishable only by their bark, others just breaking into leaf.

"Does she have anything specific in mind?" Thanet asked, eventually.

Lineham shrugged again. "She seems to think it would be a good idea to start our own business. Says that's where the money is these days and that the opportunities to do so have never been better, what with all the advice you can get free from the Government, and the ease with which you can get funding."

"What sort of business?"

"She . . . We haven't made up our minds, yet."

"But you, Mike?" said Thanet softly. "Have you made up your mind?"

Lineham shook his head miserably.

"I can see what a dilemma you must be in . . . Worrying about what your mates'll say if you leave the force, worrying about what Louise'll say if you don't, but Mike, listen"—Thanet stopped walking and turned to face Lineham, to emphasise the importance of what he was saying—"you've got to ignore all that. There's only one question you have to ask yourself and that is, 'What do *I* want to do?' "

Lineham gave a mirthless snort of laughter. "You don't think that's a somewhat selfish attitude to take?"

"No I do not! Look, Mike, you're what? Thirty? All being well you've got another thirty-five years of working life ahead of you. Now I know, as well as you do, that you enjoy your work. Really enjoy it. Oh, I know it has disadvantages, all the things you mentioned plus an awful lot of frustration, hassle and danger at times, too, but all the same you do enjoy it. As much as I do. Don't you realise how privileged we are? To wake up in the morning and actually look forward to going to work instead of waking up and thinking, Oh God, another day, how can I face it, how can I get through it? You can't buy satisfaction like that, Mike, not if you're a millionaire. Now, if there were something else you wanted to do more than this, or as much as this, and you could earn more doing it and please Louise at the same time, I'd give you my blessing, say go ahead, you've everything to gain. But if you give up work you enjoy for something in which you haven't really the slightest interest, I'm afraid you'd end up in far worse straits than you are now—not financially, perhaps, but emotionally. Because for the rest of your life you'd resent being forced into a false position, and that resentment would gradually poison your relationship with Louise."

Lineham had been listening intently, nodded now and then as Thanet made some particularly telling point. Now he said, "I know that. I know all that. But I just can't seem to get Louise to see it."

"You've actually put it to her, in those terms?"

"More or less." Lineham shook his head despairingly. "I just don't know what to do."

They had come to a five-barred gate and in mute accord they turned to lean on it, gazing out over the serene landscape below. Colours were darkening and deepening in tone, edges becoming blurred and shadows lengthening fast as the sun sank towards the western horizon.

Thanet didn't know what to do either. It was obvious that this discussion could go no further without venturing into the very private territory of Lineham's marriage, and Thanet was unsure of the wisdom of taking this step. Marriage guidance, he felt, should be left to the experts. On the other hand, now that his initial reluctance to discuss the matter had been overcome, Lineham seemed anxious to pursue it further, was even now casting anxious glances at Thanet, awaiting his response. What to do? If only he could think of a way to give the Sergeant something positive to hang on to, some new and constructive way of looking at the situation . . . Suddenly he saw how it might be done.

"Mike," he began cautiously.

"Yes, sir?"

The eager look in Lineham's eyes gave Thanet the courage to continue.

"Look, I don't want to pry, and I'll quite understand if you prefer not to answer, but I was wondering . . . Would you say that Louise is happy?"

Lineham compressed his lips, sighed and said bitterly, "No, I don't mind you asking. And I don't suppose you'll be too surprised to hear that she hasn't been happy for a long time."

"It's just that I was wondering . . . Do you think she misses her work?"

Before their marriage, Louise had been a nurse, working as a sister in Sturrenden General Hospital.

Lineham was nodding. "Oh yes. Always has. I think you've hit the nail on the head, there. She's very fond of the children, mind, but she always has missed it. If I'd had a job with regular hours, of course, she'd have been able to go back before now, do a bit of night duty, to keep her hand in. But as it is it's just not possible."

Thanet nodded, then shivered. As the light seeped out of the sky the breeze seemed to have freshened again. Perhaps there would be another touch of frost tonight. He dug his hands deep into his pockets and turned back towards the car, Lineham falling into step beside him. "Has she ever considered finding someone to look after the children during the day?"

"Not seriously, no. For one thing, she thinks—we both think—that kids under the age of five really need their mothers and that you're asking for trouble later on if you duck out of your responsibilities by dumping them on someone else—at least until they're of school age. For another, from the purely economic point of view, she'd practically be working for nothing. Nurses are so badly paid she'd have to hand over most of it to the child-minder. Then there are the hours—they're impossible, as far as child-minding is concerned. You'd really think," said Lineham bitterly, "that if they're that desperate for nurses at Sturrenden General, they'd set up a crèche."

"I agree . . . Louise has never considered doing anything other than nursing, something part-time, just until the children start school? How often does Richard go to playgroup?"

"Three mornings a week."

"And Mandy will be starting in September, won't she?"

"Yes . . . I don't know whether it would have entered her head. Nursing's her first love, always has been . . ."

"I know. But it might just be worth discussing the possibility, stressing that it would only be a temporary measure. It must be very hard for a woman like Louise, who's had a successful career, to be stuck at home all day staring at four walls and looking after two young children."

"You almost sound as if you've been through all this yourself."

Lineham was looking much more relaxed, Thanet noticed. At this point he even managed an echo of his usual cheeky grin.

"Oh, I have. Not in quite the same way. But there was a point, when Ben finally started school and Joan was contemplating a career in the probation service, when I had to do some re-thinking. Up until then I'm afraid I'd just taken it for granted that she was one hundred per cent happy looking after the house, the children and me. A real MCP, in fact. And having my eyes opened was, as I recall, distinctly painful."

"Really?" Lineham was looking at Thanet as though the confession had enhanced rather than diminished him in the Sergeant's eyes.

Thanet grinned. "Cross my heart. It took me years to adjust, really adjust, to having a wife whose career was as important to her as mine was to me. Until last year, as a matter of fact.''

"Last year? But Joan's been a probation officer for—how long?—six years now!''

"Marriage is a funny thing, Mike. People who are going through a bad patch seem to think things will never change, or if they do they can only get worse. But the fact of the matter is, none of us is static, we're all changing all the time, and when two people are involved there is tremendous potential for change, given goodwill on both sides. You know, I've often thought that in marriage there seems to be a kind of natural ebb and flow, as feelings fluctuate, situations alter and attitudes change. So that sometimes things get better and sometimes things get worse, for no apparent reason but simply because of this fundamental— what shall I call it?—groundswell, going on underneath all the time. And this is perfectly normal, perfectly natural. The trouble nowadays is that people seem to take it for granted that if they're having a bad time it means their marriage has broken down for ever. And this simply need not be true. Take your situation, now. It might seem to you that there is no way—no acceptable way, that is—out of it. But it would need only one of you to change his attitude slightly and the other would begin to react to that change, and the possibility of breaking the apparent impasse would be there.''

They had reached the car now and Lineham automatically unlocked it, climbed in and reached across to release the catch on Thanet's door. Then he sat quite still for a minute or two, gazing sightlessly out of the windscreen. "I don't think," he said slowly at last, "that I've ever really tried to look at the situation from Louise's point of view before. Oh, I know she's not happy stuck at home all the time, much as she loves the kids. But we've never really talked about it, it just comes out in other ways, as though she's trying to pin her dissatisfaction on something else . . .''

Like her husband's lack of ambition, thought Thanet.

Lineham was getting there himself. "Perhaps she feels that the only way she can change things is through me.''

"Possibly. But if so, it's quite likely that it's unconscious, she doesn't realise she's doing it. In any case, it might help if you brought it out into the open, talked about it.''

Lineham turned to look Thanet full in the face and gave a resolute nod. "I will. Yes.''

"In any case, I should stop worrying about having to make an immediate decision about leaving the force."

"I don't want to leave. I really don't. As you say, I really enjoy my work, I've never wanted to do anything else."

Thanet wondered if Lineham was remembering the battle he had fought with his mother over his entry to the police force. A widow who had brought up her only son singlehanded, she had fought long and hard against his entering what she considered to be a dangerous profession. And if he did remember, would he now make the inevitable comparison with his current situation?

"But I was beginning to wonder if there was any other way out. Now . . . Well, I think I feel there may be a light at the end of the tunnel. Thank you, sir."

Thanet recognised the note of finality in Lineham's voice. The Sergeant had had enough of discussing his private problems for the moment.

"All in a day's work," said Thanet with a grin. "And talking about work . . ."

"Ah, yes." Lineham glanced down at Telford Green, where lights were coming on in the houses. Then he gave Thanet his usual mischievous grin and said, "Well, one thing's certain, it seems to me. If Mrs. Salden didn't manage to get herself murdered, it wasn't for want of trying."

NINE

"So what did you mean, wasn't for want of trying?" said
Thanet, settling back into his seat with a mental sigh of relief
that their talk seemed to have been of some use and Lineham
was showing every sign of reverting to normal.

They had decided that it was about time they returned to
Headquarters and the car now plunged into the entrance to the
tunnel of trees which was transformed by approaching darkness
into a place of mystery; menace, even.

Lineham braked as a rabbit, momentarily transfixed by their
headlights, squatted in their path before scuttling off into the
undergrowth beside the road, white tail bobbing. "Well, OK, we
don't know yet if it was an accident or not. It could have
been—though, as I said earlier, it's unlikely. I can't see how
anyone could have been unaware of the lights and the barriers
Kimberley set up on the bridge or how Mrs. Salden could
accidentally have fallen in without being pushed. But in view of
the knack she seems to have had for stirring up trouble . . ."

"Trouble in general, or trouble with individuals?"

"Both, I should say. It's just the way she was. If she wanted
something, she went for it, regardless of what anyone else felt. It
wasn't surprising she was unpopular in the village. First she
closes off a right of way . . ."

"Her right of way, remember, Mike."

"Technically, maybe. But you can understand how the people
in the village feel, with no bus and having to walk an extra mile
or more. That's not much fun if you're an old-age pensioner or a
young mum. And they'd been using it for years. Why should she
have been so determined to close it anyway? The footpath doesn't
overlook the Manor gardens, the hedges are much too high and
thick for that. It just seems mean and petty-minded. Then there's

the business of the village hall and the planning permission. Imagine how they must have felt! They'd been slogging away raising money for years, they'd got the promise of a grant from the Borough Council, set up the purchase of the land with Mr. —what was his name?—Tiller, and then, at the eleventh hour, Mrs. Salden snatches the whole thing away from under their noses. Can you blame them for being mad at her? I bet that demonstration down there against Harry Greenleaf's eviction was as much an expression of their resentment against the way she's treated them as against the way she was treating him.''

''I thought the same thing myself. But I'm not so sure that she was just insensitive. I'm beginning to wonder if some of this provocation may have been deliberate.''

''Deliberate?'' They had reached the bottom of the hill and Lineham paused to check that the road was clear before pulling out. ''Why?''

''Ah, that's the intriguing question, isn't it? And I think I'm only just starting to get the glimmer of an answer. But if you think about Marcia Salden's background, it does all begin to make sense.''

''Not to me it doesn't.''

''Just consider, Mike.'' Thanet glanced out of the window as they entered Telford Green and then gestured at the row of cottages ahead, next to the Crooked Door. ''She was brought up there, in a farm worker's cottage. Her father was a drunk. That means that as far as this community was concerned she was the lowest of the low. Then, just as in all the best rags-to-riches stories, she finds fame and fortune—well, fortune, anyway. And what does she do? Does she go as far away as possible from the place where she suffered all the humiliations of the child of an alcoholic? No, she buys the house she fell in love with as a child, the house she swore she would one day own, and in fulfilment of all those childhood dreams comes back as Lady of the Manor. Quite a touching, romantic story, I think you'll agree. But unfortunately she didn't live happily ever after. The sequel wasn't at all what she had imagined. Country people are very conservative, Mike, and the older one's are still very conscious of hierarchy. I can't imagine that they were too pleased to see the daughter of a drunken cottager ensconced in the Manor.''

All the lights were on in the Crooked Door and the place looked warm and welcoming. As they passed, two men went in.

Thanet thought he recognised them from this morning. He resisted the temptation to suggest stopping for a pint.

"Those warning lights are clearly visible from way back up the road," said Lineham, slowing down as he drove over the bridge.

"Yes, I'd noticed."

Lineham glanced at him. "So you think they gave her the cold shoulder?"

"Let's be charitable and say that they would have been slow to accept her. Given time, they might well have done so. But I'd guess that she wouldn't have been prepared to wait. With her background she would have been hyper-sensitive to snubs, real or imagined, and when she found that they were not exactly going to welcome her with open arms she would have said, right, I'll show you, damned if I don't. And proceeded to do just that."

The Manor gates flashed by on the left. The lights were on in the lodge but the main house was invisible from the road by virtue of the curve in the drive.

"So you're saying that closing the footpath and scuppering the plans for the village hall were a way of getting her own back on them?"

Thanet shrugged. "It's possible, don't you think?"

"And evicting Harry Greenleaf?"

"Well, if what I've been saying is true, and I think it quite likely, it must have been galling for her to see Greenleaf accepted and tolerated—even liked—by the villagers, while she was shunned."

"So out he had to go."

"As good a suggestion as any, don't you think?"

"Unless she had some personal reason for wanting to get rid of him."

"Such as?"

"No idea."

"Anyway, to get back to what you were saying, Mike, about the general ill-feeling towards her, you're not by any chance suggesting that the people of the village collectively decided they'd had enough of her and grabbed the chance to shove her off the bridge?"

"No, of course not! I'm just talking about the way she steamrollered her way over people's feelings. And if she could do that on a big scale, why not on a small one?"

"Are you thinking of anyone in particular?"

"Not really. But surely you've noticed that no one we've yet met has shown any real grief over her death? They've been shocked, yes, but that's all. Mrs. Pantry obviously didn't have much time for her, Edith Phipps wasn't exactly brokenhearted even though they went way back together, Nurse Lint wasn't too impressed by her even though she tried to hide it by talking about her generosity towards her mother, and Mrs. Pepper—though she did sympathise with the rotten life Mrs. Salden had had as a girl—didn't have much to say for her either."

"Her husband seemed pretty upset."

"Well, yes. But if she treated him the way she treated everyone else, he couldn't have had much of a life. Didn't you notice Mrs. Pantry said they had separate bedrooms?"

"Lots of married couples have separate bedrooms for all sorts of reasons—he snores, she's an insomniac . . ."

Lineham's face showed that he couldn't accept this proposition. In his book, separate bedrooms meant only one thing: marital disharmony.

"So that show of grief . . . You think he was putting it on, then?"

"Not necessarily, sir. I don't know. I'm just saying he could have been."

"True. But even if you're right, and they didn't get on too well, it doesn't necessarily mean he killed her. He could still genuinely have been in shock. After all, if you've lived with a woman for—what?—twenty years, you're bound to feel something when she dies suddenly, even if the first fine careless rapture has worn off. And there doesn't seem to have been any talk about trouble between them, in the village."

"No, that's true. Miss Phipps wasn't too comfortable, though, when you asked her about them. In any case, you must admit he seems the most likely suspect so far, if only because he seems to have been in the right place at the right time."

"True."

"I mean, if he had a reason for wanting to get rid of her that nobody knows about and the opportunity to do so just shoved itself under his nose when they happened to pass each other on the bridge . . ."

"It's certainly possible, Mike, I grant you. Obviously we'll have to see him again tomorrow, when I hope he'll be in a fit state to talk . . ."

They had arrived back at Headquarters and Lineham parked the car and switched off the engine. Engrossed in their discussion, neither of them made any move to get out.

"The other likely suspect at the moment, of course, is Greenleaf," said Thanet. "You weren't there, were you, when Miss Phipps was telling me about him? Apparently he's badly disfigured after an accident, which I imagine is one of the reasons why he leads the life of a recluse."

"No, I didn't know that. Poor chap. I wonder if Mr. Salden will let him stay on, now."

"Yes, it'll be interesting to find out. I imagine it wouldn't have been easy for him to find somewhere else to go, if the eviction had gone ahead. If the disfigurement is as bad as Miss Phipps says, it's understandable that he doesn't want too much contact with other people. He'd probably have been forced into a life on the road. All of which adds up to a powerful motive for wanting to get rid of Mrs. Salden."

"Honestly, sir, I know you were trying to excuse the way Mrs. Salden behaved towards the people of the village, but with respect . . ."

"Not excuse, Mike. I was merely trying to understand her reasons. And every time you say, 'With respect,' I know you're about to disagree with me. So go on, disagree."

"No, not disagree, exactly. I was only going to say that in my opinion she sounds a nasty bit of work. This Greenleaf business was typical. Why couldn't she have left the poor man alone? He wasn't doing anyone any harm, was he? And he wasn't exactly under her nose all the time, he was tucked well away out of sight. It just seems a bit of gratuitous unpleasantness to take him to court and threaten to tip him out like that."

"Maybe. Nevertheless, Mike, if you can try to be a little more dispassionate about this, you'll concede that he has very good reason to be thankful that she is permanently out of the way."

"That's not the same as saying he might have shoved her off the bridge."

"Mike! I'm not suggesting it is, and you know it! Merely that the possibility exists."

Lineham was silent for a moment or two, then said awkwardly, "It does, of course. Sorry, sir, don't know what got into me."

"Forget it. So we'll have to interview Greenleaf tomorrow, as well. Meanwhile, there were one or two other interesting points, I thought.''

"Such as?"

"That dinner party . . ."

"Yes. A bit of a mixed bag, wasn't it? A county councillor and a hairdresser?"

"Quite. It did just occur to me . . . Isn't Lomax chairman of the Planning Committee?"

"Yes, you're right, he is, I'd forgotten that . . ." Lineham's lips pursed in a silent whistle. "You mean . . ."

"That Mrs. Salden might have been using Josie Trimble as bait in order to swing that planning permission. Yes. What d'you think, Mike?"

"Sounds quite likely to me, after what we've heard about Mrs. Salden. I wouldn't put anything past her, if she wanted something badly enough."

"It would explain why she didn't want to cancel the dinner party, wouldn't it? A quarter of a million is a high stake."

"And also why she didn't mind leaving them alone while she went down to the village to visit her mother. And," said Lineham, warming to his theme, "why the housekeeper was so sniffy when she was talking about the girl. I wondered what all that was about. I thought perhaps it was just because Mrs. Pantry was a bit of a snob, but if she was aware of what was going on . . ."

"I agree. Also, it surprised me a bit that Salden was so ready to disappear for the evening, that he didn't go back to the house to apologise to his guests and spend some time with them between his first and second visits to his mother-in-law. But if he knew what his wife was up to and disapproved of it he might have been only too glad of an excuse to keep out of the way. Anyway, if we're right, it does open up certain interesting possibilities, don't you agree?"

"I do. Blackmail, for instance. If Lomax had got himself entangled with Josie Trimble and Mrs. Salden had started putting pressure on about the planning permission . . . Lomax could have found himself in a very nasty position."

"If it had got out it wouldn't have done him much good, that's for sure."

"It'd certainly have made the headlines in the local paper. It's got all the ingredients of a first-class scandal—sex, bribery, corruption in local government . . . I can just see the headlines. BOROUGH COUNCILLOR . . ."

"All right, Mike, no need to get carried away. The point is, we'll need to pay a little visit to those two tomorrow, too."

"Don't you think we ought to see Miss Phipps again as well?"

"Ah, I wondered if you'd spotted that. Yes, she was holding something back, wasn't she, when I asked her about her movements that evening. I wonder what she'd been up to."

No doubt they'd find out, sooner or later.

TEN

After spending several hours on the "detailed, literate and accurate" reports Draco would expect next morning, all Thanet wanted to do when he got home was fall into bed and sink into oblivion. As he pulled into the drive he was surprised to see a light still on in the tiny shoebox of a bedroom which he and Joan used as a study. He went straight upstairs, pleased to note that tonight the light was off in Bridget's room.

Joan was sitting at the desk, which was strewn with papers. She turned as he came in and lifted her face for his kiss. "How's the case going?"

He shrugged. "So so. You're working late, love."

"I know." She laid down her pen, took off her recently acquired spectacles and rubbed her eyes. "I've got to finish this report by tomorrow, and I didn't have a chance to tackle it earlier on."

"Why was that?" Thanet perched on the edge of the desk. Joan, too, looked very tired. There were lines of strain around her eyes, her mouth drooped and her short fair curly hair was dishevelled, as though she had been running her hands through it. From where he sat looking down at her Thanet could see a glint of grey here and there. We're neither of us getting any younger, he thought.

She pulled a face. "Vicky was here for a good couple of hours, in floods of tears most of the time."

Vicky Younghusband lived next door. Her husband, Peter, was a travelling salesman and Vicky had given birth to their first child six weeks ago. She had worked in the offices of a local estate agent until a month before the baby was born, and had always been a cheerful, outgoing girl. She and Peter had been delighted when she found she was pregnant at last. They had been married for eight years and for the last five had been hoping

82

that Vicky would conceive. On the day the pregnancy was confirmed they had brought round a bottle of champagne, and they had all drunk a toast to the next generation of Younghusbands.

"At least three of them!" Vicky had declared, radiant with happiness.

"Wait until you've had one," Joan had teased. "You might change your mind."

Often, during the last few weeks, she had had reason to remember that light-hearted remark, for since the baby's arrival Vicky was a changed woman. Gone were the smiles, the cheerfulness, the unfailing optimism, replaced by endless tears and a dragging, debilitating depression. More than once Peter had come round to see the Thanets in despair.

"Post-natal depression, the doctor says. But how long is it going to last? I sometimes feel I can't take much more."

Joan and Thanet had made consoling noises but had felt powerless to help. What could they do, except provide a sympathetic ear and a shoulder to cry on?

Instead of the fortnight he had arranged to take off to help Vicky after the baby was born, Peter had taken a month, using up all his annual leave in one fell swoop, but at the end of this time Vicky was no better. Worried though he was, Peter had had to go back to work, and although he had tried to arrange his schedule so that Vicky was not alone more than two nights in succession it wasn't always possible; his area was large and his employers understandably becoming a little tetchy. He could not afford to risk losing his job.

Thanet and Joan had promised to keep an eye on Vicky, but at the end of a working day it wasn't always easy to call up the reserves of emotional energy which she demanded.

Joan sighed. "Honestly, Luke, I'm sure her doctor doesn't realise just how ill she is. From what she says he's one of the old school who tends to think women are a bit hysterical and everything would be all right if she'd just make an effort and pull herself together. I really am worried about her. I even wonder if . . ."

"What?"

Joan shook her head. "Oh, nothing. I'm being silly, I suppose."

"You're not suggesting she might try to commit suicide?"

"Well, it has crossed my mind, I must admit. And I feel so helpless, Luke. D'you know, I went in there the other day after I got home from work, about six o'clock it must have been, and there she was, sitting in front of the television set in a sort of

trance, still in her dressing gown. No make-up, her hair uncombed . . . I had the impression she'd been there all day. The
baby was screaming his head off, he was hungry, his nappy was
soaking wet. She really is deeply and clinically depressed."

"What about the health visitor? Surely she must be aware of
the situation?"

"So far as I can gather, Peter has always made an enormous
effort to get the house straight and make sure things look as
normal as possible when she's coming. He hasn't actually said
so, but I think he's afraid they might take the baby away if
things look too bad. Which is understandable, but very misleading."

"When's he due back?"

"The day after tomorrow."

"I'll try and have a tactful word with him, point out that
although it may have been done with the best of intentions, it's
not really in Vicky's best interest to give a false impression of
how she's coping. Meanwhile . . . Wait a minute, aren't they
with the Thompson and Merridew practice?"

"Yes. Why?"

"I heard the other day that they'd just taken on a new partner.
A woman in her thirties. One of the lads was complaining that
he'd never get used to a woman doctor. Perhaps we could
manoeuvre an appointment with her, for Vicky. She might be a
lot more understanding and constructive. We'll suggest it to
Peter, when he gets back. So cheer up, love. It's not all doom
and despair."

Joan grimaced. "That's not the only thing that's worrying me,
I'm afraid." She laid a hand on his. "Oh darling, I am sorry to
throw all this at you the second you walk through the door. You
look so tired. And I suppose your back is playing up again?"

Thanet admitted that it was. It always did, when he was tired.
An old injury had left him with a permanent weakness in the
lumbar region. It was little consolation to know that there were
2.2 million other sufferers in the British Isles. "But never mind
that. What else is bothering you? You might as well tell me the
worst."

Joan glanced uneasily towards the door and lowered her voice.
"Did you notice if Bridget's light was off?"

Automatically Thanet leaned closer. We must look like a
couple of conspirators, he thought. "Yes, it was. Why?"

"Mr. Foreman rang me at work this afternoon. He wants me
to go and see him."

Thanet frowned. Mr. Foreman was Bridget and Ben's headmaster. "Why?"

"He wouldn't say—except that it's about Bridget."

"Perhaps he's as concerned as we are that she's pushing herself too hard."

"Why wouldn't he discuss it over the phone, then?"

"No time?"

Joan shook her head. "I felt it was more . . . how shall I put it? More as if he wanted to discuss some definite misdemeanour on her part."

"What, for instance?"

"No idea."

"There you are, then. You're imagining things. Bridget isn't the type to cause trouble, you know that. In fact, she's too conscientious by half. Did you ask her if she could guess why Mr. Foreman wanted to see you?"

"Yes. She said she'd no idea. But . . ."

"What?"

"Well, I had the impression she wasn't being frank with me."

This was bad news. Thanet had great faith in Joan's powers of intuition. "Did you fix up an appointment?"

"Yes. Two thirty tomorrow afternoon."

"I'll come with you."

"No, there's no need. Really. It might look as though we're taking the whole thing far too seriously if we both turn up. And it might be about something quite trivial."

But the same thought was in both their minds: in that case, why hadn't Mr. Foreman been prepared to discuss it over the phone?

Thanet stood up. "Come on, time for bed. We're both tired."

She shook her head, picked up her spectacles and put them on. "I really have to finish this report tonight."

"How much longer will you be?"

"Half an hour or so."

For the second night running Thanet lay awake worrying about his daughter.

Next morning he set off for work early. He wanted to skim through as many as possible of the reports that would have come in on the Salden case before the morning meeting with Draco. He cast a wistful glance into his own office as he passed. Dust sheets covered the carpet and someone had been having fun spattering Polyfilla over the walls. The map of Australia on the ceiling had disappeared. Thanet found that like Lineham he mourned its passing.

It was difficult to concentrate in the main CID room, partly because the DCs were trying to be so considerate. They came and went as though walking on eggshells, held telephone conversations *sotto voce* and consulted each other in voices barely louder than whispers. It was all highly unnatural and therefore very distracting. All the reports were brief, however, and Thanet had just finished when Lineham arrived.

"Anything, sir?" said the Sergeant.

"Just a few odds and ends. There doesn't seem to be much doubt that Mrs. Salden fell from the bridge, though of course we'll have to wait to hear from Forensic before we're absolutely certain. The divers found her torch in the river below the gap in the parapet, and Mrs. Pantry identified the shoe. It was one of a pair kept for outdoor use in a small cloakroom near the back door. She also found Mrs. Salden's evening shoes, which she'd obviously discarded when she discovered her car wouldn't start and she'd have to walk to the village."

The telephone rang and Lineham answered it. He mouthed, "Tessa Barclay, TVS" at Thanet, and proceeded to apologise for the fact that Thanet had been unavailable the previous afternoon and to promise regular daily bulletins.

"Got yourself a new job then, Mike," said Thanet with a grin as the Sergeant put the phone down. "Press correspondent."

Lineham shrugged. He didn't always take kindly to being teased. "Someone's got to do it," he muttered.

"And who better?" Thanet glanced at his watch. 8:43. "Look, get on the phone and check that Mr. Salden will be at home around nine thirty, will you? As soon as the morning meeting's over we'll go out to the Manor again."

But Draco had other ideas. At the end of the meeting he once again called Thanet back and waved him into a chair.

Thanet betrayed none of his sudden unease. He had an uncomfortable feeling that he knew what was coming.

Draco sat back in his chair, picked up an elastic band and started fiddling with it, winding it around his finger, rolling it on and off his wrist. He seemed incapable of sitting still and once again Thanet wondered how a desk job was going to accommodate all that nervous energy.

"Correct me if I'm wrong," said the Superintendent in a casual manner which did not deceive Thanet for one moment, "but am I right in thinking that at the moment you haven't got one single speck of evidence that Mrs. Salden's death was anything but an accident?''

Thanet's guess had been correct. Draco wasn't the kind of man to back non-starters. He wanted Thanet to pull out. Thanet prepared to do battle, if necessary. But first he would have to cut Draco down to size in his own mind. He stared at the Superintendent. Draco's promotion was recent and his Welsh accent had been especially noticeable just now. This would be the first clash of wills with his Detective Inspector. Perhaps he, too, was a little nervous and wasn't such a formidable opponent after all.

"That's true, sir."

"So would you mind explaining to me how I can justify using the entire resources of my CID department on an exercise that could turn out to be a complete waste of time?"

Thanet noticed an involuntary twinge of jealousy at the word *my*, and his determination to win his skirmish hardened. But what ammunition did he have? None. Except . . . "Doesn't it rather turn on the word 'could,' sir?"

Draco's thick black eyebrows suddenly clamped together like two hairy caterpillars overcome by passion. "What do you mean?"

"Well, sir, we have to acknowledge that, equally, it *could* turn out that she was murdered. In which case, if we had just let the matter drop after only twenty-four hours, when there were still obvious lines of enquiry to follow up . . . The Saldens were pretty big fish in the business world down here, and were getting bigger all the time, I gather. It seems to me that you could put that question another way: Can we afford *not* to pursue the matter, for at least a little while longer?"

Draco gave Thanet a penetrating stare, pinged the elastic band a couple of times, then tossed it on to the desk. He steepled his hands beneath his chin. "Convince me," he snapped.

Thanet recognised the first sign of capitulation and breathed an inward sigh of relief.

"Well, to begin with, it's difficult to see how she could have fallen through that gap in the parapet by accident . . .''

Thanet reiterated all the conclusions he and Lineham had reached and Draco listened intently, black eyes glittering. He then asked Thanet for details of the lines of enquiry he would follow up today if further investigations were made. Finally he said grudgingly, "Well, I suppose it won't do any harm to carry on for a bit longer. When's the PM?"

"We're trying to fix it for this afternoon, sir."

"Right. We'll review the situation again tomorrow morning."

He raised a hand as Thanet started to get up. "There is just one other thing."

"Yes, sir?"

"The media. Press, television and so on. We had TVS around yesterday afternoon, claiming an appointment with you. You weren't here."

"It wasn't exactly an appointment, sir, I just said . . ."

"Never mind what you said. It's important to keep the press sweet, Thanet. It's good for our image."

"Yes, I know, sir. And TVS is particularly helpful. But you know what it's like on this sort of enquiry, it's very difficult to say you'll be in a given place at a given time . . ."

"I'm aware of that. That is why I have a suggestion to make."

Thanet waited.

"On enquiries like these I suggest that you find time, each day, in the late afternoon, to report to me, either in person or by phone, and I can make the appropriate response to the media."

So Draco was publicity hungry, too. That was fine by Thanet.

"Right, sir."

Draco reached for a file and opened it.

Thanet took the hint. He was dismissed. He hurried back upstairs still seething with resentment. If he was going to have to face this kind of hassle every morning before he could get on with his work, he'd find himself applying for a transfer before long.

ELEVEN

Mrs. Pantry showed them into the big sitting-room. "I'll tell him you're here."

While they waited Thanet wandered around, struck once again by the unsuitability of the furnishings. His work took him into many private houses and he firmly believed that a person's home said much about him. This room baffled him. Marcia Salden had obviously been hard-working and ambitious. She had made a resounding success of her business and had fulfilled her childhood dream of owning this house. Why, then, had she not made an effort to furnish it in an appropriate manner? He thought of the gracious room across the hall, downgraded to office. Surely, in a place this size, some other room could have been utilised for such a mundane purpose?

Was it insensitivity, he wondered, that had caused her to treat the house she had yearned for with so little respect? It could have been ignorance, of course, but then she would have been able to afford the best of advice, had she chosen to seek it. Perhaps she simply couldn't be bothered? But that didn't fit in with what he had learnt about her so far. She sounded a woman who paid meticulous attention to detail. Could it perhaps—unpleasant thought—have been a kind of contempt, exercised to demonstrate to the local community how little she valued what they prized so highly, the most beautiful and imposing house in the area? Or perhaps it was simply that it was her work alone that really mattered to her and it was computers and office equipment, rather than carpets and curtains, which monopolised her attention.

What had she and Salden *done* in here? Thanet wondered. There was a television set, true, and the hideous cocktail bar, but none of the clutter which gives a room a lived-in appearance—no books, magazines or newspapers, no photographs apart from the

89

one of Salden shaking hands with Princess Anne, and virtually no ornaments either. What sort of life had she and Salden led together?

The door opened and Salden came in. Thanet guessed that he had put on the first clothes that had come to hand—formal grey worsted trousers that looked as though they belonged to a suit, green open-necked shirt and a navy sweater with a pattern of blue and white diamonds and a logo of crossed golf clubs. He seemed to have aged ten years overnight. If Thanet had met him for the first time today he would have put him in his late sixties. His plump cheeks sagged, his eyelids drooped and below his eyes the pouches of slack skin betrayed the fact that after the sedative wore off he must have spent a sleepless night. But it was his eyes that revealed most clearly his state of mind. They were dazed, veiled. Salden had understandably hidden himself behind the invisible barrier erected in self-protection by those who are trying to survive the aftermath of sudden death.

Thanet experienced a twinge of self-disgust. It was going to be his job to break that barrier down. This particular type of interview, with a bereaved husband or wife who was also a suspect, was the one he hated most of all. At times it had even made him consider changing his job. If Salden were innocent, he deserved the utmost sympathy; if not, sympathy could get badly in the way. Thanet had to walk the tightrope between compassion and inexorability, knowing that whatever the outcome a human being least able to cope with life was having his defences stripped away.

"Good morning, Inspector . . ." Salden shook his head. "I'm sorry, I've forgotten your name."

"Thanet. And this is Detective Sergeant Lineham."

Salden walked slowly across to the wing chair—he was still wearing slippers, Thanet noticed—and lowered himself into it. He waved a hand at the settee opposite. "Please . . ."

Thanet complied, but Lineham retreated to the matching armchair, moving it back a little and turning it slightly so that he was at right angles to the other two and out of Salden's direct line of vision.

"Have you found out what happened?" said Salden. The dazed look was still there, but behind it was a spark of animation. The process was beginning.

"We think so. We believe she fell through the gap in the parapet of the bridge in the village, where the lorry crashed into it." Thanet was watching Salden's reaction closely. Was that alarm, or simply surprise?

"But that's not possible, surely? The gap was roped off, and there were warning lights . . ."

"You saw them when you went through the village that night."

"Yes, of course." Salden shook his head in apparent puzzlement. "I don't understand."

"I agree, it does seem odd. Obviously, we're trying to find out exactly what happened . . . You said you went for a walk that evening?"

"That's right, yes."

"What time did you leave your mother-in-law's house?"

The brief flare of interest had burned itself out and there was a pause before each answer now as if remembering were a process only to be achieved by will-power.

"Let me see . . . Somewhere around half-past eight, I should think."

"Which way did you go?"

"Through the village. I went for a drink at the pub first, then I carried on, over the bridge towards the Sturrenden road."

"The warning lights and rope barriers . . . They were all in position then?"

A long pause, this time. "So far as I can remember, yes. I think I would have noticed, if they hadn't been. But I was rather preoccupied. I was thinking about my mother-in-law. We . . ." He turned his head aside and took in a deep breath, held it. "We were very fond of each other and it always upset me, to see her as she was that night."

"Yes, I can imagine. I'm sorry, you've had a really bad time over the last few days."

The words of sympathy penetrated Salden's fragile defences and his eyes filled with tears. He blinked several times in rapid succession and brushed a forefinger across each eye. "Sorry."

"Don't apologise, please." *Remember, a man is innocent until he is proved guilty.* "I'm sorry to have to ask you all these questions, but we've been trying to talk to everyone who was out and about in the village that night . . . We understand you didn't get back to your mother-in-law's house until about half-past ten. It must have been quite a long walk."

"Well, I wasn't walking all the time. As I said, I went into the pub for a while, twenty minutes or half an hour, perhaps, then I strolled along as far as the junction with the Sturrenden road and back."

"That would have taken how long?"

Salden shrugged. "I wasn't walking very quickly. I wasn't looking for exercise, just fresh air and a chance to think."

"About anything in particular?"

Salden frowned. "Not really, no. Look, Inspector, I'm sorry, but I don't quite see where all this is leading."

"I assure you that everyone in the village is being asked similar questions."

"That may be so. But the point is, why are they necessary, if you already know how the accident happened?"

Thanet said nothing, just cast a deliberate glance at Lineham.

Salden's face changed, its slack lines firming up into much more positive contours. His eyes narrowed as the glazed look finally disappeared and he leaned forward.

Thanet could predict what was coming next. He had heard it so many times before.

"You're not suggesting . . . ? My God, you are, aren't you?"

"Suggesting what, Mr. Salden?"

"That Marcia . . . That it wasn't an accident?"

"We're treating this as a suspicious death, Mr. Salden, that's all. Before we can dismiss it as an accident we have to consider all the other possibilities. Suicide, for example."

Salden was shaking his head vigorously. "Marcia would never have committed suicide."

"You'd be surprised how many of the relatives of suicides say just that."

Salden waved a hand. "Ask anyone you like . . . The housekeeper, Mrs. Pantry . . . Edith Phipps . . . the Vicar . . . Anyone who knew her. I don't think you'll find a single person who'd countenance the idea for one second. Marcia really just wasn't the type. She had too much to live for."

"I must admit that that was the impression I had already gained from talking to people. So in that case, you see, we must at least consider the third possibility."

Salden shook his head again. There was a beading of sweat on his upper lip and he was hugging himself as if to stop himself falling apart. "I can't believe it. Who would want to do such a thing?"

"Have you any suggestions?"

Salden frowned, thinking.

There was a knock at the door. Salden appeared not to have heard. Thanet and Lineham exchanged irritated glances. Should they ignore it? But it could be important. "Come in," called Thanet as Salden, simultaneously, said, "There's only—"

Edith Phipps put her head around the door. "Sorry to interrupt, but I thought you'd want to know . . . The Vicar's on the
phone, about the arrangements for Mrs. Carter's funeral, and
he's got to go out, you won't be able to ring him later."

Salden glanced at Thanet. "Sorry, Inspector . . . Would you
excuse me for a moment?"

Thanet had no choice but to agree.

When Salden had left, Lineham burst out, "He was just going
to give us a name!"

Thanet nodded. "Yes, but I bet you anything you like it was
going to be Greenleaf's."

Lineham pulled a face. "Probably."

Thanet got up and strolled across to the window. Earlier on
the sky had been overcast but now the cloud cover was beginning to break up and patches of blue were appearing. Thanet
leaned forward to look diagonally across to the right at the
smudge of trees that was Harry's wood. It was foolish to ignore
the obvious. Greenleaf had the only discernible motive so far for
killing Marcia Salden. He would almost certainly have had
opportunity, too. He was accountable to no one for his movements and could well have been in the right place at the right
time without anyone being the wiser. Yes, a visit to Harry was
high on their list of priorities. Thanet half turned, propping one
elbow on the window ledge, so that he could see Lineham's
face. "Well, what d'you think now you've had the chance of a
second look at Salden? Still think he might have done it?"

"Might have. I don't think we're any further forward, to be
honest."

"I must admit he intrigues me, Mike."

"Why? He seems a very ordinary sort of bloke to me."

"But that's precisely it! What makes a man like that tick,
Mike? He is ordinary. So ordinary that he practically disappears
into the wallpaper."

"The last person you'd suspect of murder, in fact."

"Exactly."

Lineham grinned. "According to all the detective novels,
then, he's bound to be our man."

"Not such a joke in fact, Mike. Think of all the quiet little
men who have upped and killed their spouses when they've had
enough."

"You think Salden had had enough?"

"Not necessarily, no."

"If he did it, it looks as though he killed the goose that laid the golden eggs, doesn't it? I'd guess she was the one who was the driving force behind the health food shops and all this." Lineham waved a hand to encompass the Manor, the grounds outside. "Not that it would matter too much, I suppose. There should be a tidy little sum to keep him in comfort in his old age."

"Not necessarily, Mike. For all we know they could be mortgaged to the eyeballs. We'll have to look into it. But there's no doubt that at the moment Salden's a prime suspect. He's the only person we know of so far who was definitely in the right place at the right time."

"So far."

"True. But—and it's a big but—if his motive wasn't financial it's difficult to see what it could be."

"Does he need one, sir? As the music-hall comedian would say, he was married to her, wasn't he?"

"Don't tell me you're becoming a cynic in your old age, Mike."

"I was only kidding. No, the point I was trying to make is that, as you've said so often yourself, no one really knows what goes on between a married couple but the two people themselves. And in this case, well, they're an odd pair, you'll agree."

"True. Though they must have got on reasonably well to have worked in the same business under the same roof for twenty years or so."

"They weren't exactly under each other's feet, were they, in a place this size?"

"Maybe not, but they'd only been here eighteen months, remember. I bet that for years they were tripping over each other all day and every day in some poky little flat above the shop."

Across the hall a door slammed. Thanet strolled back to his seat.

"Sorry I was so long. There was a lot to discuss." Salden was moving more briskly, as if making decisions had nudged him one step further back towards normality. He sat down, frowning. "What were we saying?"

"I'd just asked if you could think of anyone with a grudge against your wife," said Thanet.

"Ah, yes . . . Well, as I was going to say, there's only Harry Greenleaf. I suppose you've heard about him?"

"We have, yes. In fact, we arrived yesterday just as the bailiffs were about to evict him. I hope you don't mind, but I took it upon myself to delay the eviction. I thought you wouldn't want all the fuss and commotion that would follow. A lot of the villagers turned up, you know, and formed a protest line. They'd have had to be removed bodily before the bulldozer could have got through to the hut.''

"Really? Good grief. I didn't know that. Edith—Miss Phipps—told me you'd sent the bailiffs away. Thank you. A minor riot was the last thing I'd have wanted on my hands yesterday.''

"What will you do now, about Greenleaf?"

Salden shrugged. "Let him stay on, probably. If the local people feel as strongly as that . . .''

"It was your wife who was so keen to get rid of him?"

Salden looked embarrassed. "Yes. I never did understand why. Still . . . although, as I say, he's the only person I can think of who could be said to have had a grudge against her, I really can't believe he would have gone to the sort of lengths you're suggesting. He's always struck me as being a quiet, gentle sort of chap, the kind who wouldn't squash a fly without having qualms about it. He's always taking wounded animals under his wing and patching them up before releasing them into the wild again, that sort of thing.''

Thanet decided to backtrack a little. "To get back to your walk . . . Even allowing for your time in the pub, it wouldn't have taken you an hour and a half to stroll as far as the Sturrenden road and back.''

"There's a footpath running alongside the river, on the other side of the bridge, and a bench or two here and there. I went and sat on one for a while.''

"It was freezing, that night.''

"I was well wrapped up . . . Look, Inspector, all this interest in my movements . . . I'm not stupid, I can see where it's leading . . .''

Thanet said nothing. He was interested to see how Salden would deal with this.

Salden was watching him closely. "I'm right, aren't I?" His voice rose. "That is what you're getting at, isn't it?" A rush of indignation drove him to his feet and he stood confronting Thanet, feet planted firmly apart and hands shoved into his pockets. "My God," he said, glaring down at him, "you really are the lowest of the low, aren't you?"

Inwardly, Thanet winced but, knowing that in circumstances like these silence is the most powerful weapon of all, he still did not respond.

"How can you do it?" said Salden, working himself up into a

real fury. "How would you feel if your wife had just been
dragged out of the river and some grubby little policeman came
along and said you'd shoved her in yourself, tell me that?"

This accorded so well with what Thanet himself felt that he
was stung into speech. "I said no such thing."

Salden brushed the denial aside. "Said, implied, what's the
difference? It all comes down to the same thing, doesn't it? You
think I might have killed her." He shook his head in disgust and
began to blunder blindly about the room, as if trying to find his
way out of an impossible situation.

Lineham tensed, but Thanet shook his head. *Let him be.*

Salden clutched his head. "I don't believe this. I just don't
believe it."

"Mr. Salden."

The note of command in Thanet's voice was so powerful that
Salden was stopped in his tracks.

"Mr. Salden," Thanet repeated, more gently. "Look, I know
this is an unpleasant situation . . ."

Salden gave a great bark of mirthless laughter. "Unpleasant,
he says!"

"For both of us. And for you most of all. But . . ."

"Oh, I'm glad you recognise that! Very glad! You're right, it
is *unpleasant* to be accused of murdering your wife when you're
still trying to grasp the fact that she's gone for ever. Do you have
even the first glimmering of what that can be like? Of course you
haven't. No one can, if they haven't actually been through it
themselves. There's this huge gap, this vast empty space, which
has always been filled by one person . . . And you know that no
one can fill it ever again, that you're going to have to live with
that gap for the rest of your life. How can you even begin to
understand? It's as if life itself has hit you with a sledgehammer
and you know you're never going to get over it, never . . ."

Salden was fighting for control. Thanet and Lineham sat
frozen into silence. What can you say in response to grief so raw
and unconcealed?

"And then," said Salden, his voice still shaking, "you're
expected to sit down meekly and face the allegation that you
killed her yourself!"

"Mr. Salden . . ."

"I don't want to hear any more! Get out, will you? Just get
out!"

Thanet and Lineham consulted each other with a glance.
They'd inflicted more than enough pain on the man for one day,

Thanet thought. He nodded and they both rose, walked silently to the door. Thanet had his hand on the knob when Salden said, "No!"

They turned.

Salden was chinking the change in his pockets, his restless fingers unconsciously betraying his jangled nerves. "If I don't answer your bloody questions now you'll only come back another day. I've changed my mind. I want to get it over with."

Thanet hesitated. He wasn't sure that there was any point in continuing, with Salden in this state.

Salden misread him. "Oh, don't worry, I won't blow my top again. I can see that it's in my own interest to satisfy your curiosity"—he practically spat the word out—"as soon as possible." He sat down decisively in the wing chair and folded his hands in his lap. "So I'm ready when you are."

"If you're sure . . ."

"I've said so, haven't I?"

Thanet and Lineham returned to their seats.

"Right," said Thanet briskly. "We'll be as quick as possible. This walk . . ."

"We've been over all that once," interrupted Salden impatiently.

"Please . . . bear with me for just a moment. This bench you were sitting on. How far away from the bridge was it?"

"Quite a long way. Three or four hundred yards, perhaps?"

"It was dark, of course. Would you be able to see anyone walking across the bridge, from that distance?"

"No. Not clearly, anyway, not to recognise anyone."

"There's a lamp on the pub side of the bridge, isn't there? What about on the other side? I'm not too clear on that."

"It's a sore point. We've been trying to get another one installed. The nearest one is a hundred yards away, where the houses start."

"I see . . . Now I'd like you to think very carefully. While you were sitting on your bench, did you in fact see or hear any noise at all from the direction of the bridge? Voices, for example, or footsteps?" *Or sounds of a struggle, or a splash?* Thanet shuddered at the thought of Salden's wife fighting for her life with her husband sitting innocently on a bench only a quarter of a mile away. "It was a clear, frosty night, so sound would have carried quite a long way, I imagine."

The brief, factual questions were calming Salden down. He was frowning hard, trying to remember.

"I'm sorry," he said at last. "I just can't remember. I wasn't taking any notice, you see. I vaguely remember the odd car going by, but that's all.''

It was pointless to ask if, on his way back to Mrs. Carter's cottage, Salden had seen his wife. He would obviously deny it. "On your way back to your mother-in-law's house, did you see anyone?"

"Not a soul."

"This walk you took . . . I must confess I'm a little puzzled." Salden raised his eyebrows.

"As to why you didn't go home instead? Especially as you had guests to dinner that evening."

"I just wasn't feeling particularly sociable."

"Even so . . ."

"To be blunt, Inspector, I just couldn't face the prospect of making polite conversation. My mother-in-law and I were very close, I told you . . . It really upset me to see her like that. At that particular moment I couldn't have cared less how discourteous it looked."

"That dinner party . . ." Careful now, Thanet told himself. He didn't want to set Salden off again. On the other hand, he had to find out . . . "I did have the impression it wasn't just a normal social occasion."

"Oh?" Salden's eyes were wary.

"One of your guests was Councillor Lomax, I understand."

"Yes he was."

"I believe he is chairman of the Planning Committee. And your wife was hoping to get a rather tricky planning permission . . ." The implication was clear and Thanet awaited Salden's response with interest and some trepidation. Would he pretend not to understand, feign ignorance, become angry, bluster . . . ?

Salden sighed. "Yes . . . Perhaps I should explain . . . My wife was an amazing woman. If you knew the kind of background she came from . . . Her father was an alcoholic, and they never had two pennies to rub together. I think that was why she had this tremendous drive to succeed. She was one of my students, you know, that was how we met. I was lecturing at the time on a Business Studies course, and this was what singled her out from all the rest. She was so determined . . . I couldn't help admiring her for that, it was what attracted me to her in the first place. I've always admired people who knew what they wanted and were prepared to work hard to get it. So I could hardly complain if, from time to time, she set out to do something I didn't really approve of. She never was the type to rest on her laurels, she was always looking for some bigger challenge to move on to and usually I just let her get on with it.''

"And this particular scheme?''

Salden shrugged. "I told her I didn't like it. But if you think I shoved her off the bridge to stop her going on with it, I'm afraid you're way off the mark. There were other ways to show my disapproval.''

"Like ducking out of the dinner party, for example?''

For the first time there was a flicker of amusement in Salden's eyes. "Exactly.''

"The other guest, Miss Trimble . . . ?''

"We all call her Josie. She spends quite a lot of time here. She's only eighteen and she comes from the village, her mother's a widow so they've had a bit of a struggle to manage. Josie was . . . well, I suppose you could call her a protégé of my wife's. We never actually discussed it, but I think Marcia saw herself in the girl, and was trying to help her to better herself—teaching her table manners and so on.''

"So she was often invited to dinner parties? To put into practice what she'd learned.''

"Yes. Well, not often, exactly. We don't—didn't—entertain much.''

"In that case, wasn't your wife annoyed, that you didn't go back to join them?''

Salden blinked. "How should I know? I never saw her again . . . Oh, you mean earlier, when we spoke on the phone? No, I don't think so. In fact I think at that point she was just relieved that she wouldn't have to go down to the village herself. It had been too late, earlier, to stop Lomax coming, Nurse Lint didn't ring until just before half-past seven.''

"Your wife went down to see her mother later though, leaving her guests entirely on their own.''

Another shrug. "In the normal way of things she'd only have been away ten or fifteen minutes, if she'd gone by car.''

"But she still went, even though the car wouldn't start.''

"True. But she'd have expected to find me there, remember. No doubt she thought I'd be able to give her a lift back, or that she could borrow my keys and drive back in my car . . . Look, Inspector, I really can't see why we're dredging all this up. Yes, she did go, and yes, I agree it did look odd, leaving her guests by themselves like that, but it happened and I can't see any point in discussing it further.''

"Why did Mrs. Carter want to see you?''

Salden lifted his shoulders. "She was convinced she was dying. Wasn't that a good enough reason?"

"In that case, wasn't it strange that she didn't ask for your wife in the first place?"

"She knew I'd get Marcia to come when I felt the time was right. My mother-in-law was a very proud woman in some ways, especially where my wife was concerned. It was as if she didn't want it to look as though she was making any kind of claim on her. I could never understand it myself. She really hated asking Marcia for anything. Anyway, I decided to ring Marcia from the cottage when I got back from my walk and tell her I thought she ought to come down. I knew dinner would be over by then and she'd be able to get rid of Lomax and Josie without too much difficulty. But of course, when I got back to the cottage, she'd already been and gone."

"I understand you missed her by just a few minutes."

"Yes." Salden shivered and wrapped his arms around his body. "If only I'd started back a few minutes earlier she'd still be alive . . ."

"There's never any point in saying 'If only,' Mr. Salden," said Thanet gently.

"Maybe not. But how do you stop yourself, in circumstances like these?"

The pain in Salden's eyes was so intense that it was almost unbearable to meet them and there was no doubting his sincerity.

"Just one more question, and we'll leave you in peace. When you got home, why didn't you go into your wife's room and tell her that her mother had died?"

"It was four in the morning, Inspector. Her room was in darkness and I assumed she'd been asleep for hours. What was the point in waking her up? She couldn't have done anything."

This was unanswerable.

They left.

TWELVE

"Well, that was no act, was it?" said Lineham. "He really did care about her, didn't he?"

Thanet had decided that a visit to Greenleaf was definitely next on the agenda and they were crossing the lawn towards the entrance to the footpath. It was a relief to get out into the open air, away from the claustrophobic atmosphere of the house. He sniffed appreciatively and turned his face to the sun, which had just broken through. "Mmm." His feet scuffed through the lake of fallen petals beneath the cherry tree. "Doesn't necessarily exonerate him, though." Violent crime, he knew, stirred strong passions in those caught up in its aftermath—guilt, anger and frustration as well as sorrow and regret.

"He seemed pretty cut up, to me."

"Oh yes, I agree, he is."

"And not so ordinary after all."

"True. Just shows it never pays to judge by outward appearances."

They walked on in a companionable silence, Thanet wondering if the Sergeant had yet managed to have that talk with his wife. He certainly looked much more cheerful this morning.

Lineham unhooked the gate and held it open.

A young woman was coming up the footpath from the village, leaning forward with the effort of propelling a toddler in a pushchair up the hill. She checked for a moment when she saw the two men, then came on again more slowly. It looked as though Marcia's death had encouraged people to start using the short cut again. Perhaps this girl thought she was about to be accused of trespassing. Or perhaps, Thanet thought as they stepped aside on to the grass for her to pass, she was simply nervous of meeting two strange men out here where there was no one to come to her aid if she were attacked. She had scuttled past, barely returning their greeting, and he thought how sad it was that nowadays women felt so vulnerable that even an innocent chance encounter such as this became an occasion for fear.

As they rounded the trees near the river and glanced up the grassy slope towards Greenleaf's hut, Lineham gave Thanet an excited nudge.

"He's there, sir."

It was logical to assume that the figure stooping over the vegetable patch was Greenleaf. A black and white mongrel which had been lying near him leaped up and started to bark the moment it spotted them and Greenleaf turned to look. He straightened up, shoving his fork into the ground, and, hands on hips, watched them approach. Thanet realised with surprise that the recluse was much younger than he had expected. For some reason he had visualised Greenleaf as an old man, in his sixties or seventies, but even from a distance it was obvious from the vigour of his movements that he was a good decade or two younger.

It was, of course, impossible to tell his age from his face.

Even though Thanet had been prepared for the man's disfigurement, he still experienced a shock of pity when they drew close enough to see him clearly. The fire in which he had received his injuries must have been horrendous. Despite the miracles which plastic surgery is now able to achieve, Greenleaf's face was barely human, its contours unnatural, the skin stretched and shiny, the nose virtually non-existent, the mouth lipless, the eyes mere slits. He was wearing worn but clean corduroy trousers and a collarless shirt rolled up above the elbows. His hands and arms had been badly burned too. Thanet could see why he lived in self-imposed isolation. It would be impossible for him ever to go out without attracting glances of fascinated horror, aversion or pity. Deliberately, Thanet kept his face impassive, and hoped that Lineham was managing to do the same.

The dog was still barking frantically. Greenleaf made no move to quieten it until the two men were only a few yards away, then he extended the forefinger of his right hand and pointed briefly at the dog's muzzle. It fell silent at once, sitting down close beside him. His hand moved over its head in a brief gesture of praise before he said, "Who are you?" He obviously didn't believe in wasting words. His voice was hoarse, rusty perhaps with disuse. He would have no one to talk to but the animals. He listened to

Thanet's introductions, his eyes moving to Lineham and back again. It was impossible to tell what he was thinking.

"Thought you might be more of those danged reporters. Or the bailiffs, come to chuck me out."

Thanet shook his head. "We're looking into the death of Mrs. Salden."

"Ah . . . Yes, I heard about that . . . Falled in the river, didn't she?"

"Yes, she did. We wondered if you knew anything about it."

"Knew anything?"

The dog growled low in its throat, a barometer perhaps of its master's emotions. Thanet could not remember ever having to interview a witness without being able to try to gauge his reaction from his face.

"She was drowned in the river down there." Thanet gestured at the waters of the Teale in the valley below, sparkling innocently in the spring sunshine. "We thought perhaps you might have seen or heard something."

"I heard tell that there's a lot of questions being asked," said Greenleaf. "In the village and all."

"A woman is dead," said Thanet. "Of course we're asking a lot of questions. And until we find out how and when she died, we'll be asking a lot more."

"You're thinking, perhaps, that someone might have helped her on her way."

"It is one possibility, yes."

"And you asks yourself, 'Now, who would be glad to see the back of Mrs. Salden?' And back comes the answer, 'Harry Greenleaf, that's who. Him what was about to be turned off her land and made to join the ranks of the homeless.' Am I right?"

"Of course."

"Just so long as we know where we are."

"So . . ." Thanet was brisk. "Now that we're quite clear about it . . . Perhaps you could tell us where you were, that night."

"Well now, which night was that, can you tell me?" Disfigured hand came up and rubbed travesty of a chin in a gesture of mock puzzlement.

No point in allowing yourself to be riled, Thanet told himself. "Oh, come, Mr. Greenleaf," he said lightly, "your memory can't be that short, surely. It was only the night before last."

"The night before last," Greenleaf said thoughtfully. He looked down at the dog and stroked its head. "Do you remember what we was doing the night before last, Jack?"

He and the dog gazed at each other in silence for a moment or two. "Ah, yes, that's right. Thanks, Jack." Greenleaf's slits of eyes turned in Thanet's direction again. "I was busy packing up, of course. On account of expecting to be turfed out next morning."

"It must have been a relief, to find that the proceedings had been called off."

"Oh it was, wasn't it, Jack? That Mr. Salden's all right."

"It wasn't Mr. Salden who called them off," said Lineham, interrupting. "It was Inspector Thanet here."

Thanet shot Lineham a furious glance.

Greenleaf said with mock humility, "Oh, it was, was it? Then we has every reason to be grateful to the kind Inspector, hasn't we, Jack?"

Thanet was amused to find that the last vestiges of pity for Greenleaf had vanished, to be replaced by reluctant admiration. The man was obviously more than capable of looking after himself. "So you claim you were in your hut all evening?"

Greenleaf's eyes, glittering through the narrow openings in the puffy flesh, met Thanet's squarely. "I was." He looked down at the dog. "As Jack is my witness."

He was lying, Thanet was sure of it. But it was impossible to tell whether it was because he had indeed been responsible for pushing Marcia off the bridge or because he'd been up to something else he didn't want the police to know about. In any case, it was obvious that there was no point in pursuing that particular line of questioning.

"I believe Mrs. Salden came down to see you in the afternoon."

"In a manner of speaking."

"What do you mean?"

"She did come, but she didn't see me."

"Why not?"

Greenleaf addressed the dog again. "Saw her coming, didn't we Jack." He met Thanet's eye again. "Guessed she meant trouble, so we slipped away, come back after she'd gone."

That was Harry's story and clearly he was going to stick to it. They left.

Lineham waited until they were halfway down the slope before he spoke. "Insolent so and so."

"You shouldn't have interfered, Mike."

"I know, sir. I'm sorry. But it just made me mad to see him taking the mickey out of you like that."

"I'm quite capable of looking after myself, you know. I don't need protecting."

"No, I know. But . . ."

"No 'buts,' Mike. Did it occur to you that it's probably his way of coping with his disfigurement in front of strangers? By all accounts he's popular enough with the locals."

Lineham looked a little shamefaced. "You think so?"

"Could be. If people are busy being angry at him they can't be feeling sorry for him. It works, too, didn't you notice?"

Lineham was silent for a few moments. "Yes, I suppose you're right." A further silence, then he burst out, "Why can't I ever see things like that for myself?"

"Practice, I suppose. I've been at it longer than you have."

"No point in trying to make excuses for me. It's always happening, however hard I try."

"Perhaps you're not trying in the right way."

"What do you mean?"

"Well, back there . . . You found you were getting angry, right?"

"Right."

"So, then what? You reacted by speaking out, didn't you?"

"Yes. And I shouldn't have, I know."

"So what should you have done?"

Lineham stopped walking and turned to face Thanet. "What do you mean? Kept my big mouth shut, of course."

Thanet shook his head. "No, that's not what I mean. That's a negative reaction, and I'm looking for a positive one."

"Sorry, you've lost me. I got angry, right? So I either allow myself to show it, or I don't. How else could I have reacted?"

"There are a couple of alternatives. Look, you know the anger is unconstructive, don't you? So you have to defuse it. And you do this either by trying to understand your own reaction, just why you are getting so annoyed, or by asking yourself why it is he finds it necessary to behave so provocatively. In this particular instance the answer wasn't hard to find. Nobody likes to be pitied. Better, by far, to make people angry, irritate them so that they won't come back again . . ."

"I wonder if that's why he got up Mrs. Salden's nose."

"Could be one of the reasons. I shouldn't think she'd take kindly to being made fun of . . . Anyway, as you see, it's all a question of not allowing yourself to react blindly, of trying to analyse what's going on instead."

Lineham was shaking his head. "Sounds beyond me."

Thanet moved on again, quickening his pace. There was a great deal to do today. "Nonsense. I've told you before, it's all a question of practice. A skill to be learned, like any other. The more interviewing you do, the better at it you get."

They had reached the car.

"Where next, sir?"

"I think it's time we found out how Josie Trimble and Councillor Lomax fit into all this, don't you?"

THIRTEEN

If this was the reward in the trap which Marcia Salden had baited for Lomax, Thanet thought, he wouldn't be surprised if the councillor had succumbed to temptation. Josie Trimble was a succulent morsel indeed, if you liked smooth young flesh, downy as a peach, curves that were neither skimpy nor over-generous, huge dark eyes and a tumble of luxuriant curls to match.

The proprietor of the unisex hair salon ("Call me Gary") hadn't been too pleased to see them and they had been whisked at high speed past clients and pot plants alike into a small room at the back of the premises which obviously doubled as laundry and staff room; towels whirled in a pair of automatic washer-dryers and a girl and a young man were seated at the formica table, drinking coffee and smoking.

Gary advanced, teeth bared in false bonhomie. "Sorry to interrupt your break, darlings, you'll have to tack an extra few minutes on to your dinner hours."

They cast resentful glances at Thanet and Lineham, stubbed out their cigarettes and left without a word.

"Josie hasn't been a naughty girl, I hope." The fashionable quiff at the front of Gary's head quivered with anxiety. At sides and back his hair had been cut very close, practically shaved. Thanet wondered how the hairdresser would describe the effect. "Sculptured," perhaps? He was in his mid-thirties, colourfully dressed in purple velvet trousers and canary yellow open-necked shirt.

Thanet had murmured appropriate platitudes and Josie had duly been produced. At a glance from Thanet Gary had retired, leaving the door slighly ajar behind him.

Without a word Lineham had got up and closed it.

"Now then, Miss Trimble," said Lineham.

Thanet had decided that in view of their conversation after the interview with Greenleaf it would be a good idea for Lineham to conduct this interview. From time to time the Sergeant needed a boost to his self-confidence. The girl was obviously nervous and Thanet watched with approval as, handling her gently, Lineham established the basis of her relationship with Marcia Salden ("Ever so kind to me, she was"), gradually working around to the events of Tuesday evening.

"So you arrived at the Manor at what time?"

"Mrs. Salden told me she wanted me to be there on time, so I got there dead on half-past seven."

Thanet noticed the careful aspirate. Marcia's teaching had obviously begun to pay off.

"You walked up from the village?"

She nodded. "Along the footpath. Mrs. Salden said I could use it whenever I liked."

A touch of pride, there. Josie had obviously enjoyed the privilege.

"See anyone, on the way?"

She hadn't.

When she got to the Manor, Mrs. Salden had told her that Mr. Salden had been called to see Mrs. Carter, who had taken a turn for the worse. It had been too late to contact Mr. Lomax, so they were going to go ahead with the dinner party and Mrs Salden might pop down to the village later to see her mother. At that point Mr. Lomax had arrived and they'd all had drinks.

"You'd met Mr. Lomax before." Lineham made it a statement, not a question.

Josie nodded and lowered her head a little so that her hair fell forwards to screen her face.

"Often?"

She shrugged and murmured something.

"I'm sorry, I didn't catch that."

She raised her head. "I said, a few times."

"Where did you meet him?"

"Mrs. Salden introduced me to 'im at a cheese and wine she took me to."

Interesting, thought Thanet. The aspirate had slipped. Josie was getting nervous.

"When was this?"

She licked her lips. "Christmas."

So, four months ago.

Unobtrusively, Thanet edged his chair back. He wanted to be able to see Josie's feet. Feet are often excellent registers of emotion. He was in luck, she was wearing open-toed sandals. As he expected, her toes were tightly bunched up. What was she afraid of?

Abruptly, she stood up. "Sorry, I need to go to the toilet." And without waiting for permission she blundered out of the room.

Lineham raised his eyebrows. "What was all that about?"

"Interesting, wasn't it? Lomax, d'you think? Or something else?"

But whatever it was, Josie wasn't giving it away. When she returned, Lineham continued to probe, without success. She and Lomax had met a few times at functions when she had been accompanying Marcia. Three, perhaps four times in all. She didn't know nothing about any business dealings between them. Yes, Mrs. Salden had left for the cottage at around twenty to ten, saying she'd only be gone ten or fifteen minutes and that she especially wanted a word with Josie when she got back. When she failed to return Josie and Mr. Lomax had naturally assumed that it must be because Mrs. Carter was very ill indeed.

"It must have been rather awkward for you."

"Awkward?"

"Being left to entertain Mr. Lomax on Mrs. Salden's behalf."

"Oh . . . No, not really. It wasn't as though we was complete strangers."

"I suppose not. Did Mrs. Salden ring, to apologise for being held up?"

The dark curls bounced as Josie shook her head. "We wasn't surprised, if her mum was that ill . . . In the end Mr. Lomax decided to go, but I 'ung on because I'd said I would."

"I understood that you eventually gave up and went home."

Her expression changed. "I waited for an hour or more after Mr. Salden rung up," she said defensively.

Lineham smoothed ruffled feathers. "It's all right. It's perfectly understandable that you went home. You couldn't have been expected to wait up all night."

"Didn't know what was 'appening, did I? I mean, when Mr. Salden rung about half-past ten, to ask me to tell 'er he was staying and not to wait up, we thought she must still be on her way 'ome. When she didn't come, well, I thought I must have got it wrong, some'ow. Or that she'd changed 'er mind, turned round and gone back to 'er mum's." The girl was becoming agitated and now her eyes filled with tears. "'Ow was I to know she'd fallen in the river?'' She began to cry in earnest, reaching blindly for a box of tissues on the table.

Thanet pushed them towards her groping hand. "Miss Trimble . . . Josie . . . Would you mind if I called you Josie?''

She shook her head, wiping her eyes.

"Look, Josie, I hope you're not blaming yourself for what happened to Mrs. Salden.''

"If I'd called someone right away, it might have been in time to save 'er!'' she sobbed.

"Called who?''

"Anyone! The police?''

"And what good would that have done? What would you have said to them?''

She shrugged. He had her attention now and her sobs were abating. She wiped her eyes and blew her nose.

He pressed home the advantage. "That Mrs. Salden was walking home from the village alone in the dark? D'you think they'd have taken you seriously, done anything about it? Turned out to look for a grown woman who hadn't been missing more than ten minutes? Of course they wouldn't. There's never any point in trying to be wise after the event, is there? So come on, cheer up. Whatever happened, it wasn't your fault. You do see that, don't you?''

But she was avoiding his eye, seemingly unconvinced. Perhaps . . . He glanced at Lineham, who raised his shoulders. *Carry on if you want to.*

"Josie . . . I think there's something you'd like to tell us, isn't there?''

And yes, that was an unmistakable flash of fear.

"No! What d'you mean?''

"You may have heard rumours . . .''

"What rumours?'' Her lips barely moved and she was staring at Thanet as if suddenly mesmerised.

"About Mrs. Salden's death.''

"Ah.'' A slow exhalation. She shook her head, once, a slow, almost dreamy movement. She was still gazing at him but her stare had lost its fierce intensity. Then puzzlement gradually crept into her eyes. "What rumours?'' she repeated.

"That it may not have been an accident,'' put in Lineham.

Thanet hoped they were doing the right thing in perpetuating those rumours. But the girl was frightened of something, was hiding something, he was sure of it. The affair with Lomax, perhaps?

"Not an . . . accident?" she whispered, staring at him.

"So you see, we have to ask you. Do you know if Mrs. Salden had any enemies, anyone with a grudge against her?"

You could see her working it out. Accident . . . Enemies . . .

The colour ebbed away from her face, leaving the skin chalk white. "Grudge . . . ?"

Lineham caught her as she slid off the chair.

FOURTEEN

"I always wanted to do that," said Lineham with a grin as they stepped out into the street.

They had arranged to return in an hour, when Josie would have had time to recover, having temporarily abandoned her to Gary's ministrations amidst disapproving looks which clearly hinted at police brutality.

"Catch a maiden in distress in your arms, you mean? A very pleasant experience, I imagine. And neatly done, if I may say so." But Thanet's teasing was half-hearted. He was thinking of something else.

"Sir . . ."

"Mmm?"

"Where are you going? The car's this way."

Thanet woke up. "Mike, how many times have I got to tell you?" He stopped, pointed at his feet. "You know what those are? Yes, we are going to see Lomax, but it'll be quicker to walk than drive round the one-way system. You'll lose the use of your legs before you're forty, at this rate." And he set off again, briskly.

Sturrenden was at its best on a clear, bright morning like this, the picturesque jumble of Tudor and Georgian, black and white timbering and mellow bricks and tile preening themselves to face yet another spring. A strong conservationist lobby had averted too many contemporary disasters. Thanet gazed about appreciatively. How fortunate he was to work in a place like this!

"I just like driving, that's all," grumbled Lineham, hurrying to catch up.

Thanet grinned. "Stop sounding like a five-year-old who's had his favourite teddy taken away, Mike, and tell me what you thought of the luscious Miss Trimble."

"Well, she obviously knows someone who had it in for our Marcia."

"Hmm. I wonder why she passed out just then." Thanet was satisfied that the faint had been genuine.

"A subconscious means of avoiding the issue," said Lineham with the smug smile of a conjuror who has just pulled off a particularly difficult trick. "She knows—or suspects—who the murderer is but she doesn't want to tell us."

"I'm not sure . . . I'm inclined to think it was because she had just realised who the murderer might be."

"Isn't it practically the same thing?"

"Not really, no. But whichever it is, I think it means that this person is someone close to her. She lives with her mother, doesn't she? Did Miss Phipps mention any brothers or sisters?"

"I don't think so, no. Could be Lomax, sir."

"Possibly. In fact I was wondering if what she was really frightened of, all the time we were talking to her, was whether or not we knew about her and Lomax. Ah, here we are."

Thanet had got one of his men to do a little digging on Lomax. The councillor was sixty-four, married, with two sons, both now with families of their own and settled some distance away. He and his wife lived in a bungalow on one of the more established small new estates on the edge of Sturrenden. He owned a radio and TV shop called Sturrenden Audio in one of the town's side streets.

Business wasn't exactly booming, by the look of it, thought Thanet. The place was going to seed. The glass of the window was grubby and smeared where fingers and noses had been pressed against it over a long period; dead flies which looked as though they had been there since last summer lay scattered on the faded blue paper which lined the window, and the few radios and television sets looked dusty and out of date. The shop appeared to be empty. A bell pinged as they went in.

Nothing happened. There was a distant sound of pop music.

Lineham rapped on the counter. "Shop!"

Still nothing.

The door behind the counter was ajar and Lineham put his head through and shouted. "Hello."

A sound of movement and a moment later a spotty youth appeared with a screwdriver in his hand. "Sorry."

"Mr. Lomax in?" asked Lineham.

"Just popped out. Won't be long."

"We'll wait."

The boy looked at the screwdriver, then at Thanet and Lineham. His dilemma was apparent. There was work to be done, but he couldn't leave the shop unattended with potential thieves in it. "He might be quite a while."

Lineham grinned, pulled out his warrant card. "It's all right, son, we're not going to walk off with the stock, such as it is . . . Been working here long, have you?"

"Six months."

"Like it?"

The boy pulled a face, shrugged. "It's a job, in't it?"

"Repair work, serving in the shop, that sort of thing?"

"Yeah."

"Get on well with Mr. Lomax, do you?"

The lad hesitated.

"You can be frank with us. We won't get you into trouble with him, I promise."

Another shrug. "So-so."

"No more than that?"

"Like I said, it's a job. You can't be too choosy these days."

"No . . ." Lineham leaned forward a little across the counter, glanced over his shoulder at the street as if to check that there was still no sign of Lomax, then lowered his voice as he said, "You'd have a pretty good idea of his comings and goings, I suppose."

"I suppose," said the boy, warily.

"And of his visitors, too—people who come to see him here at the shop."

"Well . . ."

"A certain young lady, now . . . About eighteen or nineteen, very pretty, long curly hair . . ."

The boy had immediately recognised the description. But there was a spark of something else in his eyes, too. What was it?

He nodded. "Can't think what she sees in him. He's old enough to be her grandfather."

Jealousy, then. And pique?

"Until the day before yesterday it was all hush-hush. They meets each other most dinnertimes, see, but she never comes in here. Ten past twelve, regular as clockwork, she walks past the shop and a few minutes later off he goes." The boy snorted. "Thinks I'm stupid or something!"

"Until the day before yesterday?" said Lineham.

The day Marcia Salden died.

"Yeah. She rings up, see, middle of the morning. Never done

that before. Wants to speak to him, urgent. Well, I tells her, he's
out, gone to pick up a TV. Half an hour later, she's on the phone
again and he walks in while I'm telling her he's not back yet.
When he hears who's on the line he sends me off to the work-
room, but I listens. Well, I wants to know what's going on,
don't I? 'I thought I told you never to ring me at work,' he
says. Then he listens for a sec, and he says, 'Oh, my Gawd,
oh my Gawd,' over and over. Then he says, 'Look, we can't
talk now. I'll see you in your lunch hour as usual. And don't
worry, I'll see you right.' '' The boy glanced into the street, then
leaned forward and said confidentially, ''D'you know what I
reckon? I reckon he's knocked her up.''

''I'll see you right.'' The most likely explanation, certainly.
Maybe this was what Josie had been afraid of revealing when
they had talked to her earlier on. And it opened up a number of
interesting avenues of speculation. If Josie was pregnant, had she
told Marcia? And if so, was the matter brought up at the ill-fated
dinner party that night? And if it had been, and Marcia had
tightened the screw on Lomax by hinting at publicity should he
fail to swing the planning permission for her, how would Lomax
have reacted? Difficult to tell, without ever having met the man.
Would he have been upset? Angry? Desperate, even? Pretty
agitated anyway, surely. Mrs. Pantry said Lomax had left the
Manor at around a quarter or twenty past ten that night. Thanet's
imagination conjured up Lomax's car speeding down the drive,
turning right towards the village . . . But no, that wouldn't
work. Lomax lived in Sturrenden. He would surely have turned
left, towards the main road. And if so, he and Marcia wouldn't
have met at all. Unless he had deliberately gone looking for
her . . .

The door bell pinged. A customer wanting a 13-amp plug.
Thanet and Lineham stood aside while she was served. Almost at
once, and before they could resume their conversation, the bell
pinged again. Thanet could tell by the way the boy stiffened that
this must be Lomax.

During the introductions he was interested to note that although Lomax tried to hide it beneath a mask of bonhomie, the
man was definitely on the defensive.

''Ah yes, I've been expecting you. What you call 'routine
enquiries,' I suppose.'' His laugh had a hollow ring. ''Go and
buy yourself a doughnut, Kevin, will you, while I talk to the
police and do my duty as a good citizen.''

A Kentish accent, Thanet noted, somewhat rough at the edges.

Kevin duly departed and Lomax flipped the notice on the door to CLOSED. Then he turned, rubbing his hands and sporting a look of bright expectancy tempered with appropriate solemnity. Quite a feat, Thanet thought. He had disliked the man on sight, slotting him at once into the category which his own father, now dead, had classified as "the type I wouldn't buy a second-hand car from."

Lomax, like his shop, had the air of going to seed. His clothes—navy blue blazer, linen trousers, striped tie, white shirt, were of good quality but slightly scruffy, his hair, although well cut, a little too long. A bright yellow silk scarf patterned with large red polka dots was draped around his neck. How did people like this get into such positions of power in local government? Thanet asked himself. Because those of the right calibre were too busy or too uninterested to stand? Thanet had met one or two truly admirable councillors, men and women dedicated to the ideal of public service, but they were all too few and far between.

Lomax now affected the hollow tones of an inexperienced newsreader reporting a disaster. "It's about Mrs. Salden, I suppose. Such a sad business. She was so young . . . and such a brilliant businesswoman. Such a waste . . ."

Such a treacly voice, Thanet parodied in his mind. Such a charming, man . . . He could hear Lineham saying, "Yuk!" But he could understand why Josie had been taken in. Lomax would be so different from the boys with whom she normally came into contact. She would look no further than the surface, be dazzled by his status as a councillor, by the apparent gloss of sophistication. A few trips in that Jaguar parked outside, a few dinners at expensive restaurants . . .

Lomax wilted under Thanet's unwavering stare. He cleared his throat, moved uneasily from one foot to another and ran a hand over his hair. His soft brown eyes, which in a romantic novel would no doubt be described as "melting," were like muddied pools with all kinds of unpleasant things stirring at the bottom.

"You were a guest at Mrs. Salden's house that evening, I believe?"

"Yes, that's right."

"Your wife was not invited?"

"No . . . She . . . It was more of a business arrangement than a social occasion."

"I see . . . May I ask the nature of this business?"

He hesitated, his eyes flickering around the room as if searching for non-existent eavesdroppers. "Confidentially, Mrs. Salden was negotiating to buy this business."

Thanet allowed his surprise to show. "She was branching out into electronics?"

Lomax shook his head and sniggered as if Thanet had made a dirty joke. "Nooo. It was the premises she wanted. She was planning on opening a vegetarian restaurant. There isn't one in the entire area. Said it was a natural progression from the health food shops and it was a good time to do it. There is so much interest in vegetarian food these days. I thought she was on to a winner, myself."

Thanet had to admit it sounded plausible. Could he have been wrong in suspecting Marcia of planning to blackmail Lomax? But even if she hadn't, she could still have intended to suborn him. Buying his shop and paying well over the odds for it could have been a neat way of handing over a bribe without seeming to do so. "These negotiations . . . They were far advanced?"

"Progressing satisfactorily, shall we say? Though whether they'll go ahead now is another matter. Her husband may want to scrap the whole idea."

"May I ask how much Mrs. Salden was prepared to offer you?"

"You can ask, but you won't get an answer. I can't see it has anything to do with . . . with the matter in hand."

"That remains to be seen. You do realise, don't you, that we are treating this as a suspicious death?"

"Suspicious death?" Lomax's ruddy complexion was turning the colour of dough.

"We have to be satisfied that it was an accident—if it was an accident, in fact."

"If?"

"Naturally, we have to consider the alternatives. Suicide, for example . . ." It would be interesting to see if Lomax took the bait.

He didn't.

"But . . ." Lomax shook his head.

"Yes, Mr. Lomax?"

"I was only going to say that Mrs. Salden would be the last person to commit suicide."

"Yes, that does seem to be the general consensus of opinion. Which leaves us with the third alternative."

Lomax was staring at Thanet like a rabbit at a stoat. "You can't mean . . ."

Thanet wondered why this particular snatch of conversation always sounded so clichéd. Simply because he had heard it so often? Yet there was no other way to put it. "Yes," he said quietly. "That's precisely what I do mean. Murder. You must see that we have to take that possibility into account. Which is why we are looking very closely into the movements of everybody she saw on Tuesday."

"You can't possibly be suggesting that I . . ." There was a strange, dry, clicking noise from the back of Lomax's throat.

"We're not suggesting anything at this stage, Mr. Lomax. Just enquiring. So perhaps you'd be good enough to answer just a few more questions. Now, what time did you leave Telford Green Manor on Tuesday night?"

There was definitely a flash of fear in Lomax's eyes before they slid away. "Somewhere around twenty past ten, I should think. Soon after I'd finished my coffee. I didn't think it was on to hang about any longer."

"Not 'on'?" What, specifically, was Lomax afraid of? Thanet wondered.

Lomax's shoulders twitched impatiently. "Not polite. With Mrs. Salden's mother being ill . . ."

"I see . . . When Mrs. Salden left to go down to the village to see her mother, did she tell you she was going on foot?"

Lomax's reaction looked genuine enough. "She *walked*?"

Thanet nodded. "Along the footpath."

"But why? We assumed she'd drive down."

"Her car wouldn't start."

"Then why didn't she come and ask me if I'd run her down? It'd only have taken a few minutes."

That was a point which, oddly enough, had not occurred to Thanet. Why, indeed? He shrugged. "No idea. What, exactly, did she say, when she left?"

"Just that she was popping down to see her mother and she wouldn't be long—ten or fifteen minutes at most. I said in that case we'd best be getting off home but she said, no, she didn't want to break up the party and that she especially wanted a word with Josie when she got back. That's why Josie stayed on when I left, or I'd have given her a lift home."

"Did you think it odd, that Mrs. Salden neither came back nor rang to explain why?"

"A bit, yes. But then we thought, well, it would be understandable if she forgot about us, if her mother was desperately ill."

"And when you yourself left, did you go straight home?"

"More or less." Lomax's voice had thickened.

"More?" said Thanet pleasantly. "Or less?"

"I'm sorry?"

Thanet sighed. "If you didn't go straight home, where did you go first?"

"For a drink." It was as though the words were squeezed out of him against his will.

Thanet suddenly understood Lomax's apprehension and he knew the answer to the next question before he asked it. "Where?"

"At the Crooked Door."

"I see . . ." Thanet allowed the silence to stretch out. Then, eventually, "So you drove through the village."

"Yes, of course." Lomax was sullen now. He resented being forced to yield up information he had hoped to keep hidden.

"Pass anyone?"

"I don't know. I can't remember. I hadn't thought about it."

"Well, think now."

Silence. Lomax screwed up his face and gazed into the middle distance.

Thanet and Lineham hid their eagerness. If Marcia had left her mother's cottage at around twenty past ten, even if Lomax had not committed the crime himself he could have been on the bridge at around the crucial time, seen something which could give them a vital lead.

"Yes . . ." said Lomax slowly. "There was . . . Yes, I remember now. There were two men, outside one of the cottages, before you get to the bridge. I had the impression they were drunk."

"Why?"

"I'm not sure. One seemed to be holding the other up."

If so, they had probably come from the pub. More potential witnesses?

"Can you tell us anything about them?"

"It was just a glimpse. And I wasn't paying much attention because I'd just spotted the first of the DANGER notices and I was wondering what was up. That bridge is difficult enough to negotiate at the best of times."

"Did you see anyone else? On or near the bridge, for example?"

Lomax was already shaking his head.

"You're sure?" But already Thanet was adjusting to the disappointment.

"No. Though . . . Wait a minute . . ."

"What?" Thanet and Lineham spoke together.

"I've just remembered. That secretary of Mrs. Salden's. I passed her just as she was turning into the gates of the Manor, near the lodge."

"You're sure it was her?" said Lineham.

"Certain, yes."

"She was on foot?"

"Yes."

"Coming from which direction?"

"From the village."

And Edith Phipps claimed she hadn't been out that night. Interesting.

"Did you see Mrs. Salden further on, in the village?" A pointless question, really, and Thanet wondered why he had bothered to ask it. Even if Lomax had seen her, he would deny it.

"No!"

"How well do you know Miss Trimble, Mr. Lomax?"

Lomax blinked at the abrupt change of topic. He was beginning to sweat, Thanet noticed. "I . . . er . . . I've met her a few times. Chiefly when she's been with Mrs. Salden."

"Chiefly?"

Lomax folded his arms, as if to put up a barrier against this new line of attack. If Josie was pregnant, Thanet could understand the man's difficulty. If he told the truth, he would lay himself open to a lot of unpleasant questions. Also, his wife might find out. But if he lied, and the police learnt the truth later, it might lead to even worse trouble. On the other hand, they might never find out . . .

Lomax shrugged. "Mostly, yes. She went about with Mrs Salden quite a lot."

"But you have met her alone, too."

"I . . ." He couldn't bring himself to utter the direct lie, for fear of future consequences. "I may have done."

Thanet didn't want to make things awkward for young Kevin by betraying the source of his information, so this was a little tricky. "Oh come, Mr. Lomax. Miss Trimble is a very attractive young woman. Surely you can remember whether you've been out alone with her or not."

"Well, perhaps on the odd occasion, yes."

"Mr. Lomax, I don't think you're being completely frank with us . . ."

Thanet waited, but Lomax said nothing, just stared at Thanet with a fearful fascination. The moment was right, Thanet judged. "I have to tell you it's common knowledge that you and Miss Trimble have been seeing a lot of each other."

Lomax took refuge in anger. "Common knowledge, my foot. I knew it! You've been listening to that madwoman, haven't you?"

Madwoman? What was Lomax talking about? Thanet knew when best to keep his mouth shut.

"I knew she wouldn't be able to resist putting her spoke in! Pretending to be so self-righteous. As if she doesn't know what her precious daughter gets up to!"

Light dawned. Lomax was talking about Josie's mother. But how did Mrs. Trimble fit in to all this?

Best to allow Lomax to go on thinking they knew all about it. Thanet looked amused. "I gather Mrs. Trimble's been having a go at you."

"Josie's nearly nineteen, you know. Nearly nineteen! And that old bat expects to be able to keep her under lock and key!"

And it looked as though Mrs. Trimble's anxiety had been justified. With a stab of fierce protectiveness towards Bridget, Thanet wondered how Lomax would have felt if it had been his daughter who was being wined and dined by an ageing Casanova old enough to be her grandfather. But, of course, he and Mrs. Lomax had had only sons.

And if Josie were pregnant, did her mother know about it?

Lomax was still being indignant. "She practically demanded Josie put her coat on and come home then and there! Of course, Josie refused. She'd promised Marcia to wait until she got back."

Thanet did a double-take. "Just a moment. When was this, Mr. Lomax?"

"When was what?"

"When did Mrs. Trimble try and get Josie to go home with her?"

"On Tuesday night, of course."

"Let me make sure I've got this straight. Mrs. Trimble actually went up to the Manor on Tuesday evening during the dinner party and made a scene?"

"Yes."

"Objecting to the fact that her daughter was going out with you?"

"That's what I've been saying, haven't I?" Lomax was, perhaps understandably, becoming exasperated.

"All right, calm down. I just wanted to make sure I hadn't misunderstood . . ."

"Here, just a minute. Didn't Mrs. Trimble tell you about this herself?"

No, *you told me yourself, just now.* "Does it really matter who told us, Mr. Lomax? We know, that's the point . . . Can we get back to Tuesday evening, please? What time was this, when Mrs. Trimble arrived?"

Lomax shrugged. "Must have been about ten or five to ten . . . The housekeeper tried to stop her, but she just came barging in . . ."

"How long did she stay?"

"Five minutes or so. Josie refused to listen to her, sent her off with a flea in her ear."

"How had she got there?"

Lomax gave a laugh that was also a sneer. "Well, she didn't drive up, that's for sure."

Thanet closed his eyes, trying to work it out. At ten o'clock Grace Trimble leaves the Manor. At twenty past Marcia Salden leaves her mother's cottage to return home via the footpath. Yes, providing Mrs. Trimble hadn't walked too quickly, it was possible that they could have met on the bridge. If Mrs. Trimble was still overwrought, humiliated at being shown the door by Josie and angry with Marcia for having encouraged the affair with Lomax . . .

Lomax was still looking aggrieved. "As soon as she'd gone, I got out, I can tell you. I'd just about had enough."

FIFTEEN

"I wouldn't trust him further than I could spit!" said Lineham.

They were discussing Lomax on their way back to Telford Green. They had returned to the hairdressing salon to see Josie only to be met by a defiant Gary. "I sent her home, poor love. There was no point in her staying on at work, was there, she was too upset . . ."

Thanet hadn't bothered to make a fuss. He wanted to go back to Telford Green anyway, to see Betty Pantry. Now that he knew more about what had happened on Tuesday night there were a number of questions he'd like to put to the housekeeper.

"Maybe not. But that doesn't necessarily make him a murderer."

"It makes him a potential murderer, though, doesn't it?"

"Oh come on, Mike. They say that everyone is a potential murderer, given the right circumstances."

"You think so? You really think so?"

"I don't know. I'd like to think not. I'd like to believe that I would never go over the edge, however hard I was pushed. But how can you ever know, unless you actually find yourself in that position? It's like condemning someone for being a thief because he steals bread to feed his starving children. If my children were starving, would I steal, to keep them alive?"

"I hope you don't mind me saying so, sir, but when I hear you talk like this it makes me wonder why you're in the police at all."

"I wonder myself, sometimes . . . But to get back to Lomax . . ."

"Well, there is just one thing in his favour."

"That he wouldn't have wanted to kill off the goose that was going to lay the biggest golden egg he was ever likely to see, you mean?"

"That's right. Unless . . ." said Lineham slowly.

"What?" Thanet could guess what was coming.

"Well, unless he found that Mrs. Salden was becoming too much for him to handle."

"Let's pull into that lay-by for a few minutes, shall we?"

Lineham glanced in the mirror and signalled left. The lay-by was empty and he switched off the engine. The sun was warm through the glass and they wound down the windows. Sweet, fresh air rushed in and the car was filled at once with the sound of birdsong. Thanet located its source, a thrush sitting on the topmost branch of a hawthorn tree in the hedge. Reluctantly he turned back to Lineham.

"Go on."

"Well, I was thinking. Suppose Mrs. Salden and Lomax set up this deal—she'll buy his shop at a grossly inflated price if he'll wangle that planning permission . . . As extra insurance she introduces him to Josie and tells Josie to keep him happy. Then, say, he gets cold feet. Perhaps someone begins to suspect what's going on, drops a few hints . . . Lomax decides to back out. He doesn't want to end up on a corruption charge and anyway power is sweet, he likes playing God on the Borough Council . . . He tells Mrs. Salden that he's changed his mind. Naturally she's furious, she can see her quarter of a million floating away out of her grasp. At this point Josie discovers she's pregnant. She tells Lomax, who is appalled and Mrs. S, who is privately delighted. Here is the lever she wanted. Out come the claws and she tells Lomax that if he pulls out of the plan he'll be seeing some interesting headlines in the local paper shortly. She's got him over a barrel. She's been careful to keep all the paperwork regarding the purchase of his shop above board, so he has nothing on her. It's his word against hers. Whereas she has Josie and the soon-to-be-obvious pregnancy on her side . . . Now, in those circumstances he'd be prepared to take pretty drastic action, don't you think?"

Lineham was looking very pleased with himself for producing such a neat and cohesive theory.

Thanet refrained from saying that he'd worked all this out himself some time ago. "Very convincing, Mike. Well done. I agree, it's a possibility we have to keep in mind."

"A very strong possibility, surely! Motive, means, opportunity, he had them all! If he left the Manor by car between a quarter and twenty past ten . . ."

"Agreed, but there is one snag."

"What's that?"

"We're basing all this on a possible false premise."

Lineham raised his eyebrows.

"That Josie is pregnant. That's pure assumption, at the moment."

"Maybe. But surely, even if she isn't, Lomax could still have decided to pull out and Mrs. Salden could still have turned nasty."

"True . . . Well, we'd better be getting on."

Lineham started the engine and checked his mirror. "Now we know about Mrs. Trimble's visit to the Manor on Tuesday night . . . You remember you said you thought Josie passed out because she had just realised who the murderer might be, that he must be someone close to her . . . D'you think it was her mother she had in mind?"

"Possibly. A bit far-fetched, though, don't you think? Plenty of parents get steamed up about their offspring's girlfriends or boyfriends, but they don't go around murdering the person who introduced them."

"Unless they're unbalanced. And Lomax seemed to think Mrs. Trimble is."

"That may have been a figure of speech. Anyway, we'll soon find out, won't we? With any luck she'll be at home."

But their luck was out, it seemed. A red-eyed Josie answered the door. The house was small, Victorian and semi-detached, built of ugly yellow brick, with a skimpy front garden in which regimented tulips stood stiffly in rows. The cramped living-room into which she led them was spotlessly clean and looked as though it was rarely used. A three-piece suite covered in brown moquette, back and arms protected by antimacassars, stood on a faded Art Deco carpet square in shades of green. There were no signs of occupation, not even a television set, and very few ornaments. Net curtains shielded the room from prying eyes.

Mrs. Trimble, Josie told them, worked as a cleaner four mornings a week. On Thursdays, like today, she always went shopping in Sturrenden and didn't get back until half-past five.

"I see . . . look, Josie, I'm sorry to trouble you again so soon, but there are some more questions we really must ask you."

She gave a tight little nod, a barely perceptible movement of her head. She was sitting perched on the edge of the armchair, arms tightly folded, legs tucked sideways. It was a stiff, uncomfortable pose, with tension in every line. She had changed into jeans, track shoes and sweater, and had caught the luxuriant mass of her hair back into an elastic band at the nape of her neck. She looked young, defenceless and forlorn. Thanet experienced a pang of conscience. Should he have brought a policewoman with him, instead of Lineham? But despite her appearance Josie was an adult, he reminded himself, and this was potentially a murder case. He would press on.

"You told us that when Mr. Salden rang at about half-past ten, and you told him Mrs. Salden had not yet arrived home, you both assumed she was still on her way."

"That's right, yeah."

"Did you know she'd had to walk down because her car wouldn't start?"

A shake of the head. "No, she didn't say."

"So you thought she'd be turning up any minute, I suppose."

" 'S right."

"So, when she didn't, why didn't you ring Mr. Salden, to tell him?"

"I told you. I thought she'd changed her mind, didn't I, gone back to the cottage."

For a moment Thanet thought she was going to start crying again, but she took a deep breath, held it and exhaled slowly.

"Look," she said, "I been thinking. It's easy to look back and say, 'I should've done this' or 'I should've done that.' But at the time you, well, you just go on from minute to minute, if you see what I mean. On Tuesday, well, it'd been an 'orrible day, one way and the other, and I was dead tired, all I wanted to do was go 'ome and go to bed. But I'd said I'd stay till she got back, so I 'ung on and 'ung on . . . And when she didn't come I just got madder and madder. I really did think she must've got part of the way 'ome and then turned round and gone back, meaning to ring us when she got there. And then she found 'er mum had taken a turn for the worse and she'd decided to stay, forgot all about us. After all, 'er mum must've been pretty bad that night, mustn't she, she died later on, didn't she? Anyway, I worked all this out, but at the same time I couldn't 'elp being mad with 'er for not ringing and letting me know . . . And like I said, the longer I waited the madder I got. So in the end I decided to come 'ome."

"Yes, I see. But if you felt like that why didn't you simply ring the cottage to say you were tired and couldn't wait any longer?"

Her eyes went blank, flickering from side to side as if seeking a means of escape. This was a question whose answer she didn't want to admit even to herself. The silence stretched out. "Didn't like to, did I?" she said at last, in a voice blank of emotion. "Didn't think it was right, not if 'er mum was that ill." She shook her head, a brief, violent movement as if to clear it of confusion. "No!" she burst out. "That in't right. I was sick and tired of being kept dangling, that's the truth. And I thought, if she can't be bothered to ring me, then I'm damned if I'll ring her. And if she's cross when she gets back and finds I didn't wait, then too bad!"

"And now you're feeling guilty."

She nodded, lips compressed, the tears starting to flow again.

"You think that if only you hadn't allowed yourself to be angry, if only you'd rung Mr. Salden, Mrs. Salden might still be alive."

More nods as she wiped her eyes, snuffled, blew her nose.

Thanet sighed. "Well, I can understand how you feel, but the fact of the matter is, there's just no reason why you should. To put it bluntly, Mrs. Salden couldn't swim, she would have drowned very quickly, and quite soon after leaving her mother's cottage. It's even possible she might already have been dead by the time Mr. Salden rang you at half-past ten. So you see . . ."

She had given an involuntary shudder of distress while he was talking, but at least she had stopped crying. "You mean that?" She gave her nose one final blow and sat up a little straighter.

"I wouldn't have said so, if I didn't. All the same . . ."

"What?"

"I'm afraid that doesn't let you entirely off the hook. Josie . . . why weren't you frank with us about your relationship with Mr. Lomax?"

A wary look crept into her eyes and the muscles along her jawline clenched. "What d'you mean?"

"You told us you'd only met him three or four times in all, and always when you were with Mrs. Salden."

She tried to bluff it out. "But I did meet 'im when I was with 'er . . ."

"Josie . . ." Thanet was reproachful. "Come on, now. We're not stupid, you know, and we do have ways of finding things out. What about all those lunch hours, for example?"

She stared at him for a moment longer and then tossed her head. "I didn't think it was any of your business."

"Maybe not, in normal circumstances. But these are not normal circumstances."

Her flash of defiance had gone and once again she was looking frightened, vulnerable. "You said . . ."

"Yes?"

"The last time I saw you . . . At the salon . . . You said, it *may* not've been an accident."

"That's right, yes."

"But you're not sure?"

"Not yet, no."

"Oh . . ." She looked relieved.

"But it's still a possibility we have to consider. Which is why I asked you if you knew of anyone who had a grudge against Mrs. Salden."

"I've been thinking . . ."

"Yes?" Thanet could see quite clearly what Josie was up to. She had decided to employ diversionary tactics in order to steer their attention away from her affair with Lomax and also, perhaps, away from her mother. All the same, this could be interesting.

"Well, I don't know if I ought to tell you . . ."

Thanet smiled. "I can't let you get away with that, now can I? Not now you've begun . . ."

"It's just that . . . Well, I was up at the Manor that afternoon and I 'appened to over'ear something . . ."

She glanced from Thanet's face to Lineham's, as if to ensure that she had their complete attention.

"Marcia—Mrs. Salden—was going on at 'er secretary, that Miss Phipps . . ."

" . . . *We've lost it, d'you realise that? Lost it! An absolutely prime site in Week Street in Maidstone, and we've lost it. And why? Because someone else got a written offer in ahead of us! And what is more, Edith, my dear, efficient little secretary, you may be interested to hear that my written offer never in fact arrived. NEVER ARRIVED! Now why do you suppose that is?*"

"*I don't understand.*"

"*Of course you don't understand. You never do understand, do you, when things go wrong because of your inefficiency? Well, it occurs to me that the reason why it never arrived could just be because it was never posted. Where's that so-called handbag of yours? Go on, get it. My God, beats me how you ever find anything in it. Now empty it out on the desk. Empty it out, go on. Ah . . . Surprise, surprise. Three unposted letters. One of which is addressed to Page and Wells, Estate Agents,*"

52–54 King Street, Maidstone. What have you got to say about that? Not a lot, obviously.''

"Marcia, I'm sorry, I really am. I can't think what could have happened.''

"Oh, but I can. It's quite simple, isn't it, Edith? You just forgot, as usual. Well, let me tell you this. I've had it up to here with your little lapses of memory, and this time they've cost me just too much. I've wanted a Week Street site in Maidstone for years, and if it hadn't been for you I'd have got it.''

"Couldn't you . . . ?''

"It's not your business to tell me what I can or can't do!''

"I was only going to suggest . . .''

"To hell with your suggestions! I don't need a secretary to make suggestions. I need a secretary who is efficient, who does what I want her to do when I want her to do it. Such as posting important letters when they're written. No, I'm sorry, Edith, I've put this off as long as I can, but I'm afraid I shall have to ask you to look for another job.''

"But . . .''

"No! I'm not going to listen. I know you're in a difficult position, but you've become too expensive for me. I have the business to think of. I haven't put years of my life into building it up to have it undermined by your inefficiency. You can have a month to find somewhere else.''

Josie stopped talking. Her eyes still glittered with the excitement of recounting the drama she had overheard.

Thanet remembered Edith Phipps's prim, tight face, the undertone of resentment, jealousy, even, as she had talked about Marcia's success. Then there was her invalid mother, the convenience of working so close to home . . . Would she have had to move out of the gatehouse, if she had lost her job?

And she had lied about not going out that night.

Like Lomax, means, opportunity and now motive, she had had them all.

SIXTEEN

"She's not back from lunch yet." Mrs. Pantry's eyes flickered in the direction of the avenue of trees, as if she half-expected to see Edith Phipps walking up the drive. Despite the fact that it was pouring with rain, she did not ask them in. The sun had suddenly clouded over and a heavy April shower had materialised with very little warning.

Thanet hunched his shoulders against the water which was trickling down the back of his neck. He and Lineham had unwisely not bothered to put on their raincoats for the short distance between house and car, and Mrs. Pantry's inhospitality had caught them unprepared. He was annoyed that she had not invited them to take shelter from the downpour and annoyed, too, that he had not thought of calling in at the gatehouse on the way. He had, after all, been well aware that Edith always spent her lunch hours at home.

Still, there were various points he wanted to raise with the housekeeper.

"In that case, I'd like another word with you, while we're waiting."

Grudgingly she opened the massive door a little wider and moved aside to allow them to pass. They stepped inside, brushing the rain off their jackets and wiping their faces.

There was a pungent smell of polish in the hall and halfway up the staircase lay an open tin and some dusters. Without asking permission, Mrs. Pantry climbed the remaining stairs, plumped down on her knees and resumed the task which they had evidently interrupted. "You won't mind if I get on with my work?"

Thanet was about to protest that yes, he did object, when he changed his mind. This was more than Mrs. Pantry's natural ungraciousness, it was a calculated snub, and it intrigued him. He would play it her way, for the moment. What had aroused

130

her hostility? he wondered. Despite Edith Phipps's brief account
of Mrs. Pantry's unhappy past, Thanet found that his dislike of
the housekeeper had not diminished. What was it about her that
provoked this instinctive recoil? It certainly wasn't her size. He
had met any number of large women in the past, and some of
them he had found very attractive. Nor was it the fact that she
was physically unprepossessing. Perhaps it was her lack of femi-
ninity, her gracelessness, her uncompromising harshness. Or
perhaps it was no one thing, but a combination of many. Irrele-
vantly, he found himself wondering about the husband who had
absconded. What sort of man would be attracted to a woman like
this?

Anxious to avoid the sight of her massive buttocks and tree-like
thighs advancing slowly towards him down the stairs, he crossed
to the oak table against the wall on the other side of the hall and
hitched himself up on to it. From here he had a good view of her
profile through the banisters. Lineham stationed himself beside
the staircase, his head just below the level of hers.

"Is Mr. Salden about?" Thanet wanted to be sure that this
conversation was not going to be overheard.

"No, he's gone into Sturrenden to make the arrangements for
his mother-in-law's funeral."

All clear, then.

She was pretending to concentrate on her work, her shoulders
moving rhythmically as she applied the polish in small circular
movements. He must begin by somehow breaking down that
barrier of hostility. But how?

By making her angry, perhaps?

"You're in a rather unique position in this house, aren't you,
Mrs. Pantry?"

She stopped polishing and cast him a suspicious glance through
the banisters. "What d'you mean?"

"Well, you come into contact with everybody, you know
what's going on . . ."

She put down her duster and knelt up, leaning her arms on the
rail and glowering at him. "I'm in a good position to spy on
people, you mean."

"If that's how you choose to put it, yes."

"How else am I supposed to put it? Oh yes, I've heard about
all these questions you've been asking." She snorted, an ugly
porcine sound. "All those nasty"—she sought the right word
and found it, triumphantly—"*insinuations*."

"What nasty insinuations, Mrs. Pantry?" said Thanet, all innocence.

"About certain people."

So that was it. She was angry with him because she thought he suspected Salden of killing Marcia. "What people? Really, you are being very mysterious, aren't you? How can I answer your allegations, if I don't know what they are?"

Anger propelled her to her feet. "You know perfectly well what I mean! And Mr. Bernard is the kindest man in the world. He'd never hurt a fly!"

"But who has suggested he would—or did?"

"And anyone who says there was any trouble between him and Mrs. Salden don't know what they're talking about! Like you said, I'm here all the time, and I know."

"As a matter of—"

"I'm not saying they was all lovey-dovey, mind, but they got on all right, they understood each other, you know what I mean? And there was never any rows or anything like that, and if anyone says any different they're lying in their teeth."

"No one has . . ."

"And you ought to have seen what he's been like since it happened! Doesn't know what to do with himself, he's so cut up about it. Can't eat, can't sleep . . ."

"MRS. PANTRY!"

She blinked. "Yes?"

Thanet crossed to look up at her, resting one hand on the newel post. "Look, I just want to make one thing quite clear. I have not come here to question you about Mr. Salden."

She frowned. "You haven't?"

"No."

She descended one or two steps, warily. "What did you want to talk about, then?"

"Chiefly about what happened on Tuesday."

"Oh." She sat down abruptly on the fourth or fifth step up from the bottom and Thanet, averting his eyes from unwelcome vistas of straining tights and large expanses of underwear, went up to sit beside her.

"We keep learning bits and pieces, you see. And we thought you might be able to fill in the gaps."

She still looked suspicious, but the frown lines on the broad, flat forehead were beginning to ease away. "What gaps?"

"Well, to begin with, I understand that Mrs. Salden had a row with Miss Phipps on Tuesday afternoon."

Mrs. Pantry's eyes gleamed. "Yes, I thought she must have. Who told you? Josie Trimble, I suppose."

"You didn't hear it, then?"

"No, but I saw Edith Phipps go home in tears."

"Do you know what it might have been about?"

"No idea." She was enjoying being so unhelpful.

Pity. He would have liked to have another version of the quarrel, to compare with Josie's. "If we could move on to the evening, then . . . I understand Mrs. Trimble, Josie's mother, came up at some point."

Questioned about this, Josie had been distinctly unforthcoming, playing down her mother's anger and making light of the whole incident.

"Been busy, haven't you? Yes, she did."

"Why didn't you tell us this when we talked to you yesterday?"

"Didn't ask, did you? Anyway, I didn't think it mattered. Oh, I *see* . . . Yes, well, I didn't know, then, that Mrs. Salden's death was anything but a straightforward accident."

"We don't *know* otherwise now."

"No, but you must think there's something fishy about it or you wouldn't still be going around asking all these questions, would you? Stands to reason, don't it?"

"We just have to be sure, that's all. So, to get back to Mrs. Trimble . . . What time did she arrive?"

"About ten, I should think." Mrs. Pantry smiled, revealing an unprepossessing row of nicotine-stained teeth. "In a fair old state, she was."

"About?"

"Mr. Lomax carrying on with that precious daughter of hers. That Josie." She almost spat the word out. "Little slut."

"Oh come on, that's a bit strong, isn't it?"

"Is it? I'm not blind, Inspector, and I'm not deaf, either, though no doubt some people like to pretend I am . . ."

Thanet suspected that if he betrayed too much interest Mrs. Pantry would dry up out of sheer perversity, the last thing he wanted now that she was starting to loosen up. He continued to look sceptical.

Mrs. Pantry leaned a little nearer. "Did you know there's a flat over the old stables at the back?"

Thanet shook his head.

She lowered her voice to a near whisper. "Mrs. Salden gave Josie a key. It's been going on for months, her and that Mr.

Lomax." Her face twisted. "Disgusting, I call it. He's old
enough to be her father—no, her *grand*father."

If Mrs. Trimble had got wind of this arrangement it was
scarcely surprising that she had been sufficiently angry with
Marcia to march up to the Manor and confront her and Lomax
together. He could imagine how enraged he would have been if
Bridget had been exploited in this way . . . Which reminded
him . . . He glanced at his watch. Yes, just about now Joan would
be entering the headmaster's study. What could Mr. Foreman be
wanting to discuss with her?

With an effort Thanet wrenched his mind back to the present.

"Was Mr. Salden aware of this . . . arrangement?"

Mrs. Pantry shook her head vigorously. "Oh no. They was
careful only to come when he wasn't here—he's out a lot with
his charity work, you know, he's on a lot of committees and
that, and does a lot of fund-raising."

"You don't think he would have approved?"

Another shake of the head. "I never did understand what Mrs.
Salden was thinking of, to allow it."

"So what exactly happened when Mrs. Trimble came on
Tuesday night?"

"She asked for Mrs. Salden. I told her she was out, that she'd
had to go down to the village because her mother'd taken a turn
for the worse, but she wouldn't believe me, thought I was just
trying to give her the brush-off. Before I could stop her, she'd
ducked under my arm and rushed into the drawing-room. I went
after her. Josie and Mr. Lomax was both sitting on the settee,
him with his arm around her. Grace Trimble started shouting at
Mr. Lomax, calling him a dirty old man and saying he ought to
be ashamed of himself, messing about with a young girl like
Josie. Then she got hold of Josie by the arm and tried to drag her
away, saying she was coming home at once, and this was the
end, the finish, she'd never see Mr. Lomax again. Josie was
struggling with her mother and screaming at her to let her go. In
the end Josie managed to get free. You should have seen her!
She looked a real sight. Hair all over the place, mascara running
down her cheeks. And all the while Mr. Lomax just sat there like
a stuffed prune . . . I tell you, I wouldn't have missed it for the
world!"

"So what happened, in the end?"

"Josie refused flat to go home with her mother. Said she was
over age and could do what she liked. Her mother could like it or

lump it." Mrs. Pantry shrugged. "There was nothing Mrs. Trimble could do about it, was there? So she just left."

"What sort of state was she in?"

"Quiet. Defeated, sort of. I felt sorry for her really. Offered her a cup of tea, but she refused."

"How long would you say all this took?"

"No more than a few minutes, I shouldn't think. I mean, a lot happened, but it was all over very quick." Mrs. Pantry shook her head reminiscently. "I tell you, we've never had a night like that since I've been here. All those comings and goings . . ." She gave Thanet a sly, knowing look. "Just like *Dallas*, it was. Real action-packed."

Surely she wasn't implying . . . "All those comings and goings?"

She smoothed the skirt over her knee, looking almost coy. "Well, first Mr. Salden going, then Josie and Mr. Lomax coming, then Mrs. Salden going, then . . ."

He had been expecting her to say, "then Mrs. Trimble coming," but she had stopped deliberately. "Then . . . ?" he prompted.

She folded her arms and leaned back against the banisters with a self-satisfied smile. "Then, of course, there was Mr. Hammer."

Hammer. The name sounded vaguely familiar. Who was he? Mrs. Pantry was enjoying this, dangling the information tantalisingly in front of his nose. Struggling to suppress his rising irritation, Thanet said, "Mr. Hammer?"

"Reg Hammer, I believe it is. His mother lives in the village— lived I should say. She died last Monday."

Thanet remembered now. The first of the three deaths the Vicar had mentioned. Mrs. Hammer, Mrs. Carter, Marcia Salden. Was there a connection?

"He came here on Tuesday evening too?"

"Just said so, didn't I?"

"What did he want?"

"To see Mrs. Salden."

"What about?"

A shrug. "No idea." She was obviously determined to make him work for the information.

"Did she speak to him?"

"No. They were in the middle of dinner."

"This was fairly early in the evening, then?"

"Yes."

"When, exactly?"

"About half-past eight, I should think."

"So what happened?"

Another shrug. "He went away."

"Before that, I mean. What was his attitude, when he asked to see Mrs. Salden?"

That sly smile again. "He wasn't too happy, I'd say."

"He was angry, you mean?"

"You could say that."

"With Mrs. Salden?"

"I suppose."

"But he didn't say why?"

"No. Just said he wanted to see her, urgent."

"And what message did she send back?"

"That he was to ring up in the morning, make an appointment."

"How did he react to that?"

"Called her some four-letter names and drove away. Wonder he wasn't picked up. He wasn't fit to drive."

"He'd been drinking, you mean?"

"Reeked of it."

"And you're sure you've no idea why he wanted to see Mrs. Salden?"

"Haven't a clue."

The front door opened and Bernard Salden came in, his eyebrows going up at the sight of his housekeeper and Thanet sitting side by side on the stairs. He didn't look too pleased to see the police again so soon and his tone was distinctly frosty. "Good afternoon, Inspector."

Thanet returned the greeting and descended to the hall. "I was hoping for another word with you, sir."

Salden gave a resigned sigh as he handed his raincoat to Mrs. Pantry. "Very well. But d'you mind if we talk outside? It's stopped raining and I could do with a breath of fresh air."

"Not at all."

Salden led the way.

SEVENTEEN

Outside the air was still charged with moisture, but the sun was just beginning to emerge from behind the heavy bank of cloud which had brought the showers, stippling the drowned landscape with random patches of brilliant light.

It was too wet to walk on the grass and they strolled across the forecourt in the direction of the drive. Salden sighed again. "What is it this time, Inspector?" He had changed out of the casual clothes he had been wearing earlier into a formal dark suit, white shirt and black tie.

"Fresh information keeps coming in, and I need your help, to understand how it fits in."

Salden gave him a wary glance. "What information?"

"About your wife's affairs—business affairs, that is," he added hastily as Salden's eyebrows shot up. "And as they're presumably your affairs too . . ."

"Not necessarily, Inspector. We were partners in the health food business, yes, but Marcia had various schemes on hand of which I knew very little. But if I can help you, I will."

"Inspector Thanet!" Mrs. Pantry had emerged from the front door, waving. "Telephone."

Could it be Joan, calling about Bridget? No. His movements at work were so uncertain that she rarely attempted to contact him during the day, except in cases of emergency. "You take it, Mike, will you?"

Lineham loped off and Thanet and Salden continued their stroll, entering the avenue of beeches which were still dripping after the rain. From time to time they had to take out their handkerchiefs and mop their faces. "Did you know that your wife had had a row with Miss Phipps on the afternoon of the day she died?"

137

Salden stopped walking. "Really? No, I'd no idea. What about?"

"Miss Phipps had forgotten to post your wife's written offer for a shop in Week Street, Maidstone, and someone else got the lease."

"She forgot to post it! No wonder Marcia was angry. I was wondering why we hadn't had a reply."

"You knew about it, then?"

"About the shop? Yes, of course. We'd been hoping to get a Week Street site for years, but they'd always been too big or too small or in the wrong position . . . This one was perfect for us."

"Apparently your wife was so angry that she fired her."

"Fired Edith? Are you sure?"

"That surprises you?"

"It certainly does. They'd known each other for years, you know. As a matter of fact, they were at school together."

"Yes, Miss Phipps told me."

"Did she tell you about this herself—about being fired, I mean?"

"No. Someone overheard the quarrel."

"Mrs. Pantry, I suppose."

"As a matter of fact, no, it wasn't."

"Then it must have been Josie."

"Does it matter?"

"Not really, I suppose. Except that you have only her word that it ever took place."

"Mrs. Pantry saw Miss Phipps go home in tears afterwards."

"Edith, in tears? Then I suppose it must be true. But I must say I'm astounded, I really am."

"The impression I had was that this was only the latest in a long series of blunders. The last straw, so to speak."

"I must admit Marcia had been complaining about her rather a lot lately, but I didn't think she was that fed up with her. In fact, I had the impression she was rather sympathetic towards her. Edith—Miss Phipps—doesn't have much of a life, you know. She's very tied to her mother, who's an invalid, and lately, for the last year or so, she's been having rather a bad time with the menopause. It's true that she has been increasingly forgetful . . ."

"But Mrs. Salden said nothing to you that evening about having fired her?"

"We hardly saw each other. I'd been out, to a committee meeting in Sturrenden, and I didn't get home until six thirty. Marcia was having a bath and I had to bathe and change as well . . . We scarcely exchanged more than a few sentences."

"I see."

There were hurried footsteps behind them and Lineham came puffing up. Thanet walked back a few paces to meet him. "You're out of condition, Mike. You should take more exercise."

Lineham rolled his eyes. "I will if you will," he managed to say between gasps.

"Anything urgent?"

Lineham glanced at Salden, who had strolled on, and lowered his voice. "Doc Mallard, with a verbal on the PM."

"And?"

Lineham shook his head. "Not a lot. Except that she was definitely dead before she went into the water. That blow to the right temple."

"Ah. Nothing else?"

"Just one interesting thing. You remember Mrs. Pepper said the Saldens had been keen to have more children after the first one died—that Mr. Salden had even suggested adopting?"

"Yes. What about it?"

"Well, according to Doc M, Mrs. Salden had been sterilised, some time ago. Had her tubes tied or something."

"Really?" Thanet glanced at Salden who had stopped walking and was waiting for them. In his dark, formal suit he looked out of place in the setting of grass, trees and parkland. Was it possible that he was unaware that his wife had had this operation? If so, and if what Mrs. Pepper said were true and he really had longed for another child, how would he react to this news?

He had evidently become tired of waiting and was walking towards them. "We might as well go back."

Thanet agreed, glancing back down the drive at the lodge. He had intended to call in and see Edith Phipps after finishing with Salden, but he could easily drive down. Why was she so late returning to work? he wondered. She should have been back an hour ago.

"I was thinking, while you were talking," said Salden. "Assuming it's true that my wife and Edith did have this quarrel . . . I hope you're not implying that this means Edith could have had anything to do with her death."

"I'm not implying anything. I told you, at the moment we're just trying to gather together as much information as we can. Though I have to tell you that we've just had the results of the *post mortem,* and I'm afraid it has been confirmed that your wife did not die by drowning."

Salden stopped walking. "She didn't drown?"

Thanet shook his head. "No. She was dead before she went into the water."

"But . . . Then how . . . ?"

"She was killed by a blow to the right temple. I'm sorry."

Salden swallowed hard, almost gulping in air as though his throat had suddenly closed up, making it difficult for him to breathe. His face was the colour of parchment. "A blow . . . ?" He swayed slightly.

Thanet put out a hand to steady him. "Yes—but perhaps not in the sense you think. You know we think she went into the river through the gap in the parapet?"

Salden nodded, a barely perceptible movement of the head, as if even the effort required for this minute movement were too much for him.

"We think she banged her head—her temple—against a sharp piece of projecting stone." Thanet decided against giving further details. Salden's skin had taken on an unhealthy, almost luminous tinge. "I'm sorry. But I felt you had a right to know."

"You're saying that this . . . blow might not have been deliberate? That it might have happened when she . . . slipped?"

"Or—it has to be said—was pushed."

Salden stared unseeingly at Thanet for some moments, apparently adjusting to this new information. At last he said, "I see." And turning stiffly like someone awakening from a dream he began to walk once more towards the house.

Thanet and Lineham fell in alongside him in silence.

They had covered more than half the distance towards the end of the avenue of beeches before Salden spoke again.

"All the same, the idea that Edith could have had anything to do with my wife's death is ludicrous. If you knew her as well as I do . . ."

Thanet wondered just how many times he had heard precisely this sentiment expressed of a murder suspect. "May I just ask . . . Will you allow her to keep her job, now?"

Salden looked at him suspiciously. "I suppose if I say yes, it won't really help her in your eyes. All the same, it's pointless to mislead you. Yes, I expect I shall—and what is more, I'm convinced that I shall be doing exactly what Marcia would have wished. I don't suppose for one moment that she really meant what she said—that is, assuming she said it. It's exactly the sort of thing one comes out with in the heat of the moment and then regrets. I've no doubt that if she'd lived she would have changed her mind by next morning and I'm sure Edith would have known that.''

''You may be right.'' On the other hand, with home, livelihood and the welfare of her invalid mother at stake, Edith might not have been willing to risk it. In any case, it was clear that at least two people who had good reason to wish Marcia dead, Harry Greenleaf and Edith Phipps, had in fact gained considerably by that death. Thanet closed his mind against the unlikely, even crazy notion that they might possibly have joined forces to bring that death about. He decided to change tack.

''This shop you were buying, to turn into a health food restaurant . . .''

''What about it?'' Salden sounded wary.

''. . . from Councillor Lomax.''

''Yes?''

''Would it have been part of the scheme we were discussing this morning, the one you didn't fully approve of?''

''It seemed a sound enough business proposition,'' said Salden stiffly.

''That isn't exactly an answer to my question.''

''I'm sorry, Inspector, I don't know what you're talking about.''

Salden had evidently decided that ignorance was the safest course.

''A sound business proposition, you say?''

''We wouldn't have been contemplating it otherwise, obviously. There isn't a single other health food restaurant in the area. We thought it had a good chance of success.''

''You'll have gone into the financial side of it, of course.''

''Naturally.''

''What price was Mr. Lomax asking for his premises?''

''I'm sorry, I can't see that that has anything to do with my wife's death. To be blunt, Inspector, it's none of your business.''

''We could examine your papers . . .''

"That wouldn't help you. Negotiations were only at the verbal stage."

"I see."

He obviously wasn't going to get anything more out of Salden on that topic at the moment. "Did you know that Josie's mother came up to the house the night your wife died?"

Salden blinked at the abrupt change of subject. "Mrs. Trimble? What on earth for?"

"Apparently she is very upset at the association between her daughter and Mr. Lomax."

"Between . . ." Salden was apparently taken aback. "You must be joking. He's older than I am."

Thanet shrugged. "Maybe. But it seems her suspicions are justified. I gather they've been meeting in the flat over the coach house."

Salden came to a dead halt again. "*Our* coach house?"

Thanet nodded.

He was shaking his head. "I don't believe it. You're making this up, aren't you? Playing games with me."

"No games, Mr. Salden. If Mrs. Pantry is to be believed, Josie has a key to the flat. She and Lomax used to meet there regularly when you were out."

"Josie has a *key*?"

Salden was silent, working it out. It was obvious that if the girl had had a key, Marcia must have given it to her.

"Understandably, Mrs. Trimble must have been rather angry with your wife."

The word *procuring* hung unspoken in the air between them. Salden gave Thanet an uncomfortable, almost shame-faced glance. "So what did Marcia say to her?"

"She didn't see her. This was latish in the evening, at about ten o'clock. Your wife was down in the village at the time."

"But Lomax and Josie were there . . ." The look on Salden's face indicated the degree of his distaste.

Perhaps he shouldn't have mentioned the matter, thought Thanet. Perhaps he should have allowed Salden to keep his illusions about his wife intact. If he had had any . . . "Yes, they were. I gather Mrs. Trimble tried to insist that Josie go home with her, but Josie refused."

Salden was shaking his head. "Poor kid. She's the loser in all this."

Especially if she's pregnant, thought Thanet. But if she were, it looked as though Salden might be prepared to attempt to make amends for his wife's behaviour by giving the girl a helping hand. In which case, he, Thanet, would have done Josie a good turn by making Salden aware of the situation. He felt a little better about bringing the matter up. Marcia was beyond help, but Josie was not.

They were almost at the end of the avenue of trees and suddenly the last of the wispy clouds which had been drifting across the face of the sun cleared away and it burst through in full strength, streaming in great shafts of light between the interlacing branches overhead.

Thanet paused to admire the effect before saying, "There's just one other point I wanted to ask you about . . . What does the name Hammer mean to you?"

Salden frowned. "There's an old lady in the village, Mrs. Hammer. Or there was. She died earlier this week."

"Do you know her son? Reg, I believe he's called. Short for Reginald, I presume."

"I didn't even know she had a son. Why?"

"Well, apparently he came here on Tuesday evening too, wanting to speak to your wife. According to Mrs. Pantry he was very angry with Mrs. Salden for some reason."

"Angry with Marcia?" Salden was shaking his head. "I can't imagine why. You'll have to ask him."

"I will, of course."

They were nearing the front door. The heat of the sun was causing ground water to evaporate so fast that a haze of low mist was rising from the paved path along the front of the house.

Salden paused with one hand on the bleached oak of the front door. "Well, if that's all, Inspector . . ."

"Mmm? Oh, yes." Thanet's mind was elsewhere, preoccupied with two questions. "May I use your phone?"

"Of course." Salden led them inside. "You can use the one in my office."

This was a small, businesslike room at the back of the house, with modern desk, computer and a couple of filing cabinets. Thanet tried the Probation office first. Joan was there.

"Luke! I was wondering if you'd ring."

Having realised that Thanet was talking to his wife, Lineham tactfully withdrew.

"How did you get on?"

"You're not going to believe this."

A stone suddenly appeared in the pit of Thanet's stomach. "What?"

"Our darling daughter has been playing truant."

"*What?*"

"True. Honestly. I just couldn't believe it. Just sat there with my mouth open. Well, we knew things hadn't been going well for her, but . . ."

"How long has this been going on?"

"For the last few weeks, apparently, on and off."

"Why on earth didn't the school let us know before?"

"That's what I said. It seems they only found out by chance, yesterday. One of the teachers had a dental appointment and saw her in the town."

Yesterday. Thanet remembered Bridget's reluctant back as she had walked towards the school gates. As soon as he was out of sight she must have turned around and headed for the town. The deception hurt. If she was as unhappy as that, surely she could have confided in them. And what about Ben? Did he know about this?

"She's been forging notes, apparently."

"She's *what?*"

"Been forging notes from me, saying that she was ill. I know. Unbelievable, isn't it? I mean, *Bridget* . . ."

"What worries me is why."

"I know. And that she couldn't trust us, to talk to us about it."

"Yes." To feel that you'd failed, as a parent, when your child evidently needed you most. That really hurt . . . Thanet said so.

"I know." Joan was subdued.

"We'll have to talk to her."

"Yes. Tonight."

Thanet rang off and then sat looking at the receiver, thinking back over the conversation. He still felt stunned.

Lineham came back in. "You all right, sir?"

"What? Oh, yes . . ." With an effort Thanet focussed his mind on the case again and remembered his other anxiety. "Anyone mention Miss Phipps? Has she rung to say why she's not back yet?"

"Haven't seen anyone, to ask."

Thanet nodded at the telephone directory. "Look up her number, will you? She should have been back a couple of hours ago.''

Lineham grinned. ''If this were an episode in one of those detective series where bodies are scattered around like confetti we'd know what's happened to her, wouldn't we?'' He spread his hands in a dramatic gesture. ''We'd dial her number and the phone would ring and ring in a silent house. The camera would pan through the empty rooms and finally come to focus on her body . . .''

''I think you'd better change your viewing habits, Mike. And look up that number before I decide to do it myself!''

It was all very well to make jokes about it, he thought, but where was she? One woman had been murdered, why not another? The palms of his hands were clammy as he dialled the number Lineham dictated to him.

EIGHTEEN

"Miss Phipps?"

"Yes?"

She sounded out of breath. The dialling tone had sounded at least a dozen times before she lifted the phone. Perhaps she had been in the garden, Thanet thought with relief.

"Detective Inspector Thanet here. I'm up at the house. Are you coming to work this afternoon? I'd appreciate another word with you."

"No, Mr. Salden gave me the afternoon off. Could you come down to the lodge?"

"Yes, of course. We'll be there shortly."

She opened the front door before they could knock and with a finger to her lips led them into a small square kitchen overlooking the drive. A door leading into a narrow walk-in larder in the corner was open and she was obviously half-way through cleaning it; a lightweight aluminium stepladder stood near by and all the upper shelves were empty, their contents stacked on the table in the middle of the room. On top of the pile of bottles and packets lay a neatly folded print apron, removed no doubt in expectation of their visit. Today her square, dumpy body was encased in a drab, rather shabby crimpelene dress in two tones of blue.

She apologised for the muddle, smoothing her hands down her skirt as if ashamed of her appearance, too. "I thought I'd take the opportunity to do a bit of spring-cleaning."

Thanet grinned. "My wife says spring-cleaning the larder is the job she hates most of all. That's why she always starts with it, to get it over and done with."

"I feel exactly the same!" She glanced at the single chair. "Is this going to take long, Inspector? If so, I'll fetch a couple more chairs. We don't spend much time in here. I think I told you, my mother's an invalid and we eat together in the other room."

She glanced nervously at the door as she spoke. Presumably she was hoping her mother would remain unaware of their presence. He wondered why, if she had nothing to hide. In his experience, housebound people welcomed any interruption of their monotonous existence. And why suggest holding the interview here at the lodge, if she didn't want her mother to know about it? Perhaps she was now regretting having done so. "No, don't worry, we can stand. But do sit down yourself."

But she, too, chose to stand and they disposed themselves about the room, leaning against various work surfaces.

"Your mother's not confined to bed all the time, then?"

"Oh, no, but movement is very difficult for her, very painful. She's badly crippled with arthritis and her heart is failing. She has a walking frame and she does try to get about a little—they say you have to, or you'll seize up altogether—but naturally she reserves the effort for essentials."

"She goes to bed quite early, I imagine."

Edith Phipps was no fool. Her eyes narrowed and she adjusted the tip-tilted spectacles as if hoping to see more clearly into Thanet's mind. "I usually settle her down about nine o'clock, yes." She paused. "Is that an . . . oblique way of asking for an alibi, Inspector?"

It was always a relief to come across a witness prepared to say exactly what she thought.

"I'll be frank with you, Miss Phipps. When we last met I asked you if you had been in all evening, the night Mrs. Salden died. You said yes. I thought at the time that you were holding something back. Now I have to tell you that you were seen, that night, walking from the village towards this house, at about twenty-five past ten."

"By whom?"

She hadn't denied it, he noted. He shook his head. "That's irrelevant. What is not irrelevant is why you found it necessary to lie at a time when there was only the merest suspicion that Mrs. Salden's death was anything but an accident."

"Do I gather that you are now sure that it was not?"

"Shall we say that at the moment it seems necessary to continue the investigation."

She stared at him in silence, thinking.

Eventually, "I'm still waiting for an answer, Miss Phipps."

She sighed and lifted her shoulders slightly. "Stupid of me not to be frank with you, wasn't it? I'd only been to post some letters. I'd . . . forgotten to do it, earlier."

And presumably hadn't wanted to risk incurring Marcia's wrath again, just in case overnight she changed her mind about firing her, thought Thanet. But although the errand may have been innocent it could have culminated in tragedy. The two women could have met on the bridge.

"Marcia! Look, you didn't mean what you said this afternoon, did you? I mean, it was just because you were angry, wasn't it?"

"You're damned right I was angry. Still am. When I think what your carelessness has cost us . . ."

"I'm sorry, Marcia, truly I am. It'll never happen again, I promise."

"It certainly won't. Because I'm not giving you the chance. I meant what I said, Edith. This sort of thing has happened once too often. Now, please let me pass."

"But what'll I do? Where shall we go? You know how difficult it is, with Mother . . . Marcia, please. I've always done my very best for you, haven't I?"

"Well, your best turned out not to be quite good enough, didn't it?"

"It's only because I haven't been well. If you knew how ill I'd been feeling . . ."

"I'm sorry, Edith, but you've used that excuse just once too often. And I've tried to make allowances, but this time . . . No, the sooner you get used to the idea that you're leaving, the better. Now, if you don't mind, let me pass. I have guests waiting . . ."

Thanet became aware that Edith Phipps was gazing at him expectantly, awaiting his reaction. "It was rather foolish of you not to admit to so innocent an errand. Why didn't you?"

"Edith?" A querulous voice calling from another room.

Edith grimaced. "My mother. Sorry, I'll have to go and see what she wants." She hurried out.

"Seems to be our day for interruptions," grumbled Lineham. "And always at just the wrong moment."

"Don't suppose it matters much. She's not going to run away, is she?"

"She didn't try and wriggle out of it," Lineham conceded. "Pretend she'd forgotten she'd been out that night."

"Quite."

"What d'you think, sir? You think she might be the one?"

Thanet lifted his shoulders. "She had a lot at stake, if Marcia Salden stuck to her guns."

"Just because she'd lost her job it doesn't mean they'd have had to leave this house, surely?"

"I've no idea. But I should think it might be on the cards. Marcia doesn't exactly sound the tender-hearted type. Look at what happened with Greenleaf."

"Sorry." Edith came back in, looking flustered. "What were you saying?"

"I was asking why you lied to us about going out that evening. Posting letters is an innocent enough occupation."

"I know." She caught her underlip beneath her teeth, shook her head. "It's just . . . I was frightened, I suppose."

"Of what?"

"You'd just told me that Marcia's death might not have been an accident. And, well, to be honest . . ." She gave him an assessing look. "I was glad she was dead," she said quietly. She shifted uncomfortably, brushed back a stray strand of hair. "Now you know," she added. Then without warning her face suddenly contorted into a mask of distress and, covering her eyes with one hand, she sank down on to the chair, fumbling in her pocket for a handkerchief to wipe away the tears. It was some minutes before she recovered sufficiently to go on. Eventually she blew her nose, shook her head and said, "Sorry."

"No need to apologise. I presume that what you're trying to say is that because you were glad she was dead you felt guilty and because you felt guilty you thought we might suspect you of having something to do with her death."

She nodded gratefully.

"Something of an overreaction, I would have thought."

She shrugged. "People don't always act logically. That was how I felt."

"Why were you glad she was dead?" Thanet awaited her reply with interest. Would she now confess that she had had a motive, that Marcia had sacked her? To her knowledge no one else knew. She must realise by now that Marcia hadn't told Bernard and she might well believe that with any luck the police would never find out. So if she did tell them it would weigh heavily in favour of her innocence.

She compressed her lips and shook her head.

"You really can't make a statement like that and refuse to amplify it," said Thanet gently. "Especially in these circumstances."

"Well, perhaps I was putting it a little too strongly. Perhaps what I really meant was that I wasn't sorry she was dead. It was a shock at first, of course, but once the news had sunk in I found I was really rather . . . relieved."

"Any particular reason?" He couldn't give her a more specific lead than that. But she was shaking her head. She wasn't going to take it.

"Not really. I just didn't like her. She was hard. Very hard. Look at the way she treated Harry Greenleaf, who never did any harm to anyone . . . And she was very difficult to work for. Very demanding, hyper-critical."

Thanet waited but she said nothing more. She had definitely decided against telling them, then. Interesting. The question now was, should he bring the matter up himself? Lineham was watching him, clearly wondering if he was going to.

"Perhaps I ought to tell you," Thanet said slowly, "that your conversation with Mrs. Salden on Tuesday afternoon was overheard."

The breath caught in her throat. "Which conversation?"

"The one you're afraid I'm referring to. The one in which she fired you."

She seemed to stop breathing, to move into a state of suspended animation. For a minute or more she gazed at Thanet unblinking. Then at last she stirred, sighed, glanced down at the sodden handkerchief in her lap. "I see . . ."

There was a further, brief silence, then she said, "How long have you known?"

"Since this morning."

"Mrs. Pantry, I suppose." But there was no bitterness or animosity in her tone, merely a weary resignation.

"Actually, no . . ."

She shook her head. "It doesn't really matter . . ." She gave a wry smile, the first glimmer of humour she had shown since the interview began. "Now all I have to do is convince you that whoever it was who pushed Marcia off that bridge, it wasn't me."

"Was it?"

She shook her head. "Even if it was, would you really expect me to admit it? But no, Inspector, it wasn't."

"It obviously wouldn't surprise you if somebody did."

"Not really, no. Marcia was the sort of person to arouse strong passions. She was very stubborn and she liked to get her own way. And she didn't really care what people thought of her."

"I gather she'd made herself pretty unpopular in the village."

Edith pulled a face. "I'll say. But you couldn't blame her, really."

"What d'you mean?"

"For not caring what local people thought. I mean, they weren't exactly welcoming when she and Bernard bought the Manor, you know. They couldn't really stomach someone from the cottages buying 'The Big House.' Honestly! In this day and age . . . Well I knew just how much that house meant to Marcia, as I told you, so I was firmly on her side, prepared to back her to the hilt. All that drawing aside of skirts made me so angry . . . And I do think that if only she'd been prepared to be patient, give them time to come round, they would have accepted her in the end. But she wasn't the patient type and I suppose her reaction was predictable. 'I'll teach them,' she said to me, after one particular snub. 'Just you wait and see.' That was when she decided to close the footpath. And then it was just one thing after another."

"So you think she did care what local people thought about her, underneath?"

"Oh yes, she did, beyond doubt. It was a shame, really. For her, buying the Manor was the proof that she'd really made it, the fulfilment of a life-long dream."

"And the dream went sour."

"I'm afraid so. And it soured her, too. She became much harder, more ruthless. And much more impatient, liable to lose her temper."

Which could be important in their understanding of this particular crime, thought Thanet. If, as he suspected, Marcia's death had happened as the result of a quarrel, her attitude could have played a crucial part in precipitating the tragedy. That barely suppressed anger and resentment simmering away just below the surface would have been all too likely to erupt if someone challenged her or took her to task.

"Can you think of anyone in particular who had a grudge against her?"

Edith frowned, shaking her head. "Strangely enough, no. Apart from Harry Greenleaf, of course, and I'm sure he couldn't have been involved. He wouldn't hurt a fly. Naturally I've been thinking about it, I've thought about it a lot, and I've come to the conclusion that Marcia tended to take on people collectively rather than individually. Which doesn't really help you, of course."

"What about her husband?" The last time Thanet had spoken

to Edith she had said that she wasn't prepared to discuss the Saldens' private life, but that she might reconsider if Marcia's death did turn out to be murder.

"Oh no. Not Bernard. He's just not the type to resort to violence under any circumstances. And although I wouldn't say they were really close, I can honestly say I never heard them quarrelling."

"I have the impression he wasn't too happy about some of his wife's business interests."

"Maybe, but you're not trying to tell me he'd resort to murder to stop her!"

"Not in cold blood, perhaps. But I'll be frank and tell you that in my opinion this was no premeditated crime. Someone quarrelled with Mrs. Salden, grabbed her by the arm, perhaps, and she tried to get away, slipped . . ."

Edith folded her arms across her plump body and shivered. "And then he just walked off, without raising the alarm, leaving her to drown."

Thanet had no intention of telling Edith that Marcia had been dead before she reached the water. "I'm afraid so, yes."

She was shaking her head. "I just can't see Bernard doing a thing like that. He's . . . well, not only is he the type of man to do everything he can to avoid a quarrel, but I just can't see him leaving anyone to drown, let alone his wife, not under any circumstances."

"What can you tell me about a man called Hammer?"

The question surprised her. "Reg Hammer?"

"Yes. His mother lived in the village. She died earlier this week."

"What do you want to know about him?"

"Anything, really."

"Well, he was born and brought up in Telford Green. He's married and lives in Sturrenden. Used to work at Chatham Dockyard, but was made redundant when it closed a few years ago and hasn't been able to get work since . . . Funny you should ask, really."

"Why?"

"I saw him in the village yesterday, for the first time in years. He and his wife were clearing out his mother's cottage."

For some reason she suddenly understood why he was enquiring about Hammer. Thanet saw the comprehension in her eyes.

"He wasn't a regular visitor to his mother, then?"

"No. Which I expect is one of the reasons why . . ." She stopped short.

"What were you going to say just then?"

"When?"

"You said, 'Which I expect is one of the reasons why . . .' Then you stopped."

She shrugged. "It was automatic, I suppose. A sort of built-in reaction. I don't normally gossip about my employers' business."

"This isn't gossip, I assure you. It could be highly relevant."

"I suppose there's no reason why you shouldn't know. It's all in the files up at the house. I was merely going to say, I supposed the fact that Reg never bothered to visit his mother was one of the reasons why Mrs. Hammer applied to join Marcia's Golden Oldie scheme."

Thanet raised his eyebrows.

"It was one of Marcia's new business ventures. Lately she'd been getting a little bored with the health food business. It was very successful, yes, but the thrill of building it up had gone."

"I thought she was contemplating moving into health food restaurants."

"That's the latest idea, yes."

"Do you know anything about the negotiations with Mr. Lomax, by the way? What price he was asking, for example?"

"I don't think they'd got as far as that, not on paper anyway. Bernard is doing a feasibility study."

"Sorry I interrupted. You were talking about Reg Hammer's mother . . ."

"Well, as I say, Marcia had been looking for ways to . . . diversify, I suppose is the best way of putting it. She spent some time considering various ideas and eventually she decided that the best investment these days is property. So she thought up this scheme."

"The Golden Oldie scheme."

"Well, that was her private name for it, yes. Officially it was Salden Investments Ltd. The idea was that she would approach elderly people living in small period village properties, terraced houses chiefly, which as you know have rocketed in price lately, and would propose to them a scheme whereby they would sell her their house but would retain the right to continue to live in it until they died. In return, instead of an outright payment of the full market value of the house, Marcia would offer them a lump sum down and a guaranteed annual income for life. It was a gamble, of course. The pensioner could continue to live way

beyond the age at which Marcia would have made a profit out of
the deal, or he could die soon after the agreement was made and
she could make a killing.''

Not the happiest expression in the circumstances, thought
Thanet. ''Perhaps you could give us an example?''

''Well, she was careful always to choose someone well into
their seventies and without any close family likely to make a fuss
if they felt they'd been deprived of their inheritance.''

Thanet was beginning to see where Hammer came into the
picture.

''Take Mrs. Hammer, for example, though she was a little
different in that, as I say, she approached Marcia, not the other
way around. She'd heard about the scheme from some friend of
hers and she was seventy-seven when Marcia first heard from her
earlier this year. She was in very good health for her age and I
know Marcia calculated on her living another ten years. The old
lady was very hurt at her son's neglect and had no compunction
about applying to join the scheme. She positively jumped at the
offer Marcia made. Marcia offered her £5,000 down and £3,500
a year for life. For pensioners these are substantial sums of
money, perhaps more than they have ever seen in their lives.
With that sort of guaranteed income on top of their pension, even
allowing for income tax they can afford luxuries they may never
have been able to enjoy before. The scheme hasn't been going
long, and of course it's all properly drawn up by solicitors, but
out of the fifteen people Marcia approached only one turned the
offer down.''

Lineham had been working it out. ''So if a cottage was worth
£50,000, she would calculate on paying out £5,000 down and a
further £35,000 over ten years, making an expenditure of £40,000
in all.''

''That's right.''

''So she'd make a tidy profit as well as cashing in on the fact
that house prices are rising by between ten and fifteen per cent a
year here in the South-east.''

''True. But you must remember that her capital would be tied
up for a period of ten years—and don't forget that the scheme
only worked because the elderly people welcomed it. And Marcia was very fair about it. She never tried to mislead them. I
always went with her, when she approached people and explained how the scheme worked, and she always presented the
snags of the scheme as well as the advantages. But it really
seemed to appeal to them. It gave them more money in their

pocket than most of them had ever had before, together with the guarantee of being able to stay on in their own homes for the rest of their lives—which is, above all, what most old people want. Given that, they just didn't care whether or not they would receive less than the market price for their properties. It really was a scheme which benefited everybody.''

"Everybody except the heirs," said Lineham.

"True. But, as I say, Marcia was careful to approach only those who appeared to have no family or were estranged from them . . . Do I gather that Reg has been kicking up a fuss?''

"Not surprising, is it?" Lineham sounded indignant on behalf of the unknown Reg. "Presumably Mrs. Salden in effect bought his mother's cottage for £5,000.''

"And half the first annual payment of £3,500.''

Lineham waved a dismissive hand. "Even so.''

"What I can't understand," said Thanet, "is why, if Mr. Salden is the accountant for all their business affairs, he didn't know about this.''

"Marcia never bothered to consult him on her pet projects. He does the annual accounts for them, of course, and keeps an eye on the books from time to time, but the payments to Mrs. Hammer only went through earlier this month, so they wouldn't have filtered through to him yet.''

"Edith?" The quavering voice again.

They had finished here for the moment. Besides, time was getting on and Thanet was anxious to get home early tonight because of Bridget. He had to ring Draco too, give him a brief progress report for the media statement. And he wanted to see Reg Hammer, first.

They thanked her, asked for directions to Mrs. Hammer's cottage, and left.

NINETEEN

"You really wouldn't believe a house like that could be worth £50,000, would you?" said Lineham.

He had parked across the road from Mrs. Hammer's cottage, which was in the middle of a terrace of eight, on the Manor side of the bridge.

It certainly had very little to recommend it in Thanet's eyes, being only about fourteen feet wide and built of ugly yellow Victorian brick with a slate roof. Prices indicated, however, that people were queueing up to buy such houses, village properties being especially in demand. "The property world's gone mad," he agreed.

"There's the Vicar," said Lineham as they got out of the car. He grinned. "Looks as though his car's gone wrong again. Can't say I'm surprised."

Fothergill had just come into sight around the bend which lay between them and the bridge, and was heading in their direction on a bicycle. Thanet and Lineham waited for him to pass, but he raised his hand in greeting and pulled up beside them.

"We really must stop meeting like this," he said with a cheery grin.

"What happened to the car?" said Lineham, grinning back.

Fothergill gave him a reproachful look. "You are insulting the vehicle I love. She is sitting in the garage at the Vicarage, resting after her exertions. We had to go to Canterbury this morning. Anyway, I never use her for visiting within the village. Much too extravagant. I told you, vicars have to be seen to be poor. Makes people respect them more. How's it going?"

"Slowly," said Thanet. "We were just talking about the ridiculous price of terraced cottages these days. Especially in the villages."

Fothergill held up a hand. "Don't start me off. That's one of my favourite hobbyhorses. People have these fantasies about living in a village, about enjoying the peace and quiet and the rural life. The young people especially are soon bored stiff and depart to the town again, looking for more excitement. They're not usually interested in village life at all. They don't join the village organisations or come to church. They don't realise that living in a village is like marriage—the more you put into it, the more you'll get out. The other thing, of course, is that it means all the old village families are disappearing. When the local young people get married they simply can't afford to buy anything and unless they're lucky enough to get a council house— and there are far too few of them—they have to move away." He grinned. "I told you, once I get launched . . . Anyway, I mustn't stand here gossiping. See you around."

He wheeled his bicycle to the last cottage in the row, propped it against the fence and disappeared around the side.

There was no reply to their knock at Mrs. Hammer's front door.

"Must've finished clearing up and gone home," said Lineham. "There's no car parked in front."

"He may not have a car. He's supposed to be unemployed, remember. Try again."

But there was still no answer and they turned away. As they were walking down the path, Thanet glanced over his shoulder and caught a glimpse of movement behind the net curtain at the downstairs window. He caught Lineham's sleeve. "There's someone in there."

They marched back to the door and knocked again, loudly. Still no reply.

"Try once more, then call 'Police' through the letterbox," said Thanet.

Lineham complied and this time they heard movement within.

The door opened a crack. A middle-aged woman peeped out. "What do you want?"

"Mrs. Hammer?"

"You want the old lady? She's . . ."

"No. We're looking for her son. Sturrenden CID." Thanet produced his identity card.

"He's out."

The door began to close, but Lineham stuck his foot in the gap, quickly.

"A brief talk with you, then," said Thanet.

Slowly, the door opened, revealing the reason for her reluctance. One side of her face was badly bruised, from forehead to chin. Avoiding Thanet's eye she stood back. "My husband said not to let anyone in." Unconsciously, her hand went up to her face, touched her cheek. She was in her late forties, wearing a tight, shoddy black skirt and a short-sleeved scarlet sweater which had seen better days. Her hair was an improbable shade of orange, a frizzy uncontrolled bush, and she was heavily made up. Despite the gaudy, defiant colours, her shoulders sagged and she exuded an aura of defeat.

Inside, the house was in good repair, freshly decorated and comfortably, even luxuriously furnished, with a thick new fitted carpet and new dralon-covered three-piece suite. Presumably Marcia would have taken over the maintenance of the fabric of the house and Mrs. Hammer would have been able to afford to indulge herself in the choice of furnishings. The curtain poles were bare and the room stripped of ornaments. Several overflowing cardboard boxes stood by the door, waiting to be taken away.

Mrs. Hammer stood in the middle of the room, arms hanging loosely at her sides, clearly uncertain as to what should happen next.

Thanet gestured at the chairs. "May we sit down?"

She shrugged. "Help yourself."

She dug a hand into her pocket, brought out a pack of cigarettes and lit one, inhaling the smoke greedily.

"I believe your mother-in-law died earlier this week."

"So?" She perched on an arm of the other chair.

Expressions of sympathy would evidently be pointless. "You've been busy." Thanet nodded at the boxes.

"Nothing wrong with that, is there?" She was very much on the defensive.

"Of course not, no. Not a very pleasant job, though."

She shrugged, drawing on her cigarette. "Got to be done, hasn't it?"

"Have you nearly finished?"

"Just about."

"Surprising how much people accumulate, isn't it, even in a small house like this? How long has it taken you?"

She gave him a puzzled glance. "We started yesterday."

"You arrived here yesterday morning, then?"

"No, Tuesday. Tuesday morning."

If Mrs. Hammer had died on Monday they certainly hadn't wasted much time moving in on what they must have thought of as Reg's inheritance. "And on Tuesday afternoon you went to see the solicitor."

She frowned. "Yeah. So what?"

"And discovered that your mother-in-law had sold the cottage to Mrs. Salden, without telling your husband."

She was scowling heavily. "Senile old bitch. Going behind Reg's back like that . . ."

So this woman's resentment was directed at her mother-in-law, not at Marcia. Predictable, perhaps. And her husband's? "I understand your husband went up to the Manor to speak to Mrs. Salden about it on Tuesday evening?"

That look of surprise was genuine, he would swear to it. "You didn't know?"

She shook her head. "He didn't tell me." There was a long grey worm of ash on her cigarette and she looked around vaguely for an ashtray. Failing to see one, she tapped it into her cupped palm.

"You knew he was out that evening."

"He said he was going to the Door."

The local name for the pub, Thanet assumed. "What time did he get home?"

Her cigarette had burned down. "Excuse me. Must go and put this out."

She went into the next room, leaving the door open, and they heard the brief hiss of a tap being turned on and off. "About half-past ten," she said as she came back in. Her eyes turned to the window as an old grey van pulled up outside. A man got out.

"There's Reg now." Her hand went up to her cheek again in that unconscious gesture.

"Don't worry, I'll explain," said Thanet hurriedly as the key sounded in the lock. He and Lineham rose as the door opened.

Hammer checked on the threshold, glancing from the two men to his wife and back again. "Who the hell . . . ?"

He was a big man, well over six feet and a good eight or nine inches taller than his wife, with a drooping grandad moustache and a belly which hung over the waistband of his trousers. Thanet disliked him on sight.

Quickly, Thanet introduced himself.

Hammer looked accusingly at his wife.

"Don't blame your wife for letting us in. She had no choice. We would have found you sooner or later anyway."

Hammer's expression changed to wariness. "What d'you want to see me about?"

"Mrs. Salden."

"What about her?"

"Shall we sit down, Mr. Hammer?"

He, too, was smoking and needed an ashtray. He flicked a glance at his wife and without a word she got up, went to one of the cardboard boxes by the door and rummaged about until she found a saucer. She put it into his outstretched hand and he took it without word or look of acknowledgement. He sat down in the second armchair, balanced the saucer on the arm and folded his arms belligerently. "Let's get on with it, then."

Thanet glanced at Lineham and the Sergeant took up his cue, opening his notebook and glancing down at some imaginary notes. "We understand you went up to the Manor on Tuesday night, to see Mrs. Salden."

"What if I did?" He stubbed his cigarette out, lit another.

"Would you mind telling us why?"

"Why should I? It was private business."

"Reg," said his wife.

"Keep your nose out," he flung at her.

"But Reg . . ."

"I told you. Shurrup."

"Mr. Hammer," began Lineham.

"Reg, they *know*," said his wife, desperately.

There was a brief silence.

"Know what?" he said to her.

"About your mum signing the house over."

He gave Lineham a venomous glare. "Trying to catch me out, were you?"

"Merely trying to give you a chance to tell the story in your own words."

Hammer gave a mirthless shout of laughter. "Want a story, do you?" He ground out his half-smoked cigarette in the saucer and leaned forward, fixing Lineham with a basilisk stare. "OK, I'll tell you one. Once upon a time there was an evil bitch who got her kicks out of making money. She got her biggest kicks of all when her victims was poor and downtrodden. She really rubbed her hands with glee the day she hit on a scheme for taking away the very roof over their heads. Now, there was one poor bloke who'd lost his job, through no fault of his own. His firm closed down, see, and he was made redundant. And he just couldn't find work 'cos unemployment was sky-high because of the bloody Conservative government what was in at the time. In the end the DHSS wouldn't go on paying his mortgage, so the building society took his house back and him and his wife and kids had to go and live with her mother in a poky little two-bedroomed flat. The council waiting list was as long as your arm, so it looked as if this situation would go on for ever. Then, unexpected-like, his mum dies. He was sorry, of course, he thought she'd go on for years, but looking on the bright side he thinks, at least I'll now have a home for my family. And what does he find? He finds that that bitch, that bloody bitch has snatched the house away from under his very nose with some crooked scheme what no one in his right mind would have taken on . . . Do you realise," he went on, stabbing the air with his forefinger to emphasise the point, "exactly how much Mrs. Salden paid for this cottage? £5,000 down and half the first annual instalment of £3,500—£1,750, that is. In other words, £6,750 in all! 6,750 quid! And do you know how much the cottage is worth? £50,000!" He clutched his hand across his stomach and groaned, as if the thought gave him physical pain.

As well it might, thought Thanet. "We're not here to discuss the rights and wrongs of the scheme, merely to . . ."

"Oh, I see," said Hammer. "The police force is no longer interested in justice."

"In this instance, what you need is a solicitor, not a policeman."

"Bloody solicitors! Fat lot of good that stuffed shirt Bassett is."

Oliver Bassett, precise, prissy, conventional and well-tailored, had been a suspect in one of Thanet's cases. He and Hammer would be chalk and cheese.

Hammer was still fulminating. "They're all the same. Make you pay through the nose just to say good morning to them. Carrion crows, that's what they are." The phrase seemed to please Hammer and he repeated it, nodding emphatically. "Carrion crows, picking over the leavings of the dead."

Thanet glanced around the stripped room.

Hammer had the grace to flush.

"You haven't quite finished your story," said Thanet.

"Oh?"

"On the night the poor honest labourer discovered the way in which he'd been cheated of what was rightfully his, the wicked witch died."

"And good riddance, too."

"But unfortunately for him, there was some doubt about her death."

A brief silence, then "Doubt?" said Hammer. He glanced at his wife, but she was staring at Thanet as if mesmerised.

It was interesting, Thanet thought, that the Hammers hadn't heard the rumours flying around the village. Perhaps it was a measure of Reg's unpopularity with neighbours who might have resented his neglect of his mother. "That it may not have been an accident."

Hammer gaped at him for a moment, then leapt to his feet. "Now look here!" he shouted. "What you getting at?"

In such a tiny room the effect was overpowering and it was difficult not to shrink back from the towering figure looming over them. "Nasty temper you've got there, Mr. Hammer," said Thanet quietly.

Hammer glowered down at him then, without a word, returned to flop down into his chair. He lit another cigarette.

"Now, if you've calmed down, perhaps we can get this over with. All I want is a brief, factual account of your movements on Tuesday evening."

Hammer's story was that he had left the house just after eight and had gone to the pub for a drink before going up to the Manor to see Marcia.

Dutch courage, no doubt, thought Thanet. "One drink? Or two? Or more?"

"May have been two." Hammer was sulky.

"Beer? Whisky?"

"Whisky."

"Singles or doubles?"

Aware no doubt that all this could be checked, Hammer muttered reluctantly, "Doubles."

He had then driven up to the Manor and had asked for Marcia. He used her Christian name this time, Thanet noticed. Of course! He was the right age. They might well have been at school together. He wanted to think about this and signalled for Lineham to take over the questioning again. They knew that Marcia and Edith Phipps had both attended the village school. Now there was Reg. How many other people still living in the village had shared their childhood and adolescence with her? Marcia had lived at home until she got married, at eighteen. Was it possible that the roots of this present tragedy went deeper into the past than Thanet had so far considered?

Listening with one ear to what Hammer was now saying, Thanet gathered that, denied entry by Mrs. Pantry ("rotten bitch"), he had resorted once more to drink, going directly back to the Crooked Door and staying there until closing time.

They would check at the pub, of course, but meanwhile . . .

"I suppose you knew Mrs. Salden well at one time, Mr. Hammer?"

He looked taken aback. "Pretty well, yes. We was at school together."

"Yes, I thought you might have been. What was she like, then?"

He gave a cynical sort of laughter. "A prig and a swot, if you must know. Always did have her sights set upwards, did our Marcia."

Mrs. Hammer stirred.

"Yes, Mrs. Hammer?" said Thanet.

"I was only going to say," she said with a nervous glance at her husband, "that she wasn't snooty, though, was she? I mean, you told me she . . ."

"Never mind what I told you," snarled Hammer.

She subsided with a little shake of the head.

"What was the name of the headmaster at the village school in your time?" said Thanet.

The unexpectedness of the question brought an immediate response. "Mr. Pringle." A brief pause, then, "Why?"

"Just wondered. He'd be retired now, I suppose."

"I suppose," echoed Hammer.

"D'you happen to know where he's living?"

"Haven't a clue."

Thanet's beeper went and Mrs. Hammer jumped. "It's all right," he said, "I'll have to get to a phone, that's all." They'd finished here, anyway. He glanced at Lineham, raising his eyebrows. *Any more questions?* Lineham shook his head.

He used the phone box outside the Crooked Door. There was a message for him to ring home. What could be wrong? He felt slightly sick as he dialled the number.

Joan answered on the first ring.

"What's the matter, darling. What's wrong?"

"It's Bridget. She's not home yet."

He glanced at his watch. "It's only half-past five. She could have gone to Amanda's house. Or Sheila's."

"I've rung around, and she's not with any of her friends. And she hasn't been at school today, remember. She could be anywhere. Oh Luke, I'm sorry to fuss, but I can't help worrying, in the circumstances. I mean, she knew I was seeing the headmaster this afternoon . . . What if she's afraid to come home?"

"I'll be there as soon as I can."

TWENTY

All the way home Thanet's unruly imagination ran riot. He was fully aware of the growing problem of runaways who, unable to cope at home, make their way to the nearest big city and end up by being sucked into prostitution or worse. And there was no point in telling himself that it couldn't happen to a girl like Bridget, from a stable, loving home. It was true that most of these youngsters ran away because of irreconcilable differences with either father or mother, but Thanet himself had dealt with at least two cases where the parents were just like himself and Joan, and completely bewildered as to what had gone wrong.

And in one of them, the child, a boy of thirteen, had never been seen again.

The very thought brought an uprush of panic and he took a deep breath and told himself to calm down. Like Joan, he was overreacting, of course. It simply would not, could not happen to them. Bridget wouldn't have expected her mother to be home before a quarter or ten to six, so there was no reason why she herself should turn up before then. After all, she wasn't a baby any more. At fifteen she shouldn't have to account to them for every minute of her time. He and Joan had always striven to strike a sensible balance between being over-protective and allowing too much freedom. No, by the time he got home she would have arrived, safe and sound.

But she hadn't. Joan came out to meet him and it was immediately obvious from her face.

"Tell me I'm blowing things up out of all proportion," she said with an attempt at a smile when they had kissed.

He put his arm around her. "Come on. Let's go inside."

Joan had rung everywhere she could think of and it was pointless to consider requesting official help from the police at this stage. Thanet knew that in similar circumstances he would expect a girl of Bridget's age to be a minimum of three or four hours overdue before mobilising his men, and probably much longer. And in any case, if Bridget were making an innocent visit somewhere, she would justifiably be furious if she discovered that an official search had been organised just because she was a couple of hours late getting home from school. Thanet said so.

"I know that. But if ever she's going anywhere, she always lets us know."

"There has been the odd occasion in the past when she hasn't."

"But not in these circumstances. I'm just worried in case, guessing why Mr. Foreman wanted to see me this afternoon, she feels she can't face us. After all, she must have felt she couldn't confide in us up to now, if things have got so bad that she's been driven to playing truant."

"Did Ben know about that?"

"I don't think so, no. He says not, and I believe him. He says he knew something was wrong, but thought it was just exams."

They were in the kitchen. Thanet sat down heavily on one of the chairs. "He's right, in a way, of course. There's no doubt that it's the prospect of GCSEs looming that's done the damage."

"But we've done everything we can to stop her getting too worked up about it."

"I know, and let's face it we've failed dismally, haven't we? Just look at the way she's been going on! Sitting up till all hours sweating over her books, and if you dare suggest she ought to give up and go to bed you either have your head bitten off or she dissolves into floods of tears . . . D'you know, the night before last she was still working at midnight and when I went along I just didn't have the nerve to tell her it was time she stopped, in case it upset her!" He shook his head in disbelief. "I suppose if we had any sense we'd have seen this coming."

"But what could we have done about it, even if we had?"

Thanet shook his head. "I don't know."

"She's too conscientious, that's the trouble. Takes things too much to heart."

"But she didn't do impossibly badly in her mocks at Christmas."

"She felt she had. She only had reasonable grades in two subjects out of seven."

"But all her teachers said she had a fair chance of achieving considerably higher grades in the summer, if she worked hard."

"Which is precisely what she's been doing, of course. Honestly, Luke, I sometimes think it would have been better if the results had been so appalling that she'd given up hope of doing any better.''

"You don't really mean that."

"I suppose not."

"After all, under this new system, her continuous assessment is supposed to be equally important, and that's been quite good."

"Let's face it, average, at best."

"Well, all right, average. There's nothing wrong with that."

"No, of course not."

"One thing's certain, we're going to have to try and work something out. If she goes on like this for another couple of months, we'll all have nervous breakdowns!"

"Just let's get her back, that's all I can think of at the moment. Oh Luke, what d'you think we ought to do?"

He stood up. "I'm going to go out and have a scout around for her. Would you mind staying here? I think one of us ought to."

"I agree. No, I'll stay."

At least he knew where to look, he thought as he set off. He'd done this often enough before. But never when it was his own child who was missing, never with quite this sense of urgency.

It was now half-past six and his task was made easier by the fact that the streets of Sturrenden were virtually deserted. It was the dead time of day between the rush home from work and the start of the evening's entertainments. He began with the cafés. In one or two there were little groups of teenagers lingering over cups of coffee, reluctant to go home, but he didn't recognise any of them as Bridget's friends and he didn't approach them. At this stage he wanted to keep things as low-key as possible, in case it was a false alarm.

After his round of the cafés he decided to quarter the town systematically. There was no point in trying the pubs. The fact that she was still in her school uniform precluded them, she wouldn't even be allowed in. It was that uniform his eyes were seeking, he realised, and once or twice his stomach lurched as one was sighted; each time he was disappointed.

Where could she have gone? He'd now been right around the town twice and there was no sign of her. It was pointless to continue.

At home Joan came to the front door as soon as she heard the car, her look of disappointment when she saw he was alone reinforcing his anxiety as he realised that she had no news either.

"No luck?"

It was almost a whisper and automatically he lowered his voice as he said, "No. Why are we talking in undertones?"

She glanced back over her shoulder along the hall. "Vicky's here."

Thanet groaned. "Oh, no." Vicky Younghusband's post-natal depression was the last thing he felt able to deal with at the moment.

"I couldn't just turn her away, could I?"

"I suppose not. It's just that . . . Have you told her Bridget's missing?"

"No. There's no point. It's not the sort of news she can cope with, the state she's in. And it would look as though I was trying to get rid of her, say, 'Sorry, I've no emotional energy to spare for you just now.' "

"Which would be true! How on earth can we deal with this situation in whispers? It's bad enough as it is without having to lurk in corners to discuss it." They were still standing in the hall. "Where is she?"

"In the kitchen. I decided to start supper. I had to have something to do."

Thanet nodded understanding. A thought struck him. Cooking . . . "Have you tried Helen Mallard?"

"No, I haven't!" She hurried to the phone and Thanet followed, hovered as she spoke into it. In a few moments she shook her head at him.

He waited while she finished the call.

She glanced at the closed kitchen door. "I thought, if I served supper . . ."

"I'm not hungry."

"No, neither am I, that's not the point. I thought, if I served supper Vicky might take the hint and go . . . Oh dear, that does sound callous, but . . ."

"Good idea," said Thanet. "Yes, do that. I suppose I'd better say hello to her."

They went into the kitchen. Vicky Younghusband was sitting at the table, hands in lap. She was almost unrecognisable as the lively, attractive, cheerful young woman of a few months ago. Her loose blouse was stained with milk and baby's vomit, her hair uncombed and unwashed. She wore no make-up and the flesh beneath her eyes was dark with the bruises of sleeplessness and despair. She even smelt, Thanet realised with a shock, sour and unwashed. Since the baby was born he had seen her only when she was with Peter, when presumably an effort had been made to make her presentable. He could now understand Joan's anxiety and resolved to talk to Peter the minute he got home.

She attempted a smile in response to his greeting, but it was no more than a mechanical lifting of the corners of her mouth.

"How's the baby?" said Thanet.

"The baby?" Her forehead creased and she looked around vaguely, as if expecting to see him somewhere in the room. "Oh, he's fine. He's asleep," she added, after a pause. "Yes." She nodded. "Yes, asleep."

"Good." Thanet heard the tone of his own voice, overhearty, and hated himself for it. "When's Pete due back?"

Another pause. "Not until the weekend."

Briefly, something frantic peeped out of her eyes, then was gone.

Had he imagined it? "Where's he gone?"

"Uhh . . ." She put her hands up to her head and pressed her fingers against her temples, as if trying to squeeze the answer out. "Scotland," she said at last.

"Scotland!" Thanet was startled. Uneasy, too. He wasn't happy about Peter being so far away, with Vicky in this state. "A bit off his usual beat, isn't it?"

"It's the annual sales conference."

"I see." Thanet glanced at Joan, who was clattering saucepans. "Where's Ben?"

"Upstairs, doing his homework."

"I'll go and have a word."

Ben was lying on his bed, reading a book. He laid it face down on the bedspread. "She not back yet?"

Thanet shook his head. "We'll be having supper soon."

Ben rolled off the bed and stood up. "I'm not hungry."

And that, thought Thanet, was a telling admission. Ben's appetite was constant and voracious. He must be very worried indeed.

"Ben, d'you have any idea at all of where she might have gone?"

"No. Unless . . ."

"What?" Thanet couldn't hide the hope in his voice.

"I was wondering . . . She did say she wanted to see *Crocodile Dundee*. She missed it first time around."

The cinema! Of course. Why hadn't he thought of that? It was dark, warm, anonymous . . . A comfortable place in which to hide, to lick one's wounds. "Like to come with me, to see?"

Ben was eager. "Sure."

They set off, Thanet careful to take the route she would follow if she were walking home from the town.

"Dad?"

"What?"

"I'm not sure this is such a good idea after all."

"Why not?"

"They have separate performances. The last one would have finished by now and the next won't start till eight. The usherettes would have checked that nobody . . . Dad, look! There she is!"

Ben was right! There she was, walking towards them some two hundred yards ahead on the other side of the road, shoulders hunched, feet dragging. He and Ben exchanged a jubilant glance. The uprush of relief, however, was immediately followed by a swell of anger. How could she have done this to them? Furious words and phrases began to run through Thanet's mind. Then, as he checked for traffic, and did a U-turn, he had a brief, vivid image of the photograph he had seen in the paper after the disappearance of a French girl in London. She had been the same age as Bridget and had been missing for over twenty-four hours before being found safe and sound, sleeping rough. The photograph had shown her struggling in the street with her father, determined, apparently, not to return home. Like other parents right across the land, Thanet had sympathised with the man's dilemma. Understandably, the Frenchman couldn't bear to let his child walk off into the London jungle unprotected, and had in fact manhandled her back into the flat. But Thanet had wondered at the time what would happen. How long would it be before the girl disappeared again?

No, anger was not the answer. This situation must be handled with kid gloves. He said to Ben, "OK, Ben, now look, we'll play it cool, right? She's in a pretty fragile state of mind at the moment . . ." He pulled up alongside her and said, "Hello, love."

She stopped, glancing from him to Ben. She looked wary, apprehensive.

As well she might, he thought. "Come on, hop in."

She hesitated a moment longer, then climbed into the back.

No reproaches, Thanet reminded himself as they headed for home. But he couldn't think of anything to say which might not be construed as such. Safer, then, to say nothing. He could see Bridget's face in the driving mirror. She looked thoroughly miserable.

The silence became oppressive.

"I went to see *Crocodile Dundee*," she said at last. She was defiant, aggressive, almost. Obviously anticipating trouble and prepared to meet it.

Ben gave his father a triumphant glance and Thanet accorded him a congratulatory nod. *Well guessed.*

"Next time, give us a ring, let us know where you are." His tone was mild, almost casual.

He caught her startled look in the mirror. *Surely they're not going to let me off as lightly as that?*

Their swift return brought Joan to the front door again. Her look of joy when she saw that Bridget was with them was one that Thanet would never forget. He sent her an admonitory glance and recognised the effort it cost her simply to say, with admirable restraint, "Ah, there you are, then, Bridget. Well timed. Supper's ready."

On the way in Joan caught Thanet's hand and squeezed it as they exchanged a look of relief.

"Vicky gone?"

She nodded.

"Good."

Despite their attempts at conversation, supper was a silent meal. Guiltily, Thanet found himself ravenous. Ben, too, was eating heartily, he noticed, whereas Joan and Bridget merely toyed with their food. Halfway through, Bridget laid down her knife and fork. "Why don't you say it?" she burst out.

Thanet and Joan glanced at each other.

Joan spoke for both of them. "Say what?"

"How can you sit there, pretending nothing's the matter?" She glowered at them. "I thought this was supposed to be a great family for talking things out, for 'communicating.' So go on, communicate!"

Joan abandond any pretence at eating. "If that's what you want."

"Oh!" Bridget jumped up out of her seat and took a few agitated paces around the room. "Why are you always so *reasonable*?"

"You make it sound like a crime," said Thanet.

"Why don't you ever shout at me, or swear, like other people's parents?" She was practically in tears.

"That's what you'd like?"

"At least I wouldn't feel so guilty." She glanced from Thanet to Joan and back. "Can't you *see*?" And she rushed out of the room.

Ben had gone on eating steadily.

"Is that how you feel too, Ben?" said Joan.

He considered, chewing away, cheeks bulging. "Sometimes, I suppose. Occasionally it's nice to have someone to kick against and have rows with, get it out of your system. But most of the time, no. Is there any pud?"

Joan shook her head. "Sorry, not tonight, no. You can be thankful you got anything to eat at all! Have an apple or an orange."

He slid out of his chair. "Right."

Left alone, Thanet and Joan looked at each other.

"Now we know!" said Joan.

"Honestly, you can't win, can you? If you shout at them you're being tyrannical, if you try to be reasonable you're not exerting enough authority!"

"I know. So what are we supposed to do now, about Bridget?" Thanet considered. "I think she wants to talk."

"I agree. Probably wants to get it over with."

He grinned. "So do I!"

Joan stood up. "Come on, then."

Bridget was lying on her bed, staring at the ceiling.

"We've come to communicate," said Thanet with a smile. "If that's what you want."

No response for a moment, then she rolled over to sit on the edge of the bed. She looked sullen, unresponsive, rebellious. Thanet's heart sank. If she continued in this mood they weren't going to get very far.

Joan evidently felt the same. "*Is* that what you want?"

Bridget shrugged. "It's up to you."

Her mother frowned. "No, it's up to you. We'll have to talk about it sooner or later, and we thought you'd prefer it to be sooner rather than later. But we don't mind, if you'd rather put it off." She glanced at Thanet and after waiting for a moment and receiving no response they began to move towards the door.

Bridget glanced up. "No. Wait. I . . ." She shrugged. "Better get it over with, I suppose."

"Look," said Thanet. "I'm not sure it's a good idea to chew it over just now, when we're all feeling a bit het up. On the other hand, we don't want you lying awake all night worrying about it. So I'll just say this. Your mother and I were naturally very upset to hear you'd been playing truant. And the reason we were upset was because you hadn't felt able to come and talk to us about it, despite the fact that you were obviously feeling pretty desperate. Now, I want to make one thing clear. As far as we are concerned, we don't care if you don't get a single decent grade in your GCSEs, if worrying about it is going to have this effect on you. Academic grades are not everything—you've got plenty of other talents and lots of qualities that employers would value. So just stop worrying about it. No exams in the world are worth this sort of stress and strain.''

"As far as we're concerned," Joan added, "this incident is over and done with. Unless you want to bring it up again some time, it's finished. So long as you understand that we both mean what your father said. Is that clear?''

Bridget nodded slowly. "Thanks.''

She said nothing more and reluctantly they left her.

"What else could we have done?'' whispered Thanet as they went downstairs.

Joan shrugged. "Nothing, as far as I can see.''

Thanet felt for his pipe. "Let's have some coffee and watch something mindless on television. I've had more than enough emotional traumas for one evening.''

They went into the sitting-room.

"Which reminds me," said Joan. "I saw your new Superintendent on *Coast to Coast* this evening, giving a statement about your case. He was . . . What's the matter?''

Thanet had just remembered: he hadn't written up a single report today.

Draco would be furious, in the morning.

TWENTY-ONE

"What sort of example d'you think you're setting?"

Draco *was* furious.

The Superintendent raked his hand through the cropped, wiry black curls and glowered at Thanet. "You heard what I said, the other day in this very room." His finger stabbed at the desk as if to impale the memory. "Reports, I said, are the key. Detailed, literate and accurate reports. Now, I can understand if, on the odd occasion, you're pushed and have to put in something a bit sketchy, but you're telling me you haven't done *any* for yesterday. And on a murder enquiry!"

Ejected from his chair by the strength of his emotion, Draco leapt up and began to pace agitatedly about. The size of the office restricted his movements and Thanet began to count: two paces from desk to window, four from window to door, three from door to desk. Draco sat down with a thump.

"What sort of excuse have you got?"

"None that you would find acceptable, I'm afraid, sir."

Draco expelled air through his nostrils in an affronted hiss. If he'd been a dragon the flames would have reached across the desk to burn Thanet to a crisp. His eyes bulged slightly. "Think I'm that unreasonable, do you, Thanet?"

Thanet saw his mistake. "No, sir, I didn't mean that. I simply meant that . . . well, I was judging by my own standards. I always tell the men that they should try not to let personal problems interfere with their work."

"Personal problems! I hope you're not sitting there telling me that the reason why these reports are late—no, the reason why they don't even *exist*—is because you're having personal problems!"

"Well, not exac—"

"My God, what's the world coming to?" Draco was up out of

174

his chair again. "When an experienced officer like you . . ." He stopped and resting both hands on the desk he leaned forward, looming over Thanet like an avenging angel. "You've got problems? Everybody's got problems. I've got problems. But do I let it interfere with my work? No, I do not. And do you know why, Thanet? Or should I say, how?"

Thanet had given up for the moment. He shook his head dumbly.

Draco straightened up, standing almost to attention. "Self-discipline, that's how. When I walk in through that door I say to myself, 'Goronwy,' I say, 'that's it. Put it all behind you now, boyo.' And I do, Thanet, I do. And so should you. Compartmentalise, that's the answer, compartmentalise."

So that was how you pronounced Draco's apparently unpronounceable Christian name, thought Thanet.

On the "p" of "compartmentalise" flecks of saliva flew across to spatter themselves over Thanet's face and he had to restrain both an urge to wipe them ostentatiously away and a desire to burst out laughing. Draco was rapidly becoming a sit-com character. Thanet almost expected him to say, like Reggie Perrin's boss, "I didn't get where I am today by . . ."

And yet, in another way, it just wasn't funny. This man had power over Thanet's career, Thanet's life. A good working relationship with him was essential to Thanet's peace of mind. And at the moment Thanet was feeling anything but peaceful. He was aware of the signs of mounting stress in himself: clenched hands, a thrumming of blood in his ears, a tension and rigidity throughout his body. Careful, he told himself. Don't let him get to you. Don't say anything you'll regret later. And, above all, calm *down* . . . Deliberately he uncurled his hands, relaxed, expelled held breath in a long, unobtrusive exhalation. "Yes, but it's not . . ."

Draco waved a hand and sat down again. "Oh, I know what you're going to say. 'It's not easy,' that's what you're going to say. Of course it's not, but it shouldn't stop us trying. A bit of practice and self-discipline, that's all . . ." His eyes narrowed. "Not marriage problems, I hope?"

"No, sir," said Thanet stiffly. "In fact, I was about to explain that it was strictly a one-off situation." *I hope*.

"I'm very glad to hear it. Crisis over now, then, is it?" Draco was visibly deflating, leaning back in his chair and steepling his hands beneath his chin.

"Oh yes."

"I see. Good. Good. Well, I've made it clear, I hope, that I don't expect this to happen again."

"Yes, sir." *Abundantly.*

It had already been decided during the briefing, earlier, that the Salden investigation was to continue. The fact that Marcia had been dead before she entered the water had ensured that. With relief, Thanet escaped. Outside in the corridor he rolled his eyes in despair. It looked as though Draco was becoming his daily cross.

Upstairs he cast a longing glance at the sanctuary of his room. The decorators had finished the woodwork and were now painting the walls. Tomorrow, they assured him, by tomorrow afternoon at the latest, he should be able to move back in.

Spirits rising, Thanet returned to the CID room. He and Lineham had already discussed the timetable for the day and there was one interview, later on in the morning, that he was especially looking forward to. Meanwhile, another visit to the Hammers was indicated. Enquiries had established that Hammer had indeed been in the Crooked Door most of Tuesday evening, for the last hour or so muttering incomprehensible drunken complaints about some bitch who had stolen what was his by right. The landlord had assumed he was referring either to wife or girlfriend. There was one interesting discrepancy, however: soon after ten the landlord, judging that Hammer had had more than enough to drink, had refused to serve him any more and had "chucked him out." Which could have placed Hammer in the vicinity of the bridge around the time when Marcia was crossing it.

"And his wife says he didn't get home till around half-past," said Lineham.

"Yes, interesting, isn't it? Twenty-five minutes to half an hour to walk a couple of hundred yards."

"Wonder what he was up to?"

"If only we could get some more precise timings," Thanet sighed as he and Lineham set off for Telford Green.

"I know. They all say 'around such and such a time,' don't they? Not surprising, of course, not many people go around checking the exact time for no particular reason. But it does mean you have to allow five or ten minutes either way . . . The one thing that does seem certain is that they were all in the right place at approximately the right time. Salden claims to have been sitting on a bench only a couple of hundred yards away, Edith Phipps was posting her letters, Josie's mother was on her way home from the Manor, Councillor Lomax was on his way to the pub and now we find Reg Hammer was around too.''

"What did you think of him, Mike?"

There hadn't been time, yesterday, to discuss their visit to the Hammers.

"I bet she didn't get those bruises by walking into a door."

"A wife-beater, if ever I saw one," agreed Thanet.

"I can never understand why women put up with it."

"It's a very complex matter, as you well know. Straightforward fear, in a lot of cases, I imagine, that they'll have to suffer even worse violence if they leave or take legal action. And we both know how justifiable a fear that is. The number of cases you hear of, where a woman is harassed or beaten up or even killed by a violent ex-husband who won't leave her alone. And it's well known that some women just seem to go for violent men, repeating the same pattern over and over again."

"Is this Mrs. Hammer his first wife?"

"That was the impression I had, from Edith Phipps."

"Anyway, it did occur to me, a man like that, who's used to hitting women around . . . We did say we thought that was probably how Mrs. Salden died, when someone just lashed out at her during a quarrel . . ."

"It's a distinct possibility, I agree." Thanet wound down his window. It was a sparkling April day with a frisky wind chasing puffy white clouds across a sky the colour of the forget-me-nots in the cottage gardens.

"In fact, the only suspect who doesn't seem to have been around at the right time is Harry Greenleaf."

"The way things are going, I shouldn't count on it."

They drove in silence for a while, then Lineham said, "Sir . . ."

"Yes?" An uncharacteristic diffidence in the Sergeant's tone alerted Thanet to the fact that this was nothing to do with work.

"I just wanted to say . . . Well, Louise and I had that talk, and you were right . . . I didn't realise just how bored and frustrated she is. As I said, it's not that she doesn't love the kids, it's just that . . . Well, we said it all the other night, didn't we? Anyway, I think we've got something sorted out. She's going to look around for a part-time job in September, when Mandy starts playgroup."

"And no more talk of you leaving the police?"

"No."

"Good. Excellent." Thanet couldn't help feeling a self-congratulatory glow.

The old grey van was drawn up in front of Mrs. Hammer's cottage. Hammer and his wife were struggling with the base of a divan bed.

"Having problems?" said Thanet pleasantly.

"Nothing we can't deal with. Hold that leg up higher, Dor, and twist it a bit to your left. To your left, you stupid cow, not to your right! Now pull!"

Pull?

The bed slid out like a cork out of a bottle and Mrs. Hammer went down on one knee. She had exchanged the black skirt for some faded jeans, the red sweater for a collarless man's shirt rolled up to just below the elbows. Hammer glowered impatiently at her and she scrambled up, putting up a hand to lift the bush of hair out of her eyes. The wide sleeve of the shirt fell back, revealing fresh bruises in the tender flesh of the upper arm. She saw Thanet noticing and flushed, quickly lowered her hand.

The van, Thanet realised, was crammed with household goods.

Hammer picked up one end of the bed. "Come *on*," he said to his wife. She stooped to lift the other end and they started off up the short path to the open front door.

"Moving in?" said Thanet.

He and Lineham followed the Hammers up the path.

Hammer dropped his end of the bed with a crash and straightened up, turning to face Thanet with a belligerent expression. "What if we are?"

"Rather pointless, in the circumstances, isn't it? I imagine Mrs. Salden was very careful to make sure the legal agreement over the purchase of the cottage was watertight. You'll only have to move out again shortly."

"Don't you believe it! Yesterday I got to thinking. What is the point in clearing the house out and leaving it empty? I'd just be handing it to them on a plate. I ought to be on the spot, defending my right to my property." Hammer cast a proprietorial glance over his shoulder. "No, if they want a fight, they can have it. I'm going to make that pouf Basset's life hell until we find a way around that agreement." He took a dog-end from behind his ear and lit it, blowing smoke into Thanet's face. He grinned. "Anyway, you know what they say, about possession being nine points of the law." He turned to pick up the bed again. "So now, if you don't mind . . ."

"Just one or two questions, Mr. Hammer," said Lineham quickly.

Hammer turned. "What now?"

"It's about Tuesday night," said Lineham. "Mrs. Hammer, you said your husband arrived home at . . ." He pretended to consult his notebook. "At about half-past ten."

She darted an uneasy glance at Hammer. "Yes, he did."

"But according to the landlord of the Crooked Door, Mr. Hammer, you were asked to leave soon after ten."

"Was I?" Hammer shrugged. "If he says so. I can't remember a blind thing about it. I was blotto." He folded his arms across his chest and a smug, self-congratulatory smile lifted the corners of his mouth.

Presumably he thought it was macho to get drunk, thought Thanet.

"We were wondering how it could take you nearly half an hour to walk a couple of hundred yards."

Hammer lifted his shoulders again. "Search me. Can't remember the first thing about it."

"Uh . . ." said his wife.

All three men looked at her and she shifted uncomfortably. "I was only going to say . . . I think someone brought Reg home, on Tuesday."

Of course! Thanet remembered the two men Lomax had seen in front of these cottages on his way to the pub that night. Why hadn't he realised before that Hammer must have been one of them? But in that case, who was the other?

Hammer and Lineham spoke together.

"You never said . . ."

"You didn't mention this before . . ."

She ignored Lineham, answered her husband. "You never asked me."

"Who was it?"

Thanet wondered if Hammer ever addressed her in anything but that rough, almost butal tone.

"Dunno, do I?"

"Stupid bitch," muttered Hammer as Lineham said, "When you say you *think* someone brought your husband home, what do you mean?"

"Someone knocked at the door. When I opened it, Reg was sitting on the doorstep, leaning against the doorpost. And a man was walking away. He was disappearing around the bend by then, on his way to the bridge."

"And you've no idea who it was?"

But she didn't reply. She was staring at her husband.

Hammer was gazing fixedly into the middle distance, mouth slightly agape, eyes narrowed, as if a thought had just struck him.

"Mr. Hammer?" he said.

Mrs. Hammer clutched at her husband's arm. "What's the matter, Reg?"

He shook her off. "Nothing."

"But you . . ."

"I said, it was nothing!"

"Remembered something, have you?" said Lineham.

Hammer's gaze focussed on the Sergeant. "If you think I've remembered shoving Marcia off the bridge, you've got another think coming. Look, we've still got a lot to do here. If you've quite finished . . ."

"You must realise that things don't look too good for you, Mr. Hammer," said Thanet. "If you remember anything, anything at all, that you might have seen or heard on your way home from the pub that night, please let us know, immediately. It could be in your own interest."

"Don't worry. I'm a lot more interested in saving my neck than you are."

"I hope you're not thinking of leaving the area at the moment."

"If you want me, you'll know where to find me."

"I should think Mrs. Hammer's mother is down on her knees praying he gets that cottage," said Lineham as they drove away. "Imagine having a son-in-law like that! Especially living in the same house!"

"Don't! It doesn't bear thinking about."

But Thanet sounded abstracted. His mind had already moved ahead to the next interview.

This was the one he was looking forward to.

TWENTY-TWO

"He's in the garage."

Mrs. Pringle, wife of the former headmaster of Telford Green primary school, was a little dumpling of a woman with sausage-like curls and cheeks as rosy as a Spartan apple. She was leaning on an aluminium walking stick with a fat rubber tip.

Thanet was intrigued by her expression as she told them where her husband was: a mixture of resignation, indulgence, and yes, he was certain of it, amused anticipation.

What could Pringle be up to in the garage?

"I'll take you across."

"There's no need, I'm sure we'll find him."

But she insisted and Thanet and Lineham followed her slow but determined progress along the concrete path in front of the bungalow. Whatever Pringle did in his retirement, it wasn't gardening. The small patch of grass in front of the house was raggedly mown and any flowers in the weed beds which surrounded it had long ago given up.

They saw the long, low pre-cast concrete structure as soon as they rounded the corner of the house. It was at least twice as long as any normal garage. On the side facing the back garden was an unusually large window and Thanet was interested to see that steel shutters similar to the type used to protect lockup shops had been fitted to roll down over both this window and the sliding entrance doors.

What could Pringle keep in there?

Possible answers flicked through Thanet's mind: a vintage car of exceptional value? Only the other day he had seen a photograph of a 1925 silver-plated Phantom Rolls in the paper. Bought for £2,000 in 1970, it was now worth £100,000. But here, in the garage of an old-age pensioner in Telford Green? Or perhaps

Mr. Pringle was one of those zany inventors who spends all his days engaged in working on some hopelessly impractical Icarus-style prototype, valuable only in his fevered imagination.

"Gerald?"

Mrs. Pringle was struggling with the heavy door and Lineham went to help.

She stood back, steadying herself on her stick as the door slid back, watching their astounded expressions with a mixture of triumph and amusement.

Lineham gasped.

The entire garage was taken up by a waist-high, landscaped model railway layout of incredible size and complexity: hills and valleys encircled a small town of houses, shops, hotels, pubs and car parks; there were tunnels, bridges and viaducts; stations and sidings; row after parallel row of rails; and, above all, dozens of exquisitely fashioned goods and passenger trains, many of which were racing around the tracks in dizzyingly impressive patterns of movement. In the centre space, supervising all this frantic activity with an expression of blissful absorption, stood a tall, crane-like elderly man with sparse grey hair and benign blue eyes which swivelled now in the direction of his wife as she spoke.

"Someone to see you, Gerald."

Lineham had forgotten about work. Like a man in a dream he stepped forward, eyes devouring the wonders laid out before him. He shook his head in amazement. "I've never seen anything like it," he breathed.

Pringle recognised genuine enthusiasm when he saw it and within seconds he and the Sergeant were involved in a conversation larded with technical terms Thanet never knew existed. Amused, he waited patiently. It would be easy this time to get the witness to open up to them; Lineham was preparing the ground beautifully.

"D'you hear that, sir? Seven hundred and fifty feet of track!" Lineham turned a dazed face towards Thanet, his expression changing as he registered the look on Thanet's face. He glanced back at Pringle, then at the layout. "Sorry, sir," he muttered. "Got a bit carried away."

"And why not?" Thanet smiled at Pringle. "It's not every day one sees something like this. To someone keen on model railways it must seem like one of the Seven Wonders of the World."

Pringle was beaming with pride. "It's taken me thirty years to build."

"And the Inspector'll be standing here for another thirty listening to you talk about it if you have your way!" said his wife, her tone that of an indulgent mother addressing a wayward child. "It's half-past ten, time for elevenses. Come into the house, Inspector, you'll be more comfortable there."

Pringle ducked out of sight and a moment or two later crawled from under the layout.

"Getting a bit old for this," he grumbled as he slowly stood up, unfolding his angular frame as if it were hinged rather than jointed. He took his wife's arm, adjusting himself to her pace as they set off along the concrete path, looking for all the world like Jack Spratt and his wife after an especially amicable meal.

"Didn't know you were keen on model railways," said Thanet to Lineham in an undertone.

Lineham looked a bit sheepish. "I don't actually collect any more. Can't afford to. But I will again one day, when the children are off our hands. I've got all my stuff packed away in boxes."

"You start the questioning," Thanet said hurriedly as they approached the front door. "After that, we'll play it by ear."

"OK."

"You go in there and sit down," said Mrs. Pringle, "and I'll make some coffee."

"There" was a cosy book-lined sitting-room overlooking the wilderness of a back garden. The three men sat down in comfortable chintz-covered armchairs, leaving a conspicuously orthopaedic chair for Mrs. Pringle if she chose to join them. Despite the warmth of the day the gas fire was full on and the room was uncomfortably hot.

"It's about Marcia, I suppose." Pringle leaned sideways to take a pipe out of his pocket and began to scrape it out, tapping the dottle into a thick glass ashtray on the table beside his chair.

Thanet immediately began to wish he could smoke as well, but it was too early in the interview, the atmosphere was not yet sufficiently relaxed for him to suggest it. Besides, two pipes in one room . . . Lineham would hate it.

"I gather you're not satisfied it was an accident." Pringle was looking at Thanet.

"Not yet, anyway."

"We've heard the rumours, of course. You can't have secrets in a place the size of Telford Green."

"What rumours exactly?" said Lineham.

Pringle blew through the stem of his pipe to make sure it was clear and flicked a mischievous glance at Thanet. "That Marcia was variously shot, strangled, stabbed or—most mundane and therefore probably true—pushed off the bridge."

Lineham raised his eyebrows. "By. . . ?"

"The most popular choice is her husband."

"Any particular reason?"

Pringle shrugged. "Not really. Because he was closest to her, I suppose, and therefore the obvious person. But there have been one or two outsiders coming up on the rails over the last twenty-four hours. Reg Hammer, for instance. Old Mrs. Hammer was as good as a public-address system and she made no secret of the fact that she'd applied to join Mrs. Salden's house-purchase scheme. Everyone was wondering what Reg would do when he found out, and the fact that you've been to see him has not passed unnoticed. Then there's Edith Phipps, because Marcia apparently gave her the sack that afternoon. Don't ask me how that whisper started. And there's Grace Trimble, too. Rumour has it that she went up to the Manor that night breathing fire. Perhaps she doesn't approve of the amount of time Josie seems to be spending up at the Manor . . ."

"Have you any particular favourite yourself?"

"Not really. Marcia always did have a talent for putting people's backs up. Well no, that isn't strictly true. Perhaps it would be more accurate to say that she always did have a complete disregard for other people's feelings. Anyway, I never could understand why she was so popular."

The door had opened and Mrs. Pringle came in, pushing a trolley. "She certainly wasn't popular when she first started school, remember. For two or three years she was practically an outcast. I used to feel so sorry for her . . ." She handed out coffee, freshly filtered by the smell of it, and homemade biscuits with cherries in the middle.

"Why?" said Lineham.

Mrs. Pringle lowered herself carefully into the orthopaedic chair and picked up her coffee. "Various reasons, really. I suppose chiefly because of her father. He used to beat her mother up, you know. And if Marcia got in the way . . .

Many's the time I've seen that child come to school covered in bruises.''

"Wasn't he reported to the NSPCC?''

"Oh yes. They were always hovering around in the background. But Marcia was never taken into care or anything like that. It wasn't the kind of deliberate and persistent cruelty you hear so much of these days, but all the same . . . I often used to think how much she must dread Friday nights, when he got his pay packet and headed straight for the Door.''

"And of course, she was badly undernourished, wasn't she, Gwen?'' said Pringle. "There was never enough money left over for food. Marcia didn't qualify for free school dinners because theoretically at least her father earned enough to pay for them. So I think she lived chiefly on bread and margarine—if she was lucky. She used to bring a bread and marge sandwich to school for her dinner and quite often she'd hide behind her desk lid to eat it before school, she was so hungry. And then, of course, she'd have nothing to eat all day and precious little to look forward to when she got home from school at night . . . She used to look so pasty and unhealthy. We resorted to all sorts of stratagems for slipping her food on the quiet, so that she wouldn't be too shamed in front of the other kids, didn't we, Gwen?''

Mrs. Pringle wrinkled her nose. "And she used to smell! I don't think her mother ever bothered to bathe her or change her knickers. And you know how cruel kids can be . . . In the end I resorted to buying half a dozen pairs of knickers for her myself and putting a clean pair on her each morning when she got to school. We never had any children ourselves, and it really used to upset me seeing that poor little scrap treated as a pariah through no fault of her own.''

No wonder Marcia had been so determined to succeed, thought Thanet. That sort of childhood puts grit into the soul.

"Didn't her mother care?'' said Lineham.

"I think Mrs. Carter was so browbeaten she'd given up caring about anything. You should have seen the state their house was in, in those days! Honestly, it seems a terrible thing to say, but it was a blessing for her when her husband was killed in that accident. After that, she was a changed woman. But that wasn't till much later, after Marcia was married. She married very young, of course. Couldn't wait to get away from home.''

"What you're saying doesn't exactly square with her being popular,'' said Thanet.

"Oh, that was later," said Pringle.

"After we'd done something about it," said his wife. "It was obvious things weren't going to improve at home, and in the end Gerald had this brilliant idea. When Marcia was about eight, old enough to bathe herself, he had a hygiene campaign at school. He got the health visitor to come and talk to the children, sent out leaflets to all the parents, that sort of thing. Well, Marcia was no fool and the message got through. Before long the improvement in her was noticeable. She was clean, she didn't smell, she even managed to wash her hair and come to school in clean clothes. We were thrilled to bits, weren't we? She looked a different child. And it was interesting to see how the other children reacted. It was such a transformation they didn't quite know what to make of it. At first they just sort of circled around, keeping their distance, then they began to make little approaches . . ."

"How did Marcia react?"

"Very wary at first, wasn't she, Gerald? Suspicious. And off-hand, always off-hand. I think that was what intrigued them, the fact that she didn't seem eager to welcome their advances. In the end she had them vying for her favours. Extraordinary, wasn't it, Gerald?"

"Fascinating."

Not so surprising, really, thought Thanet. He'd seen it so often before, the self-centred person who has everyone running around in circles trying to please him, and gets away with it every time. But in Marcia's case understandable, surely. When life is as difficult as hers had been, the one thing that matters is self-preservation. Ironic that in the end it could perhaps have been this very trait which destroyed her.

"Forgive my asking, Mrs. Pringle, but you talk as if you were very much involved with the life of the school. Did you teach there too?"

She laughed, the rosy cheeks bunching up to look more apple-like than ever, and glanced at her husband.

Pringle shook his head. "No, she didn't. But in those days we lived in the school house, which was part of the school building. Now, of course, like so many other village schools, it's been converted into a private home. A crying shame, I think. The old village schools were so much the heart of the community. Like the church, they linked village people in a way that no one at the time quite understood. Practically every household in the village used to have a child or a grandchild or a niece or a nephew at the school and even if they didn't everyone certainly knew at least one child who attended it, probably more. When they closed down, something crucial to village life was lost. Anyway, in those days, as I say, the headmaster's house was part of the school building and the headmaster's wife couldn't have got away from the children even if she'd wanted to. She was surrounded by them all day long and knew them as well as the staff did.''

Lineham said, "When the other children had got used to this transformation you were talking about, did Marcia end up with her own special little group of friends?"

"Her own 'gang,' you mean? Yes, there were four of them." Pringle ticked them off on his fingers. "Edith Phipps, Reg Hammer, Grace Gates—Grace Trimble, she is now—and Henry Gates, Grace's brother.''

"What happened to Henry?" said Lineham. "Is he still around?''

"Ah, well, that was rather sad," said Pringle. "No, he's not. No thanks, love, not for me." He shook his head at his wife, who was offering more coffee, waited while she refilled Lineham's cup, handed another biscuit to Thanet. Pringle's pipe was drawing well, Thanet noticed enviously.

"What happened to him?" said Lineham.

"Predictably, he fell in love with Marcia. This was much later, of course, when they were in their teens. At first they were all just friends, kids playing together. Edith's father was head gardener up at the Manor, and the five of them used to spend a lot of time in the Manor grounds. They used to keep well out of the way of the owners, of course, but as you can imagine they were the envy of all the other kids in the village for enjoying this privilege. And you'd often see the three girls around together, or the two boys. But of course, as they became adolescents, sex raised its ugly head and altered things between them. First Edith fell for Henry. They went out together for, oh, around six months, wouldn't you say, Gwen?''

"Something like that. The trouble was it was one-sided, really. Henry just went along with it, but it was Edith who was really smitten." Mrs. Pringle sighed and brushed some biscuit crumbs off her ample lap. "Poor Edith, I don't think she ever got over it.''

"Unfortunately, Henry then fell for Marcia, in a big way."

"Marcia shouldn't have encouraged him," Mrs. Pringle said tartly.

"Wouldn't have made any difference. He'd have left Edith anyway."

"Still, Marcia was supposed to be Edith's friend. It was all such a *pity*. As you can imagine, Inspector, Edith hasn't had much of a life, looking after her mother all these years. Henry Gates was the one bright spot in it. And," she added indignantly, "it wasn't even as if Marcia really wanted him. The minute a better prospect came along, she dropped him like a hot potato."

"Which is rather a circuitous route to answering your question, Sergeant," said Pringle. "Henry Gates left the village when Marcia threw him over, and never came back."

"And it wasn't just Edith who was upset," said Mrs. Pringle. "Grace, his sister, was in a terrible state too. Their father had died not long before and their mother had died when they were thirteen or fourteen. So when Henry went off she was left entirely on her own."

"And Reg Hammer wasn't too pleased, either. He and Henry had been bosom pals for years. He never did find another friend, and until he moved away he used to hang around the village looking like a lost sheep."

"Henry was such a good-looking boy," said Mrs. Pringle reminiscently. "Not like Reg. A great lump of a boy Reg was, wasn't he?"

Pringle laid his pipe down in the ashtray. "And he hasn't changed much, so far as I can see. Always had a foul temper, too . . . Inspector, while we've been sitting here I've been wondering . . . Why did you come to see us? I can't imagine that all this stuff that happened thirty-odd years ago is relevant to Marcia's death last Tuesday."

"Background," said Thanet. "I'm trying to understand what sort of a person Marcia was, and you've helped me immensely." He stood up. "Thank you, both of you." He smiled at Mrs. Pringle. "The homemade biscuits were delicious." He glanced at Lineham, who was still sitting down. "Sergeant? There's something else you want to ask?"

Lineham was going pink. "Er . . . yes, sir. But it's nothing to do with work."

Thanet grinned and Pringle beamed. "You'd like to come back and take a closer look at my railway! Any time, Sergeant, any time."

Thanet was anxious to be off. His hand was in his pocket, closed around the comforting familiarity of the bowl of his pipe. He was itching to take it out and smoke it. And it was lunchtime, possibly a good time to catch Grace Trimble at home, the only person in that little group that he had not yet met—apart from her absent brother, of course. Lineham was still talking and Thanet gave him an unobtrusive nudge. *Come on.*

He was eager to see if Grace lived up to her name. As mother of the luscious Josie she might well be something rather special.

TWENTY-THREE

But the genes which had given her brother and daughter their good looks had unfortunately passed Grace Trimble by. She was a tall, big-boned woman with dowdy clothes, a dour expression and prematurely greying hair scraped back into a bun. And she looked strong, easily strong enough to have miscalculated a push in anger and sent Marcia slipping backwards on the icy road through that fatal gap in the parapet.

As soon as he saw her, Thanet's pre-conceived notion of Josie as a spoiled only child and of her mother as a weak, somewhat hysterical single parent had disappeared. Far more likely, he thought, that Josie had been over-protected and suppressed and was now busy kicking over the traces.

After waving them into armchairs in the bleak sitting-room where they had interviewed Josie the previous day, Grace Trimble picked up a small upright chair which stood against the wall and placed it in front of the fireplace in the exact centre of the fawn hearth rug. Then she sat down facing them, back ramrod straight, ankles crossed, hands folded in lap.

And waited.

Thanet was tempted to wait too, see which of them broke the silence first. But he wasn't here to play games. It was irritating that she should have taken the psychological advantage by choosing an upright chair, but he had no intention of allowing himself to be disconcerted. Nor of being manipulated into going away without the information he came for.

This woman intrigued him. He had the impression that she would lose her temper rarely, but that when she did the explosion would be all the more violent because of her habitually rigid self-control.

And it was obvious that there was no point in beating about the bush.

190

"I understand you paid a visit to the Manor on Tuesday evening, the night Mrs. Salden died."

"What if I did?" She was cold, hostile, her voice grating on his ear like over-smooth chalk on a blackboard.

"Would you mind telling us of the purpose of that visit?"

"Yes, I would mind. It was private business."

"Would it help if I told you that we already know why you went and what happened when you got there?"

"If you know it all, why are you asking me about it?"

"We would like to hear your side of the story, Mrs. Trimble." No response.

"We're only trying to understand it from your point of view."

"Understand? What is there for you to understand? It's no business of yours."

"Ah," said Thanet softly, "but I'm afraid that's where you could be wrong."

"What do you mean?" Her expression changed. "Nothing's happened to Josie?"

"No. Josie's fine, so far as I know."

"Then what did you mean?"

"Mrs. Trimble, you may or may not realise that we are treating Mrs. Salden's death as suspicious. That means that we are not satisfied yet that it was an accident. Which in turn means that, until we are, we have to talk to all those people who could conceivably have had a reason for being glad she is dead."

"There's no need to wrap it up. You're saying it could be murder, and I'm a suspect."

"Possibly, yes."

Further silence. Thanet gave her a few moments to think about it, then said, "So if there's anything you'd like to tell me . . ."

"There's not. You can think what you like."

Thanet tried another tack. "I understand you used to be quite friendly with Mrs. Salden at one time, when you were children."

He saw at once that it had been the wrong thing to say. No doubt he had resurrected memories of the other injury Marcia had done her, in driving her brother away.

"I don't see what that's got to do with it."

He might as well accept that she wasn't going to unbend. Extract as many facts as he could, then, and get out.

"You left the Manor at around ten past ten on Tuesday evening, I believe."

"So?"

"What time did you arrive home?"

She shrugged. "Twenty to half-past ten, I suppose. I don't know. I didn't look at the clock. No reason to."

"Which way did you go up to the Manor? Along the main drive, or along the footpath?"

"Along the footpath."

"And you came back . . . ?"

"The same way."

"Did you see anyone, either on your way up or on your way back?"

Thanet had given up hoping for anything interesting to emerge during this interview. Grace Trimble's next words were therefore all the more a shock.

"Only Harry Greenleaf."

Greenleaf, the suspect with perhaps the most powerful motive of all! Thanet resisted the temptation to look at Lineham. He knew that the Sergeant would be remembering what they'd been saying only a couple of hours ago.

"In fact, the only suspect who doesn't seem to have been around at the right time is Harry Greenleaf."

"The way things are going, I shouldn't count on it."

It was an effort to keep his voice casual. "I see. And was this on the way up, or . . . ?"

"On the way back."

"And where, exactly, did you see him?"

"He was standing on the bridge, looking at the river."

"Leaning on the parapet?"

"Yes."

"On which side?"

"The far side."

"By 'far side,' you mean the opposite side from the broken parapet?"

"Yes."

"Are you sure it was Greenleaf?"

"Certain. He was wearing that balaclava thing he always wears when he comes into the village."

An excellent disguise, thought Thanet, if someone else had wanted to give the impression that Greenleaf was abroad that night. But that would imply premeditation, and he had been certain all along that this had been a crime of impulse, if crime it was. Marcia had simply been unlucky. Time, circumstance and contiguity had conspired to produce a fatal result.

"When he heard me step on to the road he glanced over his shoulder and then slipped away, quick as a flash. He doesn't like meeting people, does Harry." And I don't blame him, her expression said.

"In that case, it's surprising he hadn't gone before you got to the top of the steps," said Lineham. "He must have heard you coming."

She was shaking her head. "He wouldn't have heard me earlier because I was walking on grass. And while I was climbing the steps a couple of cars went over the bridge."

"Rich pickings," said Lineham, when they were outside. "Though it's a pity those car drivers haven't come forward."

Appeals had been put out on TVS and Radio Kent.

"Yes. Not that this information about Greenleaf really makes much difference in practical terms. We're no nearer to proving anything."

"We do now know that Greenleaf was lying, when he said he didn't go out that night."

"True."

"So are we going to see him next?"

"Who else? But we'll get something to eat at the Crooked Door first."

They got into the car and headed for the pub, but halfway through the village Thanet said, "Just a minute. Pull in, will you?"

They had stopped in front of what was recognisably once the school, though there were curtains at the windows and the playground had became a lawn, surrounded by flower borders. Thanet guessed that the projecting arm of the "L" had once been the school house, where the Pringles lived.

"Pringle's right, it's a shame so many village schools have closed down."

Thanet gazed at the building, imagining it as it once was, with the sound of children's voices floating through those open windows, the noise of shouts and laughter enlivening the midday hush which lay now over the village like a pall.

And it was here, within those thick stone walls, that Marcia, Edith, Grace, Reg and the long-lost Henry had spent the years of their youth, seeing each other daily, linked by the tight ties which used to bind the small rural communities. This school, this village, would have been Marcia's whole world and it was scarcely surprising that she had wanted to return to flaunt her success before the people who would once have regarded her as the lowest of the low. And her former school friends, how would they have felt when they learned that it was Marcia who had bought the Manor? None of them had made very much of their lives. Wouldn't they have found it galling, to know that the child who had once come to school bruised and hungry and smelling of stale urine had outstripped them all? And they surely wouldn't have forgotten their ancient grudges against her? She had, after all, stolen Edith Phipps's one and only chance of happiness, robbed Grace of her brother and Reg of his best friend.

And she had then proceeded to threaten to injure them further. Edith was to lose her job, Grace her daughter and Reg his inheritance.

Had the memory of those old wounds served to underline and reinforce the inevitable feelings of anger at these new and latest injuries?

Thanet suggested as much to Lineham.

"Could be, sir. In each case they were going to lose what they valued most. But unless we can come up with some evidence, whoever did it is going to get away with it."

"*Nil desperandum*, Mike. Drive on. After a certain point my brain can't function properly without food and drink."

The pub had featured so much in this case that Thanet looked around with more than customary interest when they went in, but there was nothing special about it: heavy oak beams, gaudily patterned carpet, veneered oak tables and the usual pub smell of beer, smoke and furniture polish. The food was good, though— generous portions of quiche and a salad which was rather more adventurous than the universal offering of a lettuce leaf topped with a few slices of tomato and cucumber. Apart from three young men at the bar it was deserted. The landlord recognised Lineham and they were swiftly served.

Half an hour later they were walking up the sloping meadow towards Greenleaf's hut. The place seemed deserted.

"There's no sign of him," said Lineham. "Perhaps he's out."

Thanet hoped not, but if so, there was nothing they could do about it. It would be pointless to wait, for all they knew Greenleaf could be gone all day. "Let's hope he hasn't skipped!"

"No, look, the door's open!" said Lineham. "He can't be far away."

"Try calling him."

It was evident that Greenleaf had been sawing logs. There was a wide scattering of fresh sawdust around a chunk of tree trunk which had evidently been used as a sawing horse; saw and axe lay near by, ready to be taken up again at a moment's notice. The freshly cut logs had been stacked beneath an open-sided shelter at the back of the hut.

Lineham cupped his hands around his mouth and shouted Greenleaf's name a few times, swivelling to project the sound in different directions. In the distance a dog began to bark.

"Greenleaf's dog?" said Lineham.

Thanet shrugged. He was standing at the door, looking into the hut. Greenleaf lived a spartan life. There was a canvas camp bed, a pile of neatly folded blankets at one end, a pillow at the other, no sheets; an old leather armchair with the stuffing coming out; a formica-topped table with a small Calor gas cooker on top, and an upright chair; a tall storage cupboard which probably served as a larder; a wooden box about two feet long by eighteen inches deep; and a transistor radio. A knitted balaclava helmet hung on a nail by the door.

Thanet and Lineham looked at each other.

"Are you thinking what I'm thinking, Mike?"

Lineham grinned. "Seems a pity to miss such a good opportunity."

"Call him again."

Lineham obliged, but there was still no response.

"I'm just going to take a look around out here," said Thanet. Another grin. "Right, sir."

Thanet wandered off to look at the chickens, keeping an eye open in case Greenleaf suddenly emerged from the woods. He thought that he would probably hear the man coming, though; up here it was very still. And the view was remarkable. For someone who didn't need the company of others, or who shunned it for some reason as Greenleaf did, this was as pleasant a place as he could hope to find. How badly had Harry wanted to stay here? Badly enough to kill, when the opportunity offered itself?

Thanet glanced at the hut. Lineham was kneeling in front of the wooden box.

The goat's stake, Thanet noticed, had been moved since the last time they were here, a good ten feet further away from the hut, and the animal was busy cropping the new grass near the perimeter.

"Sir!"

Thanet swung around. Lineham sounded excited. The Sergeant was hurrying towards him, waving a book.

A book?

"Look!" Lineham opened it to the flyleaf and thrust it towards him. A square label pasted inside informed him that on 18 July 1951 this book had been awarded to Henry Gates, for the best work in his class.

Henry Gates?

Henry . . . Harry . . .

Was it possible that Harry Greenleaf, the recluse, was really Henry Gates, Grace Trimble's brother? Henry, who had been Reg Hammer's best friend, Edith and Marcia's first love?

TWENTY-FOUR

Thanet stared at the label, mind racing. If Greenleaf was really Henry Gates, it would explain why he had chosen Telford Green as his sanctuary. After the trauma of the fire and no doubt many months of surgery he would have needed the comfort of familiar surroundings. Thanet closed the book, read the title. *Palgrave's Golden Treasury*. Typical of school prizes given at that time.

"What d'you think, sir? Think he could be Gates?"

"Greenleaf could have picked this up at a jumble sale in the village."

Lineham's excitement visibly waned as he considered this proposition. "Possible, I suppose."

"Likely, even. On the other hand . . ."

"If he is Gates, why d'you think he didn't go back to his family?"

"There was only his sister to go back to, remember. And frankly, from what we've seen of her, if I were Greenleaf I'd prefer to live up here by myself."

"The Pringles said she was very fond of him."

"True. Though that's not the same as saying he was fond of her." Thanet shrugged. "Perhaps he just didn't want to make himself known, wanted to hide himself away from everybody. It would be understandable, considering the degree of his disfigurement."

"You don't think . . . ? No."

"What?"

"I was wondering if his sister did know who he really was, if he might have told her. But if so, I shouldn't think she'd have dropped him in it by telling us he was on the bridge that night."

"No." Ironic, that, if Harry was Gates: brother and sister meeting on the bridge where they must have lingered so often as children, Harry knowing that the following day he would have to

leave Telford Green for the second and perhaps last time. Had he
been tempted to approach Grace, tell her who he really was? He
would then have been able to move in with her, stay on in the
village legitimately. He would have been a nine-day wonder,
true, but once the sensation became everyday reality people
would no doubt have accepted him back as Henry Gates, one of
them. Sympathy for him would have run high. He wasn't stupid,
must have realised all this. Why, then, if he was Gates, had he
not declared himself?

Perhaps he wasn't Gates after all, really had picked the book
up at a jumble sale. Thanet glanced down at it. The cover was
bent, worn and stained. If Greenleaf was Gates it must have
accompanied him through all the intervening years, perhaps the
only memento of his childhood.

Thanet suddenly became aware that the distant barking had
become louder and a few moments later Harry's black and white
mongrel shot out of the wood and tore up to them, barking
furiously. A couple of feet away it skidded to a halt but continued barking.

It didn't look as though the animal was going to attack them,
but it seemed politic to stand still. Harry couldn't be far away.

A couple of minutes later he emerged from the wood, bent
almost double, both hands clutching the rope over his right
shoulder. In a moment Thanet could see that he was dragging a
sizeable log. He lowered it to the ground and straightened up.

"Jack! Enough!"

The dog stopped barking immediately, like a radio that had
been switched off. Then it looked at its master and, nose to the
ground, ran up to the hut, sniffed around inside, then returned to
sniff at Lineham's trousers. The message was clear.

Greenleaf hadn't needed it, however. His eyes were on the
book in Thanet's hand. "Got a search warrant, have you?"

Thanet was in the wrong and he knew it. But if he admitted it,
Greenleaf could prove difficult. He was just the type to make an
almighty fuss. Better to counter-attack. If they were wrong about
his identity, of course, their ammunition would be useless. But it
was worth a try.

"Ah, there you are, Mr. Gates. We've been waiting for you
for some time."

"Gates? What are you talking about?"

Thanet held up the book. "This is yours?"

Harry glanced towards the door of the hut. "You should
know."

"Your name is inside." Thanet opened the book and held it out, displaying the label.

Harry barely glanced at it. "Ha, ha. Very funny."

"You don't deny that you are Gates, then?"

"You can think what you like, mate."

Thanet sensed Lineham tense beside him and cast him an admonitory glance. It was one of the Sergeant's weaknesses that he took it as a personal insult when witnesses were rude to Thanet. Why on earth, he wondered, had various people he had spoken to about Greenleaf said that he was a mild, gentle man, the type who "wouldn't hurt a fly?" Perhaps, in normal circumstances, he was. Perhaps it was only when he felt threatened that he threw up this barrier of implacable hostility like a hedgehog extending its bristles. Once again Thanet regretted the impossibility of reading the man's reaction from his expression. That stretched, shiny skin was about as responsive as a balloon. He heard Mrs. Pringle's voice, *"Henry was such a good-looking boy . . . ,"* and firmly suppressed the pity which once again threatened to get in the way of handling the situation correctly. If Harry, or Henry, were a murderer, he would have to take his chance with the rest. And if not, well, he seemed quite capable of looking after himself.

"If you prefer, we can go back to Headquarters to talk about it."

Harry's sudden stillness told him that this was a highly unwelcome suggestion.

"Or we can discuss it here. Providing that you are willing to cooperate."

Harry stared at him for a moment longer, then shrugged. "Let's get it over with, then, I've got work to do." He strolled across to the hut, picked up an old guernsey sweater from the chair near the door and pulled it on. Then he turned, leaned against the outside wall of the hut and folded his arms. "Well?"

Lineham took out his notebook.

Harry still hadn't either admitted or denied that he was Gates, Thanet reminded himself.

"Look, it would be a simple matter for us to check whether you really are Greenleaf or not. One phone call to the Records Office would do it." If they were lucky. "But I would like to emphasise that even if you do choose to live up here under an assumed name there is no reason whatsoever for us to make this public unless you are involved in our investigation."

"That's all right then, in't it? I'm not."

"In that case you have nothing to worry about. And nothing to hide, either. You are Henry Gates?"

Gates looked away from Thanet, down towards the village. Then, with a resigned sigh he shrugged. "Yes . . . You did mean what you said, about not telling anyone?"

It was the first sign of vulnerability he had shown.

"Of course. So long as you are not involved . . ."

"How many more times do I have to tell you? I'm not!"

"Oh come on, Mr. . . . I'll call you Harry, shall I? It'll be simpler. Come on, Harry, we both know that's not true. You were seen."

"When? What are you talking about?"

But the note in Harry's voice told Thanet that he knew quite well.

"When we were last here, you told us that you had been at home on Tuesday night, packing up, that you hadn't gone out. That was a stupid thing to do. You knew you'd been seen in the village by at least one person. Why lie about it?"

"Why d'you think? Because any fool could see that with the motive I had for wanting to get rid of her, if I told you I'd been down to the village that night, I'd be inside quicker than I could say 'Marcia!' I thought it was worth taking a chance you wouldn't find out."

"So what time did you go down?"

He had set off, it seemed, at about a quarter to ten. He wanted to take a last look around Telford Green before moving on next day. He had left Jack behind because people tended to stop and chat when he had Jack with him and he didn't feel like talking to anyone that night.

"So how long would it have taken you to get down to the village?"

"Five minutes or so."

Harry had then walked first up to the far end of the village, getting back to the bridge probably soon after ten. Pressed for a firm time he became irritable. "I wasn't looking at a bloody watch all the time, was I? Haven't even got one."

Lineham was tense, Thanet could tell. At around a quarter past ten Marcia had left her mother's cottage, only a few minutes away from the bridge, and shortly afterwards had fallen or been pushed through that gap. If Harry had been hanging about the village it was possible that, even if he hadn't had a fatal quarrel with Marcia himself, he might have seen what happened to her.

"Go on. And take your time. Tell us in detail what you saw and heard as you were approaching the bridge."

"Well, just as I was passing the pub the door opens and a coupla men come out. One of them was drunk and the other just propped him up against the wall outside and said, 'Go on then, Reg. Home.' And back he goes inside. Reg just stands there for a minute and then his knees sort of fold up and he slides down till he's sitting on the floor. Then he doesn't move."

"So what did you do?"

"Nothing. Not then, anyways. I sort of hesitated a bit, then I thought, someone else'll be out in a minute, they'll see him home. So I walked on to the bridge and stood looking down at the water."

He hadn't heard Grace coming up the steps from the footpath on the other side of the bridge because a couple of cars went by, and it was not until she stepped on to the metalled road that he was aware of her presence. He recognised her at once, and slipped away, went to hide behind some bushes near by.

"It didn't occur to you to tell your sister who you are—I'm assuming she didn't know?—and move in with her?"

Harry moved his shoulders uneasily against the wooden wall of the hut. "I did think about it, yes. But I'm used to living by myself. I like it. I like the freedom. You don't have to account to nobody, up here."

Thanet understood. Harry had escaped from his sister once and didn't want to risk being enmeshed again.

"So then what did you do?"

He could see it all as clearly as if he were there, hiding behind the bushes himself: the bridge, with the warning lights around the broken parapet; the receding figure of Grace. Any second now Marcia would come into sight . . .

"Well, Grace went off home, in the other direction, and there was Reg still sitting on the floor outside the pub across the road . . . Well, I wasn't doing nothing, and once upon a time me and Reg was best mates. So I goes across, says, 'Come on, me old mate.' I manage to get him on his feet and off we stagger."

The whole scenario sounded all too likely. Thanet remembered that curious look on Hammer's face, as if he thought that his memory must be playing tricks on him. If, in his drunken state, he had recognised the voice of the childhood friend he hadn't seen for years, he might well have wondered later if he had been dreaming. "You took him all the way home?"

"It's only a coupla hundred yards. Yeah. Rung the bell and dumped him on the doorstep."

"Mrs. Hammer says he didn't get home until half-past ten. Nearly half an hour, to cover that distance . . . ?"

"It must've taken me getting on for five minutes to get him to his feet and get him on his way. And then . . . Ever tried moving a drunk? He's a dead weight, believe me. Reg is a big man, and he kept on falling down."

"While you were helping him along, did you look back at the bridge at all?"

Harry shook his head. "Had my hands full, didn't I?"

"Or hear anything?"

"Reg was singing, on and off. And I really wasn't paying attention to what was going on behind me. If I'd known there was going to be a murder, and I was going to be a suspect . . . !"

No point in saying that strictly speaking they still weren't sure that there had been one. Harry probably wouldn't have believed them anyway.

"While you were in the village, did you see anyone else about?"

Harry frowned, thinking. "There was a woman . . ."

Thanet and Lineham spoke together.

"When?"

"Where?"

"As Reg and me staggered across the bridge. She was posting a letter."

Edith? Thanet had checked. The post box was on the Manor side of the bridge. Unless Edith had seen Marcia coming and had walked on to the bridge to accost her, there would be no reason for them to have met.

"Did you recognise her?"

"No. There's no lamp on that side of the bridge and the light is bad. And she was turning away from the box at the time. I only saw her back. Anyway, I wasn't paying much attention."

"Could it have been Edith Phipps?"

"Might have been. But I couldn't swear to it."

"Where did she go?"

"Walked away down the road."

"Towards the Manor gates?"

Harry shrugged. "I dunno. She went off ahead of us around the bend. Could've been going to the cottages for all I know."

"Did you see anyone else?"

"No."

"You're sure?"

"I told you, no!"

They left him to his sawing and walked down to the river bank.

"We need to talk," said Thanet. "Might as well sit down here for a while."

The grass was dry, the sun warm. They took off their coats and Thanet lit his pipe. They sat for a while in silence, gazing at the water. Eventually Lineham stirred, picked a piece of grass and began to chew it.

"What d'you reckon, sir?"

Thanet shrugged. "About what Harry said? It's all credible enough. Mrs. Hammer told us someone had brought Reg home, and it would be typical of Harry to ring the bell and walk away before the door opened."

"It was probably them that Lomax saw, in front of the cottages . . . If it was murder it's essential to know whether Harry's speaking the truth, isn't it? Perhaps more than any other witness so far."

"For elimination purposes, you mean. Yes."

"Both he and Hammer would be out, for a start . . ."

"Unless they were in it together."

Lineham raised his eyebrows. "Hadn't thought of that. Bit unlikely, don't you think?"

"Yes, I do, actually. Go on."

"And it would cut out Grace Trimble, too. Because she would have left the bridge before Marcia Salden arrived."

"And if the woman Harry saw posting the letter was Edith Phipps . . ."

"It certainly narrows the field down, doesn't it, sir? It only leaves us with Councillor Lomax and Salden."

"*If* Harry is telling the truth, Mike. I think we have to accept that if Marcia was murdered and he or any of his old pals were involved, he'd have very good reason for lying. He's not crying over Marcia's death, in fact it came at just the right moment for him. So if someone obliged him by getting rid of her he's not going to give that person away, especially if he or she is a childhood friend. And all those old pals had very good reasons for wanting to get rid of Marcia, remember."

"True. But let's look just for a moment at the possibility that everything he's told us is true, and only Lomax and Salden remain. As we've already said, in every case but Salden the suspect had a reason, what you always call the trigger factor.

With Lomax we think it was probably the threat of blackmail or scandal if he didn't toe the line over the planning permission; with Harry it was the threat of eviction and with Grace the damage being done to her daughter and that nasty scene with Josie up at the Manor; with Reg it was having his inheritance snatched from under his nose and with Edith it was losing the job and possibly the home which suited her and her invalid mother so well. In addition, all these people but Lomax are old mates of Marcia's and have long-standing grudges against her . . . But with Salden . . . ? Nothing, so far as I can see."

"As we've said before, in a detective novel that would automatically make him suspect number one," said Thanet with a grin.

Lineham gave a slight frown, as if to indicate that this wasn't the moment for jokes. "He stands to inherit the business, yes, but I can't see that as a reason. In fact, as his wife seemed to be the driving force behind it, he stands to lose in the long run."

"Perhaps he'd just reached the point where he was fed up with her. She does sound pretty overpowering."

"Plenty of men have overpowering wives, but they don't go round bumping them off."

Thanet restrained himself from giving Lineham a sharp glance. Had that remark been uncomfortably heartfelt?

"No," Lineham went on. "In a case like this you've got to have something which finally pushes the murderer over the edge."

Thanet remembered the scene he had envisaged between Bernard Salden and his wife, in which Bernard gets angry with her for going back to her guests at the Manor instead of staying with her mother. It all seemed rather tame, now, in comparison with the powerful motives of the other suspects. "I wonder . . ."

Lineham turned an eager face. "What?"

"Mrs. Carter, Marcia's mother . . ."

"What about her."

"Everyone's taken it for granted that she wanted to see Bernard Salden that night because she was so fond of him. Which could well be so. But what if there was another reason? What if she wanted to see him because she wanted to tell him something before she died?"

"What, for instance?"

"It would have to be something about Marcia which she knew and he didn't, something she felt was important to him . . ."

They stared at each other, then suddenly Lineham's face lit

up. "The sterilisation! What if she wanted to tell him Marcia had been sterilised?"

"It's a possibility. But why would she want to do that? It would cause him nothing but pain, and problems in his marriage too."

"Because she thought it was cruel for him to go on hoping for a child of his own, when there was no possibility of it happening? Everyone says how fond of children he is, how much he longs for one . . ."

Thanet frowned, considering. "She'd be betraying her own daughter. Would she do that, for her son-in-law?" Impossible to speculate on such a matter without knowing the people involved personally.

"Marcia and her mother weren't exactly fond of each other, were they? I mean, everyone agrees she did her duty by her, but I've never had the impression there was much feeling between them. It is a possibility, sir, don't you think?"

"Anything's possible, Mike. It would certainly explain Salden's behaviour that night—why he seemed so upset when he left Mrs. Carter's cottage, why he went for a walk and sat around brooding on the river bank instead of putting in an appearance at home." Thanet heaved himself to his feet, rubbing his backside. The grass had been wetter than he thought. "We'd better go and have another little chat with him, hadn't we?"

TWENTY-FIVE

They walked into the village to pick up the car, then drove to the Manor.

Mrs. Pantry looked harassed. She was wearing a surprisingly smart navy blue dress with white collar and cuffs and was balancing two plates of sandwiches covered in cling film in one hand. "Yes, he's in." Her usual grudging manner.

In the hall Thanet could see through an open door that a table had been set out with plates of sandwiches and cakes, cups and saucers.

Mrs. Pantry followed his glance. "Mrs. Carter's funeral is later on this afternoon, and people are coming back here."

"How is Mr. Salden today?"

Her expression lightened and she was uncharacteristically forthcoming. "He must be feeling a bit better, I think. He's been on the phone all morning."

Thanet wasn't surprised to hear it. He knew that at times like this people often found work a salvation. "Good. Where is he?"

"In his office." She put the sandwiches down on the long oak table in the hall. "I'll tell him you're here."

In a few minutes she returned. "You can go in."

She was right. Salden did look better. He was again neatly dressed, presumably for the funeral, in a well-cut grey suit and black tie. And, although there were dark smudges beneath his eyes, the dazed look was less evident. He was seated at his desk as though he had been working but there were no papers about except for a closed notebook exactly in the centre of the desk blotter.

"I hope this won't take long. I have a funeral to attend."

Thanet shook his head. "I shouldn't think so."

He and Lineham sat down.

206

"Mr. Salden, it has occurred to us that you haven't told us why your mother-in-law wanted to see you on Tuesday night."

"I don't see what possible relevance that could have to your investigation."

"You must allow me to be the judge of that."

Salden compressed his lips. "She merely wanted to say good-bye." He looked away, out of the window. "She knew she was dying, and we were very fond of each other."

"There was nothing special she wanted to tell you?"

"No." Salden's head swung back and he looked at Thanet with eyes narrowed. "Why do you ask? Was there something?"

Was the enquiry genuine? Thanet didn't particularly like the idea of breaking the news of Marcia's sterilisation to Salden, but the man would have to know some time; the information would emerge at the inquest anyway.

"I only wondered because . . . Mr. Salden, were you aware that your wife had been sterilised?"

Salden's reaction gave him the answer. Unless the man was a superb actor there was no doubt that this was news indeed. His jaw dropped and his eyes dilated, then he became perfectly still, staring at Thanet. Only the expression in his eyes changed, from shock and disbelief to pain, anger and finally to acceptance. And to something else less definable. At last he ran his tongue over his lips and said, "The *post mortem*?"

Thanet nodded. "Yes."

There was no point in prolonging the interview. And Salden had a funeral to face yet, this afternoon. They left.

Thanet glanced at Lineham's face as they got into the car. "Cheer up, Mike, it was a good idea."

"No point in having good ideas if they don't work out. You believed him then, did you, sir?"

"Didn't you? Yes, I'd swear it was a complete surprise to him. A terrible shock, in fact." He wondered how Salden would feel about Marcia now, knowing that she had deceived and betrayed him over something which meant so much to him.

"I agree," said Lineham gloomily. "So where does that leave us?"

"Up a gum tree as far as Salden's concerned, I should say."

They had reached the end of the drive and pulled in to allow the funeral cortège to pass by. Mrs. Carter was going to set off for her last resting place from the Manor. Bernard was doing her proud.

Thanet could see Edith Phipps watching from the kitchen

window. She was wearing a black hat with a feather in it. No doubt Bernard had offered to pick her up on the way past. "I suppose we could console ourselves by the fact that, even if he had known about the sterilisation and even if we had got him to admit that it was in order to tell him about it that Mrs. Carter sent for him that night, there is still no way that we could prove that it was he who committed the murder. And at the moment the same thing applies to all the others. We've got to come up with something concrete, Mike."

"What, for instance?"

"Your guess is as good as mine. We'll really have to put our minds to it."

They drove in silence for a few minutes, then Thanet said, "Perhaps we've been barking up the wrong tree all along. It's happened before. Perhaps Marcia wasn't murdered at all and it was a simple accident."

"Difficult to see how it could have been, under the circumstances. Anyone passing that gap in the parapet would have been hyper-careful."

"Oh, I don't know. She could have been crossing the bridge towards the footpath entrance, which is right alongside the broken section. A car could have come along too fast and she could have jumped back to avoid it, slipped on the icy road . . ."

"Are you suggesting we give up, then, sir?"

"Not yet, no. But I'm beginning to wonder if we might have to. If we don't come up with any better ideas . . ."

"Meanwhile, what?"

"Bring Draco up to date and then it's time for a session on reports, I think. And there's no point in groaning. Have you got a better suggestion?"

In the past they had often found that if they were stuck a thorough sifting of everything that had come in so far was a useful way of breaking the impasse. Up until now reports on the Salden case had been read as they came in, in dribs and drabs. Now, with any luck, discrepancies might be spotted that had earlier been missed and a fresh overall view would suggest new insights, new avenues to explore.

"It'll be impossible to concentrate in the main CID room," said Lineham hopefully.

"Then we'll commandeer one of the interview rooms," said Thanet.

So they did. But to no avail. At seven o'clock, Lineham put

his head in his hands and groaned. "I don't know about you, sir, but I can't think straight any more. I'm just not taking this in."

Thanet closed the file he was reading and tossed it on to the desk. "Neither can I. We'll call it a day." He pressed his fingers into the deep, dull ache across the small of his back. He longed to lie down, preferably flat on the floor, and allow his muscles to relax. He decided that when he got home he'd go up to the bedroom and do just that.

Joan was in the kitchen, busy with supper. "Twenty minutes," she said, after one look at his face. "Plenty of time, if you want to crash out for a while."

At the door he turned. "Bridget in?"

Joan nodded. "In her room."

"How is she?"

Joan pulled a face. "Subdued."

"Only to be expected, I suppose."

In the bedroom he lowered himself to the floor and began his relaxation routine. Right leg, stretch . . . and relax. Left leg, stretch . . . and relax . . . Breathe in, breathe out . . . He was beginning to float when the back door slammed, interrupting his concentration. He tried to ignore it. The telephone pinged in the hall, then there was a rush of feet on the stairs and Joan's voice, jagged with emotion.

"Luke! Luke!" She burst into the room.

His eyes snapped open. "What?"

"It's Vicky. I think she's taken an overdose."

"Oh God." Thanet rolled over, got up. "Is she still alive?"

"Just, I think. I've rung for an ambulance."

Bridget appeared at the door, looking frightened. "What is it! What's the matter, Mum?"

There was no way she could wrap this up, protect Bridget from the harsh reality. "It's Vicky, darling. I'm afraid she's . . . well, it looks as though she's taken an overdose." She glanced back at Thanet. "I heard the baby. He was screaming his head off, that's why I went across . . . I must go and get him."

And she was gone.

Bridget said: "Dad, how awful! What can we do?"

They started downstairs.

"Not much, at the moment. We'll have to look after the baby, obviously. I expect he's hungry. Go and put the kettle on. Just as well she isn't breast-feeding."

Everything seemed to happen quickly. Joan arrived with the screaming baby and within minutes had changed his nappy and

made his bottle. Meanwhile the ambulance arrived. Thanet let
them in next door and watched them take away an unconscious
Vicky. He then took a quick look around to see if there was any
clue to Peter's whereabouts. To his relief, by the telephone he
found a clear list of dates, times and places; Peter had wanted to
be certain that Vicky would at least be able to contact him each
evening. But it hadn't been enough, Thanet thought sadly as he
dialled. At this particular time in her life Vicky had needed a
much stronger lifeline than a voice on the telephone once a day.
It was unfortunate that both sets of parents lived some distance
away. They were all good, decent people and would be desperately upset about this. Thanet didn't envy Peter, having to break
the news to them.

At home peace had descended. Bridget was nursing the baby
and Joan was putting on her coat.

"I managed to get hold of Peter," said Thanet. "He's coming
straight home."

"Good. What time will he be here?"

"In the early hours, he thinks. You're going to the hospital?"

"Yes, I must. You do realise, don't you, that it's my fault
she's there? The least I can do is be with her."

"What do you mean, your fault?"

"I just didn't make enough time for her. She was sending out
all the signals and I just ignored them. If only I'd—"

"Joan!" Luke took her hands. "When will you learn that you
are not responsible for the well-being of the whole world? You've
spent a lot of time with Vicky, taken endless trouble over her.
It's her illness that has put her in hospital, not you."

Joan bit her lip. "That's not how it feels to me at the moment.
I should have gone over to see her as soon as I got home from
work. I'd have found her that much earlier and she'd have had a
much better chance." She snatched up her bag. "I'll see you
later."

"Ring me," Thanet called as she hurried to her car.

Ben arrived home soon afterwards and they had supper. Thanet
fetched further supplies for the baby from next door and at ten
o'clock he and Bridget between them fed and changed him,
Thanet remembering ruefully how adept he had once been at
handling his own children.

At eleven Joan rang. "She's come round."

"Thank God." Thanet was relieved not only for the sake of
the young family, but for Joan. If Vicky had died . . ."Are you
coming home now?"

"No, someone must be here with her, for moral support. I'll wait until Peter arrives. Is he coming straight to the hospital?"

"I don't know, he didn't say. I imagine so . . . How is she?"

"Drowsy. She doesn't really know what's hit her yet. Poor Vicky. When I think how happy they were, when she first knew she was pregnant . . ."

"I know. Well, I suppose the only good thing to come out of this is that now she will at last get some psychiatric treatment. The hospital will make sure of that before they release her."

"True. That doctor of hers ought to be struck off!"

"I'm sure Peter'll see that she's transferred to that woman doctor I was telling you about."

"I do hope things improve for her." Joan suddenly sounded very low.

"Cheer up. They will. Post-natal depression doesn't go on for ever."

They chatted for a few minutes longer, then Joan said she must get back to Vicky.

In bed, Thanet could not get to sleep. Without Joan beside him he felt bereft, incomplete, and found himself listening out all the time for her return.

Eventually, after an hour of tossing and turning, he decided to get up. He went downstairs, made himself some tea and sat down at the kitchen table to drink it. A moment later he decided he might as well wait in comfort in the sitting-room. He didn't feel like reading, and although he had never watched television at this hour before he switched the set on. They were showing a film of a nineteen fifties musical. Sinking into an armchair he drank his tea then slipped into a half-awake, half-asleep state in which he drifted in and out of consciousness. Images from the dramatic events of the evening mingled with sentences read during the report session this afternoon and snatches of conversation from the last few days. Some time in the small hours he fell asleep and dreamed that Marcia was floating down the river towards him, that he was reaching to pull her out. But when he finally got her out of the water he discovered that she was Vicky. "What shall I tell Peter?" he moaned. "What shall I tell Peter?"

Someone was shaking him by the arm and he blinked awake. Joan's concerned face hovered over him.

"You were dreaming."

He shook his head to clear it. "Yes, I . . ." He stopped, groping to recapture the dream before it faded.

"What?" She looked exhausted. "Luke, what is it?"

He didn't reply, scarcely heard her. An astounding thought had just struck him. Was it possible?

"Luke?" Joan was tugging at his sleeve.

He glanced at his watch. Half-past three. Louise would not appreciate it if he rang Lineham now. And this certainly wasn't the moment to start propounding theories to Joan. Somehow he would have to wait until morning.

Suppressing his excitement, he shook his head. "Just an idea," he said. "Come on, let's get you to bed."

TWENTY-SIX

At half-past nine next morning Thanet and Lineham were knocking at Mrs. Pepper's door. The pink and scarlet tulips in the tiny front garden were looking somewhat the worse for wear after the torrential rain the other day. The weather today didn't look too promising either; the early morning sunshine had long since faded and ominous-looking clouds were building to the west.

Mrs. Pepper looked surprised to see them. She was even smaller than Thanet had remembered. She had exchanged the green tracksuit with orange trimmings for a purple one with yellow trimmings. Thanet was glad to see that beside her was Spot, old Mrs. Carter's dog. Nurse Lint must have persuaded Mrs. Pepper to take him on.

"No, we won't come in, thank you. There's just one question we wanted to ask you."

He told her what it was and her eyebrows went up. "What on earth d'you want to know that for?"

"I'm sorry, I can't say. But if you could just tell us . . ."

Her answer was just what he wanted to hear. He and Lineham exchanged jubilant looks.

They left her gazing after them, puzzled.

Next stop was the Vicarage.

"Let's hope he's in," said Thanet as they walked across the green. "If I hadn't had to attend the daily meeting . . ."

"We couldn't have left any earlier anyway, we had to make that phone call."

"True." Thanet was edgy. What if Fothergill were out? They already had sufficient confirmation of his theory—Fothergill's evidence would really just be the icing on the cake. But he had a feeling amounting almost to superstition that he must have the answers to every single query he had listed before tackling the murderer; he wanted to be as sure of his ground as possible.

Telford Green Vicarage was a compact modern house which had been built in the grounds of the large, draughty, Victorian vicarage next door.

There was no response to their ring.

Thanet shifted impatiently from one foot to the other. "Come *on*, Mr. Fothergill."

"I'd settle for Mrs. Fothergill. At least she could tell us where he's likely to be."

"Vicars!" said Thanet, scowling. "He could be anywhere. He could be away at a conference."

"Or at the Diocesan Synod."

Thanet raised an eyebrow. "Didn't know you even knew such a thing existed, Mike."

Lineham grinned. "Just a little information I picked up." He rang the bell again. "I haven't the faintest idea what it is, though. What is it?"

Thanet was saved from having to reply by the young woman who now walked through the gate. She was wearing jeans and a sweatshirt and was pushing a pushchair with a baby in it. "Can I help you?"

"Mrs. Fothergill?" said Thanet with relief. He introduced himself. "We'd like a word with your husband."

"I'm sorry, he's out." Then, looking at their faces, "But he should be back shortly. He'd better be! I need the car to go to Sturrenden and do the weekly shop. Would you like to wait inside?"

She showed them into the sitting-room, made them cups of coffee, then excused herself. "I'm sorry, but there's rather a lot to do before I go."

"Just forget we're here," said Thanet, smiling.

Ten minutes later a series of explosions heralded Fothergill's return. Lineham jumped up and went to the window. Thanet joined him. Fothergill spotted them and raised a hand, ostentatiously patting the car before coming into the house.

"Is she really going shopping in that?" said Lineham.

"Don't suppose she has much choice."

"Sorry!" Fothergill breezed in. "Hope I haven't kept you waiting too long."

"Not at all. We've only been here ten minutes and your wife very kindly gave us some coffee."

"Good. Excellent. So?" Fothergill looked from one to the other. "How can I help you?"

"There was something we wanted to ask you . . ."

Five minutes later they were back in the car.

Lineham's eyes were sparkling. "Pretty conclusive, don't you think, sir?"

"I hope so, Mike. I hope so." Over the years Thanet had learned to trust his intuition. "Never underestimate those gut feelings," he had once been told by a policeman he very much respected. And he was certain about this now, in his own mind. But to satisfy the law was another matter. He said so.

"So what do we do? Wait until we have some evidence that'll clinch it?"

"The trouble is, I don't see much prospect of getting any. No, I think our only hope is to try and manoeuvre a confession."

"And if one isn't forthcoming?"

Thanet shrugged. "We'll just have to play it by ear."

Back, then, through the village which had become so familiar to them, past the cottage where Marcia had spent the miserable childhood which had spurred her on to success beyond her dreams; past the pub where Salden, Hammer and Lomax had in turn drowned their sorrows on the night of what Thanet was now convinced was a murder; over the bridge—now being repaired, Thanet noticed—where Marcia had met her death; past the Hammers' cottage and the lodge where Edith lived, to the house with which Marcia had fallen in love all those years ago.

As they emerged from the avenue of trees, huge spots of rain began to spatter the windscreen. Remembering their previous experience when Mrs. Pantry had kept them standing on the doorstep in a downpour, this time they pulled raincoats on. By the time they reached the front door it was pouring.

Mrs. Pantry was as unwelcoming as ever. "He's out."

It was an anticlimax. Hunching his shoulders against the water trickling down his neck, Thanet tried to suppress his disappointment.

"Where's he gone?"

She planted herself a little more firmly on her solid legs, as though preparing herself against an onslaught, and folding her arms across her chest said belligerently, "Can't you leave the poor man alone? After all he's been through."

"I assure you we wouldn't be wanting to talk to him if it weren't absolutely necessary. Where is he?"

"You're the detective. Well then, detect."

Thanet suppressed his rising anger. "Mrs. Pantry . . ."

"What is it, Mrs. Pantry? What's going on?" It was Edith Phipps. "What on earth are you thinking of, keeping the Inspector and the Sergeant standing out there in the pouring rain? Look at them, they're half drowned. I can't think what Mr. Salden would say. Come in, Inspector!''

Thanet shook his head. ''Thank you, no. We wanted to speak to Mr. Salden, and I believe he's out. Do you know where he is?''

Edith gave Mrs. Pantry an admonitory look. ''He's gone fishing.'' She wrinkled her nose. ''Not exactly ideal weather, but it never seems to bother him. He's got one of those big umbrellas.''

''Where does he go, do you know?''

''Not really. Down to the Teale, that's all.''

''So he'll be somewhere in the grounds.''

''Oh yes, I'm sure of it.''

''Great!'' said Lineham when they were back in the car. ''So all we have to do now is walk along about a mile of river bank in the pouring rain.''

''I don't know about you, but I couldn't get much wetter than I already am.''

''True.''

''So we might as well do it.''

''Why not?''

They decided to drive back to the bridge and start from there. He'd been wrong in thinking he couldn't get any wetter, thought Thanet as they trudged along, their wellingtons swishing through the sodden grass. He must be mad. Why couldn't he have waited? The rain would stop soon enough and then they could have made this trek in comfort. But having come this far he certainly wasn't going to turn back now.

Ten minutes later they spotted the blue and yellow segments of a big umbrella tucked under the lip of the river bank fifty yards ahead.

''It might not be him,'' said Lineham.

But it was. Salden looked cosy enough, well wrapped up in waterproof jacket and trousers, a steaming cup of coffee in his hand. Thanet looked at it enviously. He could hardly expect to be offered a cup, and even if he were he wouldn't be able to accept, in the circumstances.

''You look a little damp, Inspector.'' There was a glint of amusement in Salden's eyes. ''This is surely devotion well beyond the call of duty. Would you like to share my umbrella? I'm sure we could all squeeze underneath.''

''There are some trees over there,'' said Thanet.

He and Lineham waited while Salden reeled in his line and

propped his rod against the overhanging bank, then they headed for the trees. It was only marginally drier here; the leaves were not yet fully unfurled, the summer canopy not yet established.

Thanet decided that there was no point in wasting time. Shock tactics might in any case prove more effective. He nodded at Lineham.

"Bernard Salden, you are not obliged to say anything unless you wish to do so, but what you say may be put into writing and given in evidence."

Salden looked—what? astounded? appalled? It was difficult to tell, with the rain streaming down his face.

He looked from one to the other. "What?"

"Mr. Salden. Before you tell us exactly what happened on Tuesday night, let me say off the record that I'm sure you will find any jury sympathetic to your case. Any man who suddenly discovers that his daughter has been murdered . . ."

Salden was galvanised into life. "Murdered? What are you saying? Who told you that?" He grabbed Thanet by the shoulders and shook him. He looked frantic.

Thanet was nonplussed. He didn't know what to say. In a matter of seconds his neatly constructed edifice had been demolished. His whole case rested on the premise that, in an abnormal state of mind as a result of severe post-natal depression, Marcia had killed her baby daughter and disposed of the body. With no one else to turn to she had then run to her mother for sanctuary, confessed her crime and sworn Mrs. Carter to secrecy. This, he had been convinced, was what Mrs. Carter had wanted to tell Bernard before she died and this, he had been certain, was what had prompted that fatal quarrel between Salden and his wife. But if Salden hadn't known . . . ? He stared at Salden. Should he back down, apologise? No. Facts were facts. Doggedly he re-counted them.

"That charade your wife played, when she came back to Telford Green, claiming the baby had died. We checked with the Records Office, and no death certificate exists. We spoke with Mrs. Pepper, who attended the 'funeral.' The 'ashes' were not buried in the churchyard. In that case the vicar would have needed a copy of the death certificate, and of course Marcia didn't have one. A convincing little ceremony was held on the village green instead. No doubt your wife intended to deceive her mother, too, but somehow she must have let the truth slip out. Mrs. Carter might have carried the secret with her to the grave, but her conscience wouldn't allow her to. She . . ."

"Just a minute, let me get this straight. Are you suggesting my wife *murdered* Clare?"

"I told you, the death certificate doesn't exist . . ."

Something was happening to Salden's face. The flat planes were cracking, breaking up. He collapsed into a sitting position on the ground, hunched forward with hands over face, shoulders heaving.

Thanet and Lineham looked at each other. Now what? They stood staring down at Salden. And then Thanet realised. Those snorts and sniffles were not the sounds of grief.

Salden was *laughing*.

Oblivious of the rain, Thanet realised that at last it really had happened; his famous intuition had let him down and one of his theories truly was just as preposterous as it sounded. He remembered the struggle he had had to convince Draco of its credibility, and his soul shrivelled with embarrassment. He cursed himself now for not keeping his mouth shut until he was certain. Yes, he had to face it. He had made a fool of himself in a big way. He risked a glance at Lineham, but the Sergeant was avoiding his eye.

Salden was wiping his eyes, shaking his head. He held out a hand and Thanet helped him to his feet. "Sorry about that. But you really had me worried there, for a minute, Inspector."

"I'm sorry," said Thanet stiffly.

"Oh, it's OK. Don't worry. As soon as I realised you were talking about the past, not the present . . ."

"What do you mean?"

"I thought," said Salden, with the patient air of someone spelling something simple out, "that you meant you'd just heard that my daughter had been murdered."

Just heard? Thanet tried to remember exactly what he'd said. *Let me say off the record that I'm sure you will find any jury sympathetic to your case. Any man who suddenly discovers that his daughter has been murdered* . . . But if Salden had thought that . . . And Salden hadn't queried what Thanet had said about the death certificate . . . A tiny bud of hope began to unfurl in his chest as he adjusted to new possibilities.

"You did know that your daughter is still alive, then?"

There was a brief silence. In Salden's eyes was the look of a man who suddenly realises that he has said too much.

"So that was what Mrs. Carter wanted to tell you on Tuesday night. I see." Thanet did see. He saw that here was another motive as strong as the last. Whatever Marcia had done with the child, Salden would have been furious with her for deceiving him so, for depriving him of almost thirty years of fatherhood.

"I don't know what you're talking about."

"Oh come, Mr. Salden. I'm not stupid. You gave yourself away there, didn't you? What did your wife say she'd done with the baby? Given her to a childless couple, perhaps, who were so desperate for a child that they would take her with no questions asked? No? Surely she didn't just abandon her?"

Despite his attempt at self-control, Salden's expression gave him away.

"No," said Thanet firmly, knowing that if this bluff failed all was lost. "That can't be true."

"Why not?" The words seemed forced out against Salden's will.

"Because in that case your wife would have been traced. A woman can't just disappear, leaving a child behind her . . . No, I'm afraid you've been badly deceived."

"What do you mean?"

"That your wife was desperate enough at that time to have been driven to take far more drastic action than that. Naturally she wouldn't have told her mother the truth."

"You're trying to tell me you have proof that Clare is . . . dead?"

Thanet said nothing.

"No!" said Salden. "That's not true! There's some mistake! She left her, I know she did. In the foyer of a hospital, where she would be found and looked after."

The fear that Thanet could be right had made Salden throw discretion to the winds. Even now he did not realise that he had betrayed himself.

It was essential to press on without allowing Salden time to think. Hating himself, Thanet said, "Where was this? In the town where you were living?"

"No. She wanted to get right away. She couldn't risk leaving her anywhere in Bradford, she was afraid she might be traced."

"Where, then?"

"York. She caught a train to York. She'd heard it was a nice city, she said."

She said?

They had him! There was only one possible occasion when Salden and Marcia might have discussed this subject: after he had seen his mother-in-law on Tuesday night.

"Who said? Your mother-in-law?"

"No! Marcia! My wife. She told me herself and I believed her."

"When?" said Thanet softly. "When did she tell you?"

Salden opened his mouth to reply, then closed it again. His face betrayed the fact that he knew he had given himself away.

TWENTY-SEVEN

"So what happened then?" said Joan. "Here, mash these potatoes, will you, while I do the sauce?"

Thanet took the saucepan, added margarine, black pepper, milk. With two cooks in the house you couldn't help learning something.

"He just caved in, confessed."

"He needn't have, of course."

"Why not? He'd given himself away, hadn't he?"

"He hadn't actually admitted that he'd heard about all this from his mother-in-law that night."

"True."

"So all he had to do was say that his wife had told him ages ago."

Thanet froze. "That's true. You're right! I didn't even think of that! How stupid can you get!" If Salden's wits had not been blunted by pain, grief and confusion he could have got away with it, at the very point when Thanet thought he had him. Thanet's scalp prickled with sweat as he realised how close a shave he had had.

"You're lucky he didn't think of it either! Have you finished with that?"

Thanet held out the saucepan. "Will this do?"

"Fine, yes." Joan was stirring vigorously. "Put the lid on, I'm not quite ready."

Thanet was recovering. "We caught him off balance and he wasn't thinking straight. And also I think it was a relief to him to confess, get it off his chest. He's not the sort of man to live comfortably with a secret like that on his conscience."

Joan took the plates out of the oven and began dishing up.

"So what did happen that night, exactly?"

"Well, if you remember, Salden had been sitting brooding on

221

a bench on the river bank a few hundred yards away from the bridge on the other side from the Manor. Around twenty past ten he decided he really ought to get back to his mother-in-law's house. He was worried about her and, besides, there was an unseasonable frost that night and he was feeling thoroughly chilled.

"He was climbing the steps from the footpath when he heard footsteps approaching from the direction of the village. As he came up on to the bridge he saw that it was his wife. Because of the broken parapet she had been walking on the side nearer to him, but now she was crossing the bridge diagonally, making for the opposite flight of steps which lead down to the footpath to the Manor. He called her name and hurried to intercept her. When they met she was standing right next to the warning lights with her back to the gap in the stonework."

"Marcia! What are you doing here?"

"What d'you think? I've been to see my mother."

"Did she tell you why she wanted to see me?"

"No, she was asleep. Anyway why should she?"

"Because it concerned me."

"Concerned you? What d'you mean? What are you talking about? Look, couldn't we discuss this later? We've got guests, in case you've forgotten. I can't think what they'll think of us. You don't turn up at all and then I walk out on them."

"To hell with them! Who cares what they think? I don't. But I can tell you this, Marcia. I cared about what your mother told me. I really did care about that . . . What did you do with her, Marcia? What did you do with our daughter? With Clare?"

"Clare's dead. She died thirty years ago . . ."

"Don't give me that! I won't let you get away with any more lies. To think I believed you, unquestioningly . . . What a fool I was . . . So tell me. What did you do with her?"

"Let go of my arm. You're hurting me."

"What did you do with her? Tell me!"

"I . . . took her to York."

"York? Why York?"

"I don't know."

"There must have been a reason why you chose York."

"I think . . . Someone once told me it was a nice place . . ."

"Where did you go, in York?"

"My arm . . . Please . . ."

"Where?"

"A hospital. I left her . . . in the foyer . . ."

"Which hospital? Which hospital?"
"I can't remember. I don't know. I didn't notice. Please.
"You're really hurting me. Let go . . ."

"He claims he can't remember very clearly what happened then. She was struggling to get away, pulling and tugging, and he thinks she gave an especially violent wrench just as he finally let go. The road was slippery and she lost her balance, doubling up as she fell backwards through the rope barrier. She'd disappeared through the gap in the parapet almost before he realised what was happening."

"You believe him?" Joan had finished serving and had put the plates of food in the oven to keep warm while Thanet finished his story.

"I don't know. I'm not sure, how can I be? He may have shoved her away, in disgust or anger . . . Whatever happened, I do believe it was an accident, a result of the quarrel."

"In that case, why didn't he try to do something to save her, call for help?"

"He says that for a moment or two he couldn't believe his eyes. One moment she was there and the next she was gone. He'd been so wrapped up in what they'd been saying that he hadn't been aware of the gap in the bridge wall behind her and he couldn't understand what had happened. For a moment he just stood there. Then he rushed to the parapet and looked over. There was no sign of her. Neither of them could swim, the river was running high because of the rain and he realised at once that it would be pointless to go for help, it was already too late."

"He should have, all the same."

"Of course he should. I think the truth is that, even though he may not deliberately have pushed her, at that point he still felt so angry and cheated that he just didn't care if she was alive or dead. A child of his own would have meant so much to him. If his wife had lived I don't think he could ever have forgiven her for what she did."

"I expect he'll get a verdict of manslaughter. I wonder if he'll go inside."

Thanet shrugged. "Depends on the judge. He might get a suspended."

"Highly probable, I should think. From what you say, he isn't likely to be a danger to the public." Joan grinned. "Though I wouldn't say that was exactly the impression conveyed by Superintendent Draco on *Coast to Coast.*"

"You saw him?"

"Wouldn't have missed it for the world! Anyone would think he'd conducted the entire investigation single-handed!" Joan came and put her arms around Thanet's neck. "It's not fair. You should have got the credit."

"Some credit! When I think how I was within a whisker of it going the other way, and I didn't even realise. . . !"

Joan kissed him. "Well, it didn't. Tell me, what put you on to him in the first place?"

They moved apart and sat down.

"Oddly enough, it was Vicky, poor girl. I was thinking about her a lot last night, of course, while you were at the hospital. While I was waiting for you to come home I dozed off and I had a rather nasty dream in which she turned into Marcia. I suppose that, subconsciously, I had spotted the similarity between them: they'd both had severe post-natal depression. Vicky had been driven to try to kill herself. What if Marcia actually had killed her baby?

"You see, I knew she hadn't wanted that baby. I also knew that she'd been very ambitious, that she'd hated living up North and that when her husband was posted abroad and she was left alone there with the baby it must have been the last straw. Looked at like that, the baby's death had been very convenient for her. It had meant that she was free again to pursue whatever career she wanted, and that she had an excuse to run away from the area she hated and return to Kent. In the circumstances no one would blame her.

"Well, we checked, and discovered that the death had never been registered. The fact that there'd been a funeral, presided over by the vicar and witnessed by at least one neighbour who couldn't possibly be suspected of complicity, was a bit of a stumbling block. Until we discovered that it hadn't been a proper burial service in the churchyard at all—the vicar would have needed a death certificate for that—but a simple sort of blessing ceremony, a scattering of the ashes on the village green . . . Stupid of me, really. I just assumed the baby was dead, it never occurred to me that she could have just abandoned it. I can imagine how Salden felt when he found out. He adored that child, by all accounts."

"So how is he taking this now?"

"All he can think of is how to trace his daughter. He'd already started making enquiries."

"That won't be an easy road. And if he does succeed, who knows if she'd want to be found?"

"Quite. Still, that's his affair. As I say, I can understand how he feels . . . Which reminds me . . . I think I've had a brilliant idea, about Bridget's problem."

"Oh?"

"What if we said to her, 'Look, what if you planned, afterwards, to do something for which you don't need to do particularly well in these exams, would that help you to stop worrying?' "

"Such as?"

"Well, we've always thought in terms of catering college, haven't we? But there's no reason why we shouldn't consider sending her to one of the private cookery schools. Some of them have excellent reputations. And I read somewhere that their academic entrance requirements aren't too exacting. In any case, with all Bridget has already achieved in the cookery field, I'm sure they'd be only too delighted to take her."

"Could we afford it? They're terrible expensive."

"But wouldn't it be worth it?" Thanet took Joan's hands. "I know it wouldn't be easy, we'd have to make economies, but later on, if Ben manages to get to university, we'll have to help him through, and over the three years that would mount up. Most of these Cordon Bleu courses are only a year, or less. Surely we ought to be prepared to spend the same on Bridget."

"True. It's just that it's a new idea . . ." Her tone became more positive. "It would certainly take the pressure off her as far as these exams are concerned."

"Exactly! Then, if she did pass . . . Well, I suppose then we'd have to leave it to her to choose which she wanted. We could hardly offer her the chance then take it away if she passes!"

"Quite. Oh darling, the more I think about it . . . Let's go and talk to her now, before we have supper, shall we? She badly needs cheering up."

"If you like."

Faced by the sight of both parents entering her room, Bridget's look was less than welcoming.

"It's all right," said Thanet. "This isn't what you think."

"No *post mortem*," said Joan. "Daddy's come up with a brilliant idea."

"Oh?" Bridget was wary. She looked ill, Thanet thought, pale and listless. He couldn't bear the thought that his bright, lively daughter had been reduced to this. He began to explain his idea. "Your mother and I wondered . . ." He watched her face as he talked. Almost at once her cheeks became tinged with colour, her eyes began to sparkle and before he had finished she jumped up out of her chair and flung her arms around his neck. "Oh Dad, what a wonderful idea. That would be terrific!" She turned to her mother, hugged her too. Then she stood back to study their faces. "You mean it, don't you? You really mean it!"

Thanet and Joan, relieved and delighted at her reaction, beamed at her and at each other. They both nodded. "We certainly do," said Joan. "We thought it would take the pressure off you. As Daddy says, even if you didn't do too well in your exams, you'd be sure to get in, after winning that cookery competition and writing the column for the *Kent Messenger*."

"Terrific!" Bridget's look of excitement faded. "But wouldn't it be terribly expensive?"

Joan explained what Thanet had said about Ben's education. "It won't be easy, there's no point in pretending it will. But we see no reason why you shouldn't have the same chance as Ben, in a different way."

Bridget burst into tears.

Joan got up and took a handkerchief from a drawer, handed it to her.

She wiped her eyes, smiling and biting her lip. "It's such a relief . . ."

Joan reached for Thanet's hand and squeezed it.

He smiled and returned the pressure. It looked as though another of life's minor crises was over.

ABOUT THE AUTHOR

DOROTHY SIMPSON is a former French teacher now living with her husband and three children in Kent, England. This is her eighth Luke Thanet novel. Her fifth, *Last Seen Alive*, won the 1985 British Crime Writer's Association Silver Dagger award. Her other books are *Element of Doubt, Dead on Arrival, Close Her Eyes, Puppet for a Corpse, Six Feet Under*, and *The Night She Died*.

If you enjoyed SUSPICIOUS DEATH, you'll want to read Dorothy Simpson's next Luke Thanet mystery, DEAD BY MORNING. Here is a special advance preview chapter from DEAD BY MORNING, which will be available as a Bantam paperback in August 1990, at your local bookseller.

DEAD BY MORNING
Dorothy Simpson

And don't miss these other Dorothy Simpson titles, all available now in Bantam paperback from your local bookseller:

ELEMENT OF DOUBT

DEAD ON ARRIVAL

LAST SEEN ALIVE

CLOSE HER EYES

PUPPET FOR A CORPSE

SIX FEET UNDER

THE NIGHT SHE DIED

As soon as he opened his eyes next morning he was aware of the difference in the quality of the light. There must have been more snow overnight. He hoped that the fall had not been heavy. Snow was very picturesque but it brought problems. However hard the local authority tried, it never seemed to make adequate preparation for bad weather. A mere skim of snow brought its crop of traffic jams and minor accidents; anything over six inches, severe disruption. And, of course, there was the cold. Thanet hated the cold and the tip of his nose told him that the temperature in the bedroom was at a far from acceptable level. February was definitely bottom of his personal popularity chart of favourite months. He allowed himself the indulgence of a few more moments in the warm cave that was the bed, then braced himself and slid out, careful not to allow a gush of cold air to disturb Joan, who was still sleeping peacefully. He padded across to the window. Might as well know the worst.

Despite his dislike of the inconvenience snow brought in its wake he could not escape the inevitable sense of wonder at its transforming beauty. Beneath its mantle of pristine white, his familiar world preened itself in the first rosy light of a clear winter dawn. He peered at the roof of the garage, trying to gauge the depth of the fall: not more than a few inches, by the look of it. Good. It shouldn't take too long to clear the drive, with Ben's help. And the gritting lorries had been out last night, so the roads shouldn't be too bad.

Three-quarters of an hour later, fortified by the porridge that Joan had insisted on making, he and Ben had almost reached the front gate. Up and down the road warmly clad figures shovelled and swept drives and pavements. In the road cars seemed to be making slow but steady progress.

Joan appeared at the front door. "Luke? Telephone."

"Finish it off, will you, Ben?"

Ben, thirteen, gave a reluctant nod.

"Sergeant Pater," said Joan, handing over the receiver.

The Station Officer. Something out of the ordinary, then, to necessitate an early morning call, in view of the fact that Thanet was due at headquarters in half an hour or so.

"Thanet here."

"Morning, sir. Just had the report of a body in a ditch at the side of the road, out at Sutton-in-the-Weald. Found by a man walking his dog."

As in his last case, Thanet thought. If you were a dog owner you certainly seemed to run a greater risk of stumbling over a corpse than most.

"You've reported it to the Super?"

"Yes, sir. He says he's going out there himself." Pater's tone was carefully non-committal.

"Ah." Thanet's heart sank. This was new. What was Draco up to now? He remembered wondering, when Draco first arrived, just how long the new Superintendent would be content to sit behind a desk. All that restless energy needed numerous outlets. Thanet hoped that active participation at ground level wasn't going to be one of them. It would be impossibly inhibiting to have Draco breathing down his neck.

"Apparently there's been quite a bit of snow out there, fifteen inches or so, with some pretty deep drifts in places, so it's going to make transport a bit tricky. The Super's put through a request to the Council to clear the road as soon as possible and he's asked for a couple of Land Rovers to be laid on for you. He wants you to meet him here and he'll go out with you."

"I see. What time?"

"Eight-thirty."

"Right, I'll be there. Have you contacted Sergeant Lineham?"

"I'll do that next, sir. I'll arrange for the SOCOs and the CCTV sergeant to come in the other Land Rover, and pick up Doc Mallard on the way. I thought I'd let you know first."

So that Thanet wouldn't be late for Draco, no doubt.

"Thanks."

Grateful that he had already had breakfast and that the driveway was clear, Thanet put on thick socks, wellington boots, sheepskin jacket, gloves and woolly hat in anticipation of hours of standing around in the snow. "I feel like the Abominable Snowman," he said as he kissed Joan goodbye.

She grinned. "You look like him. Here." She handed him a thermos.

"Thanks, love. Oh, hang on. Better take some shoes, in case. I can't go tramping in and out of houses in these."

"Sure you wouldn't like me to pack a suit-case for you?"

"All very well for you, in your nice, cen-trally heated office."

Joan worked as a Probation Officer in Sturrenden.

"Courtroom actually."

"Courtroom, office, what's the difference, it'll be *warm*."

"Stop grumbling," she said, pushing him out of the front door. "Go on, you don't want to keep Draco waiting, do you?"

Thanet rolled his eyes. "Heaven forbid."

As he got into the car he realised that he had been so put out by the prospect of Dra-co's presence that he had forgotten to ask whether the body was that of a man or a woman.

It was another couple of hours before he found out.

The journey out to Sutton-in-the-Weald had been irritatingly protracted. The first few miles hadn't been too bad but then the snow had begun to deepen and a little further on they had caught up with the snow plough sent out at Draco's request. After that they had resigned themselves to travelling behind it the rest of the way, at a snail's pace. Fortunately a local farmer with a snow-clearing attachment on the front of his tractor had eventually turned up coming the other way and after a certain amount of manoeuvring they had been able to proceed more quickly.

There then followed a long wait for the second Land Rover bringing Doc Mallard and the Scenes-of-Crime officers. Meanwhile, there had been little to do. The body lay in a roadside ditch backed by a high stone wall, only a few yards from the lion-topped pillars at the entrance of the driveway to Longford Hall Country House Hotel. From the road nothing could be seen but the upper surface of a sleeve in distinctively bold black-and-white-checked tweed, lying along the edge of the ditch as it had been uncovered by the dog. Although the arm was patently stiff with rigor mortis, PC Yeoman, the local policeman who had been first on the scene, had understandably cleared the snow from the man's face, to make quite sure that he was dead. The rigid features, pallor of the skin and open, staring eyes had told their own tale and thereafter he had left well alone, winning Thanet's approval by erecting a temporary barrier of sticks stuck into the snow and linked by string.

Despite his years in the force Thanet had rarely been able to overcome a dread of his first sight of a corpse, but today, uncomfortably preoccupied by Draco's presence, he had approached the body with no more than a twinge of trepidation and, gazing down at the dead face set deep in its ruff of snow, he felt no more than his usual pang of sorrow at a life cut short. Blurred as the man's features were by snow, it was difficult to estimate his age with any accuracy, but Thanet guessed that he had been somewhere between forty and sixty. Time, no doubt, would tell.

No further attempt had yet been made to clear the snow from the rest of the body. Thanet wanted photographs taken first. Not that he thought this very important. Covered with snow as it was, the body had obviously been placed or had fallen into the ditch before or around the time the snow started. Still, one never knew. It paid to be scrupulously careful and, with Draco taking in every move, Thanet had every intention of playing it by the book.

In any case, the marks in the snow told their own story: a scuffled, disturbed area betrayed the dog's excited investigation of this interesting and unusual find and there were two sets of approaching and departing footprints, belonging to Mr. Clayton, the dog's owner, and PC Yeoman. Thanet, Draco and Lineham had been careful to enquire which were Yeoman's tracks, and to step into his footmarks when they approached for their brief inspection of the body.

As yet the snow had kept most people indoors and there had been little traffic up and down the road. Half an hour ago a tractor had begun clearing the hotel drive and any minute now Thanet expected someone to arrive and demand an explanation of the activity just outside the gates.

"Where the devil are they?"

Draco, who along with Lineham and Thanet had been stamping up and down the road in an attempt to keep warm, was finding it difficult to contain his impatience. "They should have been here half an hour ago."

"Perhaps Doc Mallard was out on a call."

Draco snorted, two dragon-like puffs of condensation emerging from his nostrils. Short, square and dark and sporting an astrakhan hat and a heavy, fur-lined overcoat, he looked like a Russian statesman awaiting the arrival of foreign dignitaries. The backdrop of snow served to heighten the illusion.

"Like some coffee, sir? I've got some in the Land Rover."

"Thank you. Excellent idea. Should have thought of it myself."

"My wife's, actually."

Thanet fetched his thermos from the Land Rover and he, Draco and Lineham took it in turns to sip the steaming liquid. Lineham had been very quiet so far, subdued no doubt by Draco's presence. Thanet had to suppress a grin at the memory of Lineham's face when he had seen Draco climb into the Land Rover. The sergeant evidently hadn't been warned.

A vehicle could be heard coming down the hotel drive and a moment later a Range Rover pulled up between the stone pillars. A man and a woman jumped out.

"What's going on here?"

It was, unmistakably, the voice of authority, cultured and self-assured. Its owner, clad in country uniform of cords, thick sweater, Barbour and green wellies, was in his late forties, tall and well built with slightly receding dark hair and slate-grey eyes which quickly summed up the situation and unerringly selected Draco as the person to approach. "What's happened?"

Draco handed the thermos cup to Thanet and, drawing himself up to his full height, announced, "Superintendent Draco, from divisional police headquarters at Sturrenden . . ."

But the man wasn't listening. He had caught sight of the arm in its boldly checked sleeve and his expression changed. "My God, that's . . ."

He spun around, putting out his hand to prevent the woman behind him from coming any closer.

"What is it, Giles? What's the matter?"

Clear, ringing tones, another Barbour and more green wellies. A beautiful woman, this, a little younger than her husband, in her early forties, Thanet guessed. She, too, was dark, her long hair swept back into a thick French plait, accentuating the classic bone structure of her face. She would look much the same, he thought, twenty years from now.

"I think you ought to get back into the car, darling," said her husband.

She shook off his restraining arm impatiently. "What do you mean, what are you talking about?"

The movement gave her a clear view of the arm for the first time and she gasped. "My God, that's Leo's coat."

Draco stepped forward. "Leo?"

"My brother." Her gaze was riveted to the arm, her eyes appalled. She clutched at her husband, who put an arm around her. "Is he . . . ?"

"Dead?" said Draco. "I'm afraid so. If it is your brother, I'm sorry that you had to learn of it like this."

"But why are you just standing around drinking coffee, for God's sake! Why aren't you trying to get him out? You can't just leave him there!" She grabbed the stick marker nearest to her, tugged it out of the snow and, tossing it impatiently aside, started towards the ditch.

The three policemen darted forward to stop her, but it was her husband who grabbed at her coat and tugged her back. "No, Delia. Can't you see? If it is Leo, there's nothing anybody can do now."

"But it's awful! It's . . . inhuman, just leaving him buried in the snow like that!" She turned on Draco, her eyes blazing. "How dare you!" Her contemptuous gaze swept around the little group of policemen and returned to Draco. "The Chief Constable is a personal friend of ours. I shall report you to him. Immediately!"

Thanet studiously refrained from looking at Lineham.

She turned to her husband. "Come on, Giles. We'll go back to the house and get something done about this absurd situation."

And with another furious glance at Draco

she swung herself up into the car and sat gazing stonily through the windscreen as her husband manoeuvred the Range Rover around and drove off.

"A lady who's used to getting her own way, I presume," said Draco, apparently unruffled. "You're going to have your hands full with her, Thanet."

Just what Thanet had been thinking. Though the prospect intrigued rather than dismayed him. He raised an eyebrow at PC Yeoman. "Who are they?"

"Mr. and Mrs. Hamilton, sir. Owners of Longford Hall. She runs the hotel, he runs the estate."

"There are the others now, sir," said Lineham.

"About time, too," growled Draco.

Doc Mallard's half-moon spectacles glinted through the windscreen as the Land Rover drew up.

"Where the devil have you been?" snapped Draco as Trace, the SOCO sergeant, got out, followed by his team.

Mallard accepted Thanet's steadying hand. "My fault, I'm afraid, Superintendent. Blame it on a doctor's irregular lifestyle. I was out at a confinement. Woman was on her way to hospital, but the ambulance got stuck in the snow. Luckily I just got there in time." He beamed. "Bouncing baby boy, mother and child both right as rain, I'm glad to say. Nothing like bringing life into the world to cheer you up, you know."

"I'm sure." Draco turned to Trace. "Well, let's get on with it now you are here. If we have to stand around out here much longer we'll all turn into blocks of ice."

Kinsey Millhone is...

"The best new private eye." —*The Detroit News*

"A tough-cookie with a soft center." —*Newsweek*

"A stand-out specimen of the new female operatives."
—*Philadelphia Inquirer*

Sue Grafton is...

The Shamus and Anthony Award winning creator of
Kinsey Millhone and quite simply one of the hottest
new mystery writers around.

Bantam is...

The proud publisher of Sue Grafton's Kinsey Millhone
mysteries: